ZONE

Titles by Jack Lance published by Severn House

PYROPHOBIA
ZONE

ZONE

A Paranormal Thriller

Jack Lance

This first world edition published 2015
in Great Britain and 2016 in the USA by
SEVERN HOUSE PUBLISHERS LTD of
19 Cedar Road, Sutton, Surrey, England, SM2 5DA.
Trade paperback edition first published
in Great Britain and the USA 2016 by
SEVERN HOUSE PUBLISHERS LTD.
Originally published in the Netherlands as Zone
by Luitingh-Sijthoff in 2012. This English edition
translated from the Dutch by Lia Belt, with
additional editorial input from Bill Hammond.

British Library Cataloguing in Publication Data

Lance, Jack, author.
　Zone.
　1. Air travel–Fiction. 2. Suspense fiction.
　I. Title
　839.3'137-dc23

ISBN-13: 978-0-7278-8569-2 (cased)
ISBN-13: 978-1-84751-677-0 (trade paper)
ISBN-13: 978-1-78010-735-6 (e-book)

All Severn House titles are printed on acid-free paper.

Severn House Publishers support the Forest Stewardship Council™ [FSC™],
the leading international forest certification organisation.
All our titles that are printed on FSC certified paper carry the FSC logo.

Typeset by Palimpsest Book Production Ltd.,
Falkirk, Stirlingshire, Scotland.
Printed and bound in Great Britain by
TJ International, Padstow, Cornwall.

Asmara, Alexander and Rina
You're showing me worlds I couldn't have imagined.

A 747 is coming down in the night
There's no radio, no sign of life
We were strangers in the night
Strangers in the night
Going nowhere

Saxon, *747*
(Strangers In The Night)

Prologue

Everything changed on a balmy day in March when the first flowers started to bud. She returned home at three o'clock in the afternoon, after cheering on her boyfriend Ross's baseball team. Two patrol cars were parked outside her house, one in the driveway and one at the curb. Bad news, she thought when she saw them. This can only mean bad news.

She went inside, heard people talking in the living room. Her father, sitting in his big green armchair, was leaning forward, hiding his face in his hands. Standing in the room with him were two uniformed police officers and a man dressed in a gray pinstriped suit. The pinstriped man, his hands folded as if in prayer, was speaking softly to her father.

Her father lowered his hands and glanced over his shoulder. His red-rimmed eyes met hers. He reached a hand out to her.

'Sharlene,' he croaked. 'Come here.'

Hesitantly she shuffled closer to Dean Thier, the father she had always known to be so strong and who now appeared utterly broken. As she did so, the policemen and the man in the gray suit stepped aside to make way for her.

'What's wrong?' Sharlene whispered.

She was strangely convinced she already knew the answer, but that didn't mean she was prepared to believe it. She kept hoping that what she was experiencing was some kind of nightmare, a terrible dream from which she would soon awaken.

Her father embraced her. She felt the damp of his tears on the side of her face.

'Would you like us to step outside, sir?' the man in the suit asked.

Dean shook his head. 'No. That won't be necessary. I can handle this.'

He cast Sharlene a look of utter despair. 'It's . . . It's your mother.'

That was what she had feared. Instead of her mother, the police were here.

'There's been an accident,' Dean went on quietly. 'A very serious accident, I'm afraid. It wasn't even your mother's shift today. She was covering for another crew member. If she hadn't . . .' He swallowed hard and turned his face away.

Sharlene couldn't speak. She just stood there listening to words that her brain could not process. She wanted her father to stop talking. She wanted him to take back his words, to say that it wasn't so, to admit this was all a horrible misunderstanding.

Her father turned back to her, his eyes bright with unshed tears. 'She had a flight to Phoenix this morning,' he managed. 'But something went terribly wrong. We still don't know what happened. Engine failure, perhaps. The plane crashed just outside a Phoenix suburb. There was a fire . . . There are no known survivors. My beloved Claudia . . . Your mother . . . She's . . .'

Dean was unable to complete the sentence. His voice broke, he buried his face in his hands, and he wept openly.

Sharlene went cold. She felt as if a tub of ice water had been dumped on her. She stood there, trembling, staring first at her father sobbing uncontrollably, and then toward the uniformed officers and the man in the suit, their own eyes filled with sadness and sympathy. She was only fifteen years old, and she had no idea how to handle this.

She ran up the stairs to her bedroom and locked herself inside. For a span of time impossible to measure she sat there, staring with glassy eyes while her body shook uncontrollably as if from an epileptic fit.

Then the dam burst, and it wasn't until the next morning that the tears subsided.

Several relatives dropped by to see her and her father. The last thing Sharlene wanted to hear was how very sorry they all were. She only wanted her mother to come home from the airport in her red Camry LE as she always had.

Sharlene rejected the notion that her mother would never be coming home again. This had to be a nightmare. When was she finally going to wake up?

She told her father how she felt. He put a hand on top of her head and kept staring in the distance, his eyes hollow and empty, void of emotion.

It was a balmy day in March, and the first flowers were starting to bud.

I

6:32 P.M. — 2:36 A.M.

ONE

Sharlene and Aaron

A wave of panic washed over the white bungalow at 94 Howland Avenue, located near Pacific Avenue and a mile-and-a-half from Venice Beach.

If it wasn't exactly panic, it was something close to it. Sharlene Thier, wearing nothing but a white G-string and a silver necklace with a gold crucifix around her slender neck, was searching for her makeup kit. Her clothes were still in the dryer and her uniform was wrinkled. If they weren't in the car in fifteen minutes, they wouldn't make it to the airport on time.

Aaron Drake, already wearing his airline purser's uniform, snapped the lid on his suitcase. Shaking his head, he glanced toward Sharlene's open suitcase, and then folded out the ironing board to quickly press her crew shirt and slacks for her. She would have to iron the rest of her clothes after they arrived in Sydney, and she could buy makeup at the airport.

That afternoon, on Venice Beach, they had lost all track of time, as most newly minted lovers do. A phone call from an acquaintance had interrupted their carnal intimacies and brought them back to reality. A dash back to her bungalow, a shower, a few minutes to change into work clothes, and he was ready to go. She, however, was still padding around in her underwear.

'I thought you liked me for my charm and my body,' he called out as he carefully ironed her slacks. 'But you're only using me as your maid.'

'Maids are important people,' she quipped in a voice tinged with fluster. Crouching down in front of the dryer, she turned off the machine even though the cycle was not finished. As she tossed her moist clothing into a hamper, she added, 'Unlike many other women, I can appreciate a man who won't shirk his household chores.'

'Yeah, go ahead,' Aaron groused. 'Rub it in. Is that all I'm good for? Nothing else?'

Sharlene brushed back a lock of golden hair, and gave him a

fetching smile and an alluring view of her apple-shaped breasts. 'Come on, now. Is it really that bad?'

His eyes feasted on her. 'Damn, I wish we had more time,' he said devoutly.

'Men!' she sighed, shaking her head. 'You really do all have a one-track mind. Have you forgotten the beach already? The spot behind the boulder?'

'That was ages ago.'

'That was only a few hours ago,' she countered. 'Just wait till we're in Sydney. I hope you aren't planning to spend your time there chasing kangaroos and wallabies.'

'They're cute, but actually I'm becoming very much attached to something far cuter.'

'Good. Now get back to work. Just so you know you won't be getting something for nothing.'

He heaved a sigh. 'Keep this up, and I'll stuff you into a kanga-roo's pouch once we're in Australia.'

Sharlene hid a smile. 'Well, that would be fine, as long as you get stuffed in there with me. I imagine things could get quite cozy.'

In recent weeks Aaron had discovered many new sides to Sharlene. Her routine – or rather, her lack of routine – had not escaped his notice. But it mattered not. It matched her personality, and was high among the reasons he had fallen in love with her. That, and her physical attributes. He found everything about her irresistible, from her wavy, silky hair cascading down to the small of her back, to her round ass and long sexy legs and perfectly formed feet.

They both worked for Oceans Airways, based in Los Angeles. He had risen to the rank of purser and she to the rank of assistant purser. Unfortunately, their schedules didn't assign them to the same flights as often as he would have liked. For six months he had been trying his damnedest to get her to notice him whenever they did find themselves together. Finally, after a flight to Tokyo nine weeks earlier, he had succeeded – putting it mildly.

Since then they had been alternating between her place and his. Last night had ended in her bungalow. The next bedroom they would share would be in Sydney, thousands of miles away from Los Angeles.

But first he had to get her uniform ready.

*   *   *

Sharlene could not seem to get a grip. Her thoughts were bouncing all over the place, like a nest of startled hares. She glanced at her small, empty Samsonite suitcase. Then she turned and snatched her toothbrush, a tube of toothpaste, her Helena Rubinstein day cream, and a few other jars and bottles from the shelf beneath the bathroom mirror. These items she tossed into her toiletry bag.

'What else?' she mumbled to herself.

'What was that?' Aaron called from the bedroom.

Sharlene frowned. Normally adept at multi-tasking, this evening she felt like a sieve.

Aaron switched off the iron. 'Your uniform's ready,' he called to her.

Sharlene strode into the bedroom, her eyebrows arched in surprise. 'You're the best.'

'How much longer do you need?'

'Five minutes. You go on ahead and start the car. I'll be right out.'

He nodded and grabbed the car keys.

After she donned her uniform, she shoved her feet into her pumps. Now all she needed to do was pick out some leisure wear from her wardrobe and find the rest of her makeup. She felt certain she had not yet collected everything she needed. At the very least, she would have to cram some essentials into her smaller case in order to apply lipstick and some rouge to her cheeks on the way to the airport. All she needed then was to make a quick final tour of the house to make sure all appliances had been turned off, tidy up in the kitchen a little, and lock the front door behind her.

Muted, but still audible, she heard the tune of 'Love Is in the Air' emanating from her purse in the living room. It was a ringtone she had downloaded after that special night with Aaron in the Tokyo Grand Hotel.

As Sharlene turned on her heel, she heard it snap off from her right shoe.

Shit! That's all I needed!

In that instant she lost interest in the phone call. Whoever was calling her, he or she would have to wait.

By the time the phone stopped ringing, she had taken off the pump with the broken heel. She stood staring at it pensively. Which pair of shoes should she wear now? She was not one of those women who had a closet full of footwear. Pumps, high heels, and bootees held little interest for her. To the surprise of every female friend she had ever had, she owned only a few pairs of shoes, and what she had was stored in a cramped, wedge-shaped attic located above the guest room.

Sharlene sighed, removed the other pump, and walked in stocking feet into the guest room.

The scene awaiting her in her small storage space, the place she jokingly called her personal archive, was, as always, a complete mess. Boxes, folders, clothes she never wore anymore, knick-knacks of every description – a disorganized mountain of clutter and debris. Since she had no choice, and no time, she leaned into the unlit space and, with more desperation than courage, groped about in search of another pair of shoes. She moved some stuff aside, cursing out loud when she scraped her knee on a bent nail.

'Sharlene, what the hell are you doing?' she scolded herself.

She needed to keep her mind off Aaron for a moment. He was waiting in the car for her, no doubt thinking she was almost ready. It would never enter his mind that what she was actually doing was wading into her own private labyrinth of chaos and confusion.

Finally she saw it, a white shoe box. Inside, she was sure, was a pair of pumps.

'Thank goodness,' she mumbled.

She drew the box toward her and started crawling backwards out of the crawl space.

Suddenly the meager light in the space turned to pitch black.

The tiny door leading out behind her must have closed, she thought.

Sharlene inhaled sharply. Cold sweat oozed from her pores. She was afraid to move; she *couldn't* move.

She not only disliked the dark.

She *detested* it.

Aaron dumped his suitcase on the back seat of his blue Chevrolet Malibu and drove in reverse from the driveway on to the street. He had negotiated a good deal on the car at one of Tommy Jones's dealerships, the self-crowned 'Automobile King' of greater Los Angeles. He got out of the Malibu and started pacing up and down the sidewalk, his hands shoved into the pockets of his trousers. He kept glancing at his watch. A little after 6:40. The hours had zipped by. Officially their shift started at 7:15. He would have to floor it once they were on the road. How was it possible, he wondered, that after an entire day together they *still* risked being late for work?

'Hurry up, Sharlene,' he muttered.

The five minutes she had said she needed had come and gone. She should be coming out the front door any moment now. He fought the urge to go back inside and drag her out of the house. Hardly the most gallant of moves, he knew it would only lead to further delays. And her being pissed off at him.

The hot August sun slowly dipped below the rows of white bungalows on Howland Avenue. He wiped the sweat from his brow with the heel of his right hand, continuing to look at the front door of Sharlene's house.

Aaron started pacing again. He did not want to be late and keep fourteen other crew members waiting. Even as it was, they would not have much time to prepare for their flight.

He checked his watch one more time. Ten minutes had elapsed since he had left to start the car. Maybe he should check on her progress after all.

Just let her do her thing, it'll be faster, another thought cautioned him.

Squinting, Aaron peered up into the sky, where he would be later this evening. In frustration he planted his fists on top of the Malibu's hot roof. Sharlene still hadn't appeared. From the corner of his eye he spotted a small red sports car approaching. The car drove past, turned into Pacific Avenue, and disappeared from view.

He stood his ground for a moment longer, and then walked resolutely back to the bungalow.

'This is taking far too long,' he mumbled as he let himself in.

As he had expected, she was attending to last-minute details.

'Just leave me be,' she growled at him.

Aaron took a step back and decided not to hassle her. Clearly, he was being more of an obstacle to her than a help.

Her earlier good mood had evaporated.

But he had seen her like this before.

He turned around, ambled back outside, and continued pacing.

At length she had been able to move about in the enclosed dark space that had suddenly enveloped her as if in a tomb. As quietly as possible, holding her breath, she had turned around and crawled forward a few inches. Nothing in the darkness appeared threatening.

But she wasn't out of the tomb yet: a lot could still go wrong until she was back out in the light. As she paused a moment to breathe, a drop of sweat slithered down her cheek. She was afraid to tempt fate and look around. Because she *might* see something fearful and freeze.

Gathering her courage, she shuffled forward. But she felt rigid with fear, and she had to struggle to avoid screaming for help.

Screaming was the worst thing she could do, she reminded herself. She mustn't make a sound. She must remain deathly quiet.

Were *they* keeping still, lurking in the deep shadows until she came close to the tiny door that was blocking out every shard of light? Were they waiting until then to strike? Sharlene's fingers touched something, and she almost *did* scream before realizing it was the door.

This was it. She had to get out of here now. She took another deep breath and began groping for the door handle. But she couldn't find it. *God dammit to hell*, she silently cursed.

Any second now a cold claw would burst from the pitch black, grab her ankle, drag her back, and then—

Finally she felt cool metal. She twisted the handle, the door opened, and she threw herself into the bright evening daylight flooding into the guest room.

But she would not be safe until the door was firmly closed. She kicked it shut with a loud bang.

Immediately she was overcome by another unsettling shock.

I left my shoes inside!

But then she felt the box she held pinned under her left arm, and she almost wept for joy.

After that, her waves of panic had subsided, to be replaced by a sour mood. She snapped at Aaron when he came back into the house to see what was taking her so long, and she felt badly when he turned around and walked back outside.

Sharlene finished packing, and close to 6:55 she wheeled her Samsonite suitcase on to the pathway leading from her front door to the sidewalk. On each side of the pathway stretched sixteen feet of sun-bleached gravel: her version of a maintenance-free garden. *What good is having a green thumb*, she had often said to her friends, *when all I do is travel*?

She locked the door, strode toward the car, and put her suitcase beside Aaron's in the back seat. She then slid into the passenger seat.

'That took a while,' Aaron said, unable to mask the pique in his voice. 'Everything OK?'

'Sure,' she deadpanned. 'Why shouldn't it be?'

As they drove off, Sharlene glanced back at her house. For a reason she could not explain, she sensed that she might never see it again. She didn't want to fly today. Today had turned into a bad day.

Keep your cool, she chided herself. *For God's sake, keep your cool.*

Olive shrubs and palm trees slid past the car window. The August heat shimmered in a sky colored azure blue like the Pacific Ocean.

'Are we going to make it?' she asked at length.

'I'm doing my best,' he replied gruffly.

She looked askance at him. 'Are you mad at me, Aaron?'

She could not blame him if he was. She had spoiled the mood by keeping him waiting and by snapping at him.

'No, I should have kept better track of time,' he said, unjustly taking the blame and not wanting to create a scene.

'I had to find another pair of shoes in the attic,' she explained, 'but the door closed behind me. I was suddenly trapped in the dark, and my imagination started running away with me, as usual.'

Aaron nodded, seeming to understand. 'You're OK now?'

'I think so.'

He fell silent after that.

Sharlene stared out the passenger window, immersed in her own thoughts. She clenched the crucifix on her necklace, took a deep breath, and exhaled slowly. It was a familiar ritual. Breathe quietly, stay calm, she reminded herself as if it were a mantra, and perhaps her wounds would eventually heal. But no, she told herself for the hundredth time. Her wounds would never heal.

In the other lane an endless line of cars stood impatiently idling on the hot tarmac. Up ahead must be either roadworks or an accident.

Aaron took the exit for Los Angeles Airport. Without her being aware of it, they had almost reached their destination. While Aaron steered the car toward the employee parking area, she unzipped her compact cosmetic bag and searched for her lipstick.

On an impulse, she kept throwing worried glances up at the sky above them. Her next shift was waiting for her on a flight from Los Angeles, California to Sydney, Australia.

Flight 582.

TWO
Pilots

At 6:35 sharp, Jim Nichols stepped into the Oceans Airways crew center at LAX, shoving his shirttails deeper down his pants. His stomach had started to protrude in recent months, and his uniform was feeling a little snug. He was an hour early, as was his wont. Unlike some of his colleagues who made a sport out of clocking in the minute their shift started, Jim was always early. And today was no exception.

Even today was no exception.

Jim had assumed he would be the first crew member to check in, but someone he knew very well was perusing the newspaper while sitting in one of the lounge's maroon lazy chairs. Upon spotting him, Jim pushed his worries aside and walked toward him with his hand outstretched.

'And here I was thinking *I* was the early bird,' he chirped.

'We both are, I guess,' the man said solemnly. Dressed in the same navy-blue uniform Jim was wearing, he arose and shook Jim's hand.

'Everything OK, Ben?'

'Fine. You?'

Jim sat down without answering the question.

In his early forties, his hair cut short and dark without a trace of gray, Ben Wright was nearly a head taller than Jim. Not an ounce of fat sullied his lean physique. Today he was serving as the relief pilot who would be taking over from the cockpit crew at set intervals. Jim flew with Ben frequently, as well as with Greg Huffstutter, the copilot on this flight.

Oceans Airways was a smaller company than Delta Airlines, where Jim had launched his career. At Delta it was not uncommon for crew members to meet each other for the first time during a flight. On some flights, Jim was well underway toward his destination before he determined whether or not he liked a fellow crew member.

At Oceans, Jim knew most of his co-workers. He had long ago pegged Ben and Greg as thorough and dependable professionals. Ben tended to be down-to-earth and candid, while Greg could sometimes be a little obstinate. But he too was a kindly soul.

'So, what have you been doing with yourself these last few days?' Jim asked.

Ben shrugged. 'Nothing much. I had a cold. Must've left the air conditioner on for too long.'

He coughed as if to prove his diagnosis. 'So I stayed home most of the time and caught up on some reading. You?'

Jim paused a moment to choose his words carefully. 'I've been working in the garden. Jody was mighty pleased.'

Ben gave him an amused grin. 'Were *you*?'

Jim chuckled with him. 'Oh, you know, maybe it'll grow on me someday.'

'Have you given anymore thought to . . . Well, you know.'

Jim did know what Ben was referring to. He had confided in Ben several months earlier, and that may have been a mistake. Ben didn't need to know everything.

Least of all about the last few hours.

That was something best kept to himself.

'Well, it's been on my mind a lot,' he said vaguely. 'But I haven't made a decision yet. I know I'll have to soon, though. I can't keep postponing it forever.'

The grin disappeared from Ben's face. 'If you need someone to talk to, I'm your man.'

'Thank you, Ben. I'll keep that in mind.'

'I'm serious, Jim.'

Jim pushed his unease away and slapped his colleague on the shoulder. 'Believe me, Ben, if I need advice, I know where to find it.'

In the crew center Jim fetched the flight plan from a dispatcher – the airport's ground crew – and sat down beside Ben. He checked the weather and other current information for their departure airport LAX and arrival airport SYD – Sydney Kingsford Smith

International – and also for Canberra, their alternate airport located thirty minutes from Sydney by air.

Their estimated flying time was thirteen hours and thirty-eight minutes, with a theoretical fuel burn of 324,024 pounds. They would carry more than that on board, of course: they needed extra fuel to reach their alternate airport in case for any reason they were unable to land in Sydney, and they needed enough fuel to keep flying for at least another thirty minutes should they need to circle an airport before they were permitted to land. In addition, a specific quantity of spare fuel was mandatory. In sum, his calculations amounted to an FOB – fuel on board – estimate of 361,703 pounds. Later, in the cockpit, he would be able to adjust variables based on these estimates after he had seen the actual payload. If they took on more or less weight than expected, they would need to make a correction in their fuel consumption projections.

Jim studied weather reports for his route. Everything looked in order. Wind directions and velocities indicated a favorable jet stream, something any airline appreciated since it meant less fuel consumption and therefore lower fuel expense – an increasing concern for all airlines. His one concern upon final review of the various reports was a rather large stationary storm front hovering between Tahiti and the Cook Islands. An unusual phenomenon for this time of year, and one that could cause considerable turbulence.

As Jim leafed through the flight plan, other crew members started coming in and going about their business. For intercontinental flights they had ninety minutes preparation time, and every second counted. The airline gave them time to do what needed to be done, without much wiggle room.

Around 7:15 all sixteen members of the crew were assembled in Oceans Airways' crew center at LAX, except for Greg Huffstutter. Sharlene Thier smiled when Jim's eyes met hers. Jim knew her better than anyone else present, save for Aaron, and he had heard through the grapevine that she and Aaron had become an item. He shook her hand first, then welcomed the others, who introduced themselves. Some faces Jim recognized, others he did not. He may have flown with them before but there were many more flight attendants than pilots, and cabin crews normally suffered a large turnover.

Aaron Drake finished the introductions assisted by Sharlene, who as assistant purser was responsible for Tourist Class. Jim had a tendency to call the purser *chef de cabine*, as they did in French airlines. To him, it was a classier-sounding title.

As required by flight protocol, Aaron and Sharlene then discussed the service and rotation system with the cabin crew and reviewed the so-called 'disaster scenario,' agreeing on who would manage which exit in case of an emergency. After the briefing, Jim took time to chat with Sharlene.

Greg Huffstutter was last to arrive, which was unlike him. He had been stuck in traffic, he explained apologetically. Ever since he had received his pilot's license two decades ago and was hired by Oceans Airways, he had been as dependable as Old Faithful. He had his routines, from which he never deviated. Greg did not like change, it was as simple as that. Maybe, his co-workers conjectured, that was why he had remained single. Now in his fifties, he no longer anticipated meeting the right woman. It didn't matter to Greg, Jim knew. His copilot had a passion for Superman, Batman, Spiderman, the Fantastic Four, and other superheroes. He was addicted to comic books and his attic was crammed with thousands of boxes full of them, collected since early childhood. Ben, one of the few people who did not get along famously with Greg, called them 'fairy tales' and had asked him once when he planned to finally grow up. Greg had responded that everyone had *some* kind of idiosyncrasy, and there was no need to worry until and unless you acquired more than one.

Jim warmly greeted his partner on this flight. The last time they had been inside a cockpit together had been two weeks prior, during a flight from LAX to Bangkok. On that flight, Greg had served as commander and Jim as copilot.

'Well, Australia awaits,' Greg said. 'No matter how often I go there, I can't get enough of the place.'

'Isn't that the truth?' Jim said with a smile.

And it's far, far away from my problems, he added to himself.

Aaron had parked his Chevrolet Malibu and he and Sharlene had hurried into the terminal building together. Inside, after going through security, they hurried on to the crew center.

The first person Sharlene saw was Jim Nichols, and when she did, her eyes lit up.

Life is a congruence of coincidences, and her friendship with the captain was evidence of that. After one of her first flights with

Oceans Airways, long before Aaron had entered her life, Jim had approached her in a hotel bar in Singapore. Neither of them had viewed the encounter as another episode in the never-ending love sagas involving an airline pilot and an attractive, single flight attendant. All they had done that evening was talk, which had been therapeutic for her. Maybe she owed it to Jim and to that night in Singapore that she hadn't immediately quit her new career as a flight attendant. What would her life have been like if she had? It would probably have remained cheerless, and she would never have met Aaron.

She shook Jim's hand and chatted with a few co-workers. The crew briefing was a routine matter and she felt herself calming down, largely because she was working and had other things to occupy her mind. After the briefing, Jim approached her again.

'It's been a while since we flew together, Sharlene.'

'A couple of weeks,' she agreed.

'You're radiant,' he said, nodding toward Aaron, who was talking to a crew member named Jessica Orrigo.

She blushed prettily.

Jim grinned, but Sharlene noticed that the circles beneath his eyes had darkened since their last flight together. He looked tired, worn down by something or someone. When Greg Huffstutter entered the room, Jim turned his attention to him.

Aaron finished his conversation with Jessica and walked over to Sharlene. 'Thank goodness!' he said cheerfully. 'I'm glad to see you smile again.'

'Like I told you, I was just nervous because I locked myself in the attic. I'm fine now.'

He grinned in relief. 'Everything's going to be fine in the end, you'll see.'

That was typical of Aaron, Sharlene mused. He always thought everything would turn out all right. If only she could feel that way.

Although she managed to be the flawless, smiling, friendly assistant purser, the feeling that she should not be flying today persisted, shadowing her like an ominous squall hovering on a distant horizon.

But she had a job to do, and there was no going back.

THREE
Passengers

As the evening sun faded over LAX, the heat became more bearable. But the still air, suffused with kerosene fumes and other toxic cast-offs, remained damp and clammy. Taxis, shuttle buses, limousines, and cars drove on and off the gray, desiccated tarmac outside the Oceans Airways terminal.

Inside, long lines formed before each of the three counters that had opened. The check-in procedure was slow, since suitcases needed to be checked one by one before being set upon the conveyor belt taking them out to the loading dock. Carry-on luggage went through a similar screening process. Security staff kept an eagle eye out for anyone acting suspicious. Today there was a disturbance caused by one of the last passengers to arrive. His name was Joe Tremain.

At five foot two, Joe was a small man who had endured any number of disparaging nicknames: leprechaun, toddler, midget, hobbit, and Shorty, to name but a few.

The only thing big about him was his mouth, and he used it to compensate for his pint-sized appearance. His big mouth had landed him his first job as an assistant buyer, where he was on the phone all day, mouthing off to everyone, and no one needed to see his diminutive size. Later, he moved into telemarketing, another job at which he was successful. Years later, after Joe launched his own thriving business, he started receiving what had always eluded him: respect. Today, more than two hundred people worked for him.

An official at the luggage-inspection desk was, however, unimpressed.

'Would you mind opening your suitcase for me, sir?' he asked Tremain.

Joe, wearing a brown suit with a matching brown necktie, felt insulted by what he took to be the supercilious tone of 'the Uniform' – his name for everyone on security staff. With an angry gesture he complied, whereupon the official started rummaging through his personal belongings.

He had hated the Uniforms in airport security ever since one of them had confiscated his letter opener. It was just a bloody souvenir, for God's sake. He had lost his temper, and why not? The bastards had no right to root around in his belongings.

Joe's dudgeon soared to new heights when the official, his expression inscrutable, continued searching through the contents of his green Samsonite suitcase. He zipped open Joe's toiletry bag and moved his black boxers around, groping for hidden compartments inside the piece of luggage.

'Having trouble finding it?' Joe asked.

The official glanced up. 'Excuse me, sir?'

'What you're looking for. You must be looking for something specific, otherwise you wouldn't be doing this. What's your problem?'

Unperturbed, the blue Uniform continued his inspection of the suitcase.

'Jesus Christ, man!' Joe exploded. 'I don't have all day. I have a plane to catch.'

It was like talking to a prison wall. The security officer continued doing what he was doing. 'What's your destination, sir?' he asked, glancing up.

'Sydney,' Joe hissed between his teeth.

'Business or pleasure?'

None of your fucking beeswax, Joe was tempted to respond. He felt the stares of other travelers burning holes in his back.

'I'm a businessman,' he said instead, struggling to keep a lid on his temper. 'So I'm going there on business.'

To make money so my tax dollars can pay for your fucking salary, asshole.

'What kind of business?' the uniform asked calmly.

'Am I obliged to tell you that?'

Joe inadvertently clenched his fists. This man was seriously getting on his nerves.

'Did you pack this suitcase yourself?'

'I did.'

'And no one else has touched it?'

'No one. Except you. And you've been touching it long enough now, if you don't mind my saying so.'

The Uniform's face split in an evil grin, like a bloodhound smelling a wounded prey. 'Sir, I could make this very hard on you if I wanted to. I could make this so hard on you that you might even miss your flight. Is that what you want?'

'Wouldn't you like that,' Joe nearly spat. His eyes flashed; he doubted not for a moment that the Uniform was taking pleasure in harassing him.

'What's your problem, sir?' the official asked, turning the tables on Joe.

Two of the Uniform's co-workers were watching them. Joe heard someone coughing behind him; other people waiting in line were getting impatient.

Joe took a deep breath. This was no time to get angry. He had important things to do in Sydney. He *had* to get to Australia. It wouldn't do to be held up at LAX by some cork-brained official who was having a bad day. Joe managed to paste a smile on his face.

'No problem at all, sir.'

The striking blue eyes of the Uniform remained fixed on Joe for a moment, then he shoved the suitcase back toward him. At last Joe could move on. It had been a close call, but everything had turned out all right. He had managed to keep his cool despite the Uniform's unjust provocation.

But when he reached the waiting area, he glanced down at his right hand and noticed blood on the palm. In his anger and frustration, he had pressed his fingernails into his flesh.

Apparently he had not been as cool and collected as he had assumed.

Phyllis Kirby sat jammed tight in her seemingly tiny bucket seat. Sitting next to her, Jerrod Kirby had more room to move than his wife, only because there was a 150-pound difference in weight between them. He was like a slender, nimble catamaran, while she resembled a beamy river barge.

He would never dream of uttering such a comparison if she could hear him, of course: she reacted badly to people who commented on her weight. Jerrod had long ago learned to consider every word he said to her carefully. Bitter experience had taught him that colliding with a river barge could cause considerable damage.

Phyllis claimed that her metabolism went haywire every time she went on a diet. No matter her low-calorie regimen *du jour*, it only made her bigger and heavier. Jerrod seriously doubted whether it was purely her internal systems that had fashioned her into such a formidable battle-axe in recent years. He often caught her snacking every hour of the day while she was theoretically on a diet, and he suspected that she raided the fridge even more when he was away from home. But he had learned not to offer comments about that, either.

'Did you remember to bring my book?' she demanded to know.

'Yes, dear,' he said meekly.

Her firm, steady glare indicated that she wanted proof. In reply, Jerrod picked up the overnight bag tucked under the seat in front of him and retrieved her latest Danielle Steel. This he waved at her triumphantly, as if showing off a prize.

'See? Didn't I tell you?'

A low growling noise emanating from Phyllis's throat indicated conditional satisfaction. Jerrod knew all her sounds and the likely import of each. He knew when to tread carefully, and when he was permitted back in her favor.

His friends sometimes asked him to divulge the secret of their marriage. It was a question he could have answered with confidence when he knelt at the altar beside her. Now, twenty years later, she was simply the woman to whom he was committed. Nothing more, nothing less.

He tried not to notice that she had turned from a slender reed into a wide oak tree. Usually he was successful. He was resigned to her sudden shifts of moods, just as he accepted the variability of the weather. Sometimes it rained, sometimes it stormed. What was a man to do?

'I hate flying,' she griped.

Now she had her book, Phyllis moved on to the next item on her list of complaints.

'We'll have a great time in Australia,' he said in as pleasant a voice as he could manage.

'Sure,' she responded without enthusiasm. 'But first we get to spend twelve hours on a bloody plane. My butt already hurts and we're not even on the plane yet.'

Jerrod was tempted to point out that Phyllis was the one who had picked their destination. She always decided where they would spend their annual vacation. The two weeks in Australia they had booked were costing him an arm and a leg. If it had been up to him, their travel plans would have been a lot simpler and cheaper. It was what it was, but he sure as hell had no desire to listen to her grouse for hours about all her discomforts while crossing the Pacific. Nevertheless, he managed to restrain himself.

For better or for worse, Phyllis was his life. He *had* no other life.

Sometimes he dreamed of turning back the clock and standing with her at the altar again. Only this time, when the vicar asked his solemn question in his holier-than-thou tone, Jerrod would turn around and bolt down the aisle – as fast and as far away from her as he could.

But this was a pipe dream, an illusion, and nothing more. Unfortunately, time elapsed in an unrelenting straight line. On its way to inevitable destinations, always onward.

Just like flying.

One by one, the late arrivals among the 327 passengers for Flight 582 entered the stark waiting area enclosed by glass partitions. The large windows around the next security station, with a monitor overhead displaying the destination SYDNEY and the flight information, afforded a view of the white shape of the *Princess of the Pacific* parked at the end of the jetway.

The waiting area was filled with men, women, and children of all colors and descriptions. Among them was a gray-haired man in a checkered blue shirt and a fiftyish woman with short hair, without a strand of gray or white. For them, this trip to Sydney was the dream vacation they had anticipated for years. For a broad-shouldered man and his attractive fair-haired bride, Australia was their honeymoon destination. An Asian family – husband, wife, and two young sons – were planning to visit family.

When the boarding call was announced, Evelyn Hooks – a hefty woman who according to friend and foe alike was an unshakeable Dragon Lady – looked up.

'They're letting us on the plane,' she told her adopted daughter, Cassie, who was sitting beside her. Cassie was fourteen, slender to the point of being skinny, and short for her age. Her long dark-brown hair was tied back in a ponytail. She and her mother occupied seats in one of the last rows in the waiting area, and Evelyn kept a close eye on her. Not only was this Cassie's first flight, this was the first time in two years she was leaving the vicinity of Sugar Creek, a neighborhood which had gradually become a familiar place for her. Evelyn prayed there would be no trouble.

The passengers were invited to board. Business Class first, followed by parents with infants and young children, and anyone needing assistance. Evelyn remained seated with Cassie, waiting for their turn to join the line. Normally she would not have been nervous before a flight. But this time, for a reason she could not explain, she was. When the attractively uniformed employee announced that all other rows were now permitted to board, Evelyn stood and picked up her purse.

'Let's go,' she said to Cassie.

Cassie slowly rose to her feet. Evelyn took her by the hand and led her toward the boarding desk. Cassie glanced around skittishly, as if she was looking for an opening to make a run for it. Evelyn tightened her fingers around her thin wrist. With Cassie, you never knew what to expect.

Before they reached the desk, where two Oceans Airways employees were checking tickets, a man in uniform strode toward them, his eyes hard on Cassie. 'Young lady,' he said to her, 'would you come with me, please?'

Cassie stared back at him, with a look suggesting she had just been caught with her hand in the proverbial cookie jar.

'I'm her mother,' Evelyn said calmly. 'If you have any questions for my daughter, *I* will answer them.'

The man nodded. 'In that case, would you *both* please come with me?'

He gestured toward another desk, slightly set back from the line of passengers. Behind it stood two other men in uniform. If they had been singled out for an extra security check, they must have signaled something questionable. Although Evelyn had grown accustomed to such treatment, it still frustrated her. They stepped from the line.

As they did so, a burly security officer with a bald head stepped forward. 'What is your travel destination?' he demanded to know. He towered over her, and she felt pinned down by his piercing gaze.

'Sydney,' she said forthrightly.

'On business or pleasure?'

'Both,' Evelyn explained 'My daughter and I are attending a minerals exposition there. But we hope to travel about the area, too.'

'May I see some ID, please?'

Evelyn handed him her passport and Cassie's identification card.

'She's my adopted daughter,' she added, before the officer could ask.

She hoped the man wouldn't force her to tell him their entire life story. If he did, they would be here a while. She felt the curious glances of other passengers shuffling by behind her.

'How long will you be staying in Australia?'

'One week.'

'And what's your destination after that?'

'Back home to Los Angeles. We have round-trip tickets. Would you like to see them?'

'If it's no trouble.'

Evelyn showed him their tickets for the return flight.

'One moment, please,' the man said.

He handed their documents to the two men behind the counter, who spent several minutes checking the validity of her passport and Cassie's ID. It seemed to take forever for the men to be convinced that Evelyn Hooks and her adopted daughter had nothing to hide.

This time Cassie kept quiet while they waited. By the grace of God she did not make a scene. That was the very last thing Evelyn wanted right now. Another horrible scene.

At length the bald security officer waved them on. Their boarding passes were checked, and they walked down the gangway and boarded the plane. Their seats were located in the middle section of row 31, seats D and E.

As Evelyn stowed her purse in the luggage bin above her seat, she temporarily blocked the aisle for a flight attendant with long blonde hair, who waited patiently. Her task done, Evelyn moved aside, allowing the flight attendant to continue on her way. Which she did, but not before throwing Cassie a strange look similar to the one the security officer had given her a few minutes earlier in the terminal.

Let her have some peace, finally! Evelyn mused, her mood turning sour and angry.

She took her seat.

'Sit down, Cassie,' she said quietly, pulling on her daughter's arm, forcing her to sit down in the aisle seat.

Cassie complied, staring fixedly ahead, ignoring everyone. She pinched her lips into a tight line and made not a sound.

Evelyn settled in, saying nothing further. Her neighbor on the other side in seat F was a beautiful young woman with shoulder-length brown hair. The last seat in their row, seat G, remained unoccupied.

Evelyn prepared for the long flight. *Please God*, she silently prayed, *may Cassie see it through the next twelve hours, or however long the trip might take.*

'Everything's OK. I'm here,' Evelyn said to her daughter. She gave her a reassuring squeeze on the arm, but it did not have the desired effect. Cassie began glancing around furtively, casting nasty looks at passengers stowing their cabin luggage and taking their seats. She seemed frightened, petrified.

Evelyn sighed inwardly. What was it *this* time?

Sharlene was conducting a quick check to see if she could assist any of the passengers when that portly woman blocked the aisle. A young girl standing behind her, probably her daughter, suddenly turned and touched Sharlene briefly.

The girl moved her lips, murmuring something that Sharlene could not make out. She considered asking the girl what she had said, but thought better of it.

The mother, who couldn't have overheard her daughter, turned sideways to make room for Sharlene to pass. Sharlene maintained eye contact with the girl until the mother gave her a surly look, signaling her displeasure.

Although Sharlene found this odd, she decided to leave it be. A passenger down the aisle looked as if she required assistance. She was a short, heavy-set woman wearing a long black dress and an oversized pair of Ray-Bans, as if she were either a nun or a Goth in a midlife crisis. At least that was Sharlene's first impression. The woman clearly was too short to lift her cabin luggage up into the overhead bin.

Sharlene strode up to her. 'Do you need some help, madam?' she offered pleasantly.

The woman curled her lips. 'Thank you, I would appreciate that,' she said in a thin sing-song tone of voice. Sharlene could not see the woman's eyes. They were hidden behind the enormous pitch-black lenses of her sunglasses.

FOUR
Princess of the Pacific

The airplane dubbed *Princess of the Pacific* was 230 feet long from stem to stern, and almost as wide from wingtip to wingtip. Her skin was aluminum, and without fuel, cargo, and passengers she weighed 400,000 pounds. She could hold 63,400 gallons of fuel, and her maximum take-off weight was 800,000 pounds. Her nose, high above the ground, was awe-inspiring, even in the gathering dusk of the day. Coiled inside her belly were 170 miles of wiring and 5 miles of vein-like tubing. The first of her breed had flown in 1969, thirteen years after the death of her creator, William E. Boeing, founder of the Boeing Company.

The *Princess of the Pacific*, type 747-400, was ready for her next crossing of the ocean, on this run to Sydney, Australia. In the twelve years since her construction, she had transported hundreds of thousands of people to every corner of the world, across every sea and continent.

She had always been good to her passengers and had suffered few defects. On one memorable occasion, one of her four engines had stalled over the Atlantic Ocean. That had initiated a precautionary emergency landing at JFK Airport in New York. The passengers hadn't noticed anything amiss. After all, the plane could still fly smoothly with only two engines functioning.

Tonight, proud and ready, she was set to welcome yet another shipload of passengers.

'Start pushing in 330,000 pounds, but keep the fuel hose locked,' Jim Nichols told the fuel-truck driver, who was standing next to him in the cockpit. 'I have yet to determine exactly how much fuel we'll need.'

'Will do,' the man said, before turning and walking away.

Next, Jim received a visit from two LAX mechanics for a routine check of the 747-400 and to sign off on the technical manuals. After they left, Jim inspected the overhead panel inside the cockpit indicating the status of fuel, hydraulics, and air conditioning. He paid special attention to the flight instruments and the EICAS display. EICAS – an acronym for the Engine Indication and Crew Alerting System – supplied the pilots with information on engine power, speed, and temperatures. To the right of EICAS were red and yellow readings for details that still needed resolution. Protocol dictated that this screen had to be empty before the plane could take off. Greg's job was to ensure that it *was* empty.

The cockpit of a 747-400 houses two pilots: the commander and the copilot, also referred to as the first officer. The two pilots can hold the same rank – Jim Nichols and Greg Huffstutter were both captains – but during a flight there is a specific chain of command that has to be followed.

For today's flight, Oceans had appointed Jim commander, with primary responsibility for navigation and the autopilot. Greg would serve as the airplane's first officer; as such he was responsible for radio contact with air-traffic control as well as the internal equipment.

While Greg checked the systems, scrutinized the cockpit from top to bottom, and set the devices, Jim prepared their heading. Reserve pilot Ben Wright, meanwhile, stood by quietly, with no specific duties for the moment.

'I'll check on the refueling,' Jim said after they had reviewed the hydraulic system and oxygen levels, and activated the cockpit-window heating and the lighting inside the aircraft. Refueling did not demand supervision by the captain, but he had made a habit of being present, regardless. Every pilot had his own routines, and this was one of his.

Jim left the aircraft and stood beside the wing, watching as the fuel was pumped aboard. 'Add another 30,000 pounds,' he requested.

Every airline pilot understands that several factors are involved in the consumption of fuel on an airliner. Distance flown and the weight of the aircraft are critical factors, of course, but so is temperature. Airline fuel has a tendency to expand as it heats and can trickle out from the wings – a phenomenon that can frighten a passenger looking out a window. In winter, the tanks hold more fuel weight because the gallons contract.

The refueling finished, Jim went back inside the plane. His next job was setting the electrical system in the auxiliary power unit, a smaller engine in the tail of the aircraft which operates as a power generator. The APU also generates air to start the massive jet engines and to power the air-conditioning system.

The time was 8:25, twenty minutes before takeoff. Time for the cockpit briefing – another pre-flight routine. Some airlines dictate exactly what needs to be addressed in the briefing, but Oceans Airways was less formal and left it to the pilots to set the agenda. That pleased Jim, who preferred to tell his own story chronologically.

'OK, here's how I want it done,' he said to Greg and Ben. 'We've taken on 360,000 pounds of fuel, so we can leave as soon as everyone is on board and the doors have been closed. A pushback truck will push us . . .' He paused briefly. '. . . We haven't arranged for pushback yet, let's not forget to take care of that. During the pushback, we'll start the engines and taxi to 2-4 left. If a problem should arise, we abort before V_1, at 150 knots.'

He was referring to the threshold speed to abort a takeoff. At any speed below V_1 an aircraft can stop before takeoff if need be. At V_1 it is still possible to abort takeoff, but only for such emergencies as engine failure, a fire, or a configuration alert. The flaps may be positioned the wrong way, or the aircraft may pull in the wrong direction. Sharp braking during this phase can cause overheating in the brake discs, which in turn can melt the valves and deflate the tires. In such circumstances there is also the danger of a brake fire. After V_1 is attained, however, the pilot no longer has options: he *must* take off. An aborted takeoff above this critical speed renders the aircraft incapable of stopping before it reaches the end of the runway.

'Should we continue with an engine defect, we'll climb to 985 feet at V_2. Then we'll accelerate to 250 knots, pull up the flaps, and climb to a safe altitude of 2,000 feet. There, we'll see if we can fix the problem. If I decide to turn back, we'll climb to 5,000 feet to dump fuel over the ocean. If there are no problems after V_1, however, we'll first climb to 5,000 feet, then to cruise altitude of 30,000 feet. We'll take a westerly course toward Hawaii, across Tahiti, the Cook Islands, and Fiji. Then we'll pass the date line and fly on to Sydney. Weather reports confirm clear conditions except over the Cook Islands. There's a slow-moving typhoon in the area moving southward. Sustained winds are at 65 knots, so I'm expecting some heavy turbulence there.'

Jim had never experienced an aborted takeoff, but like most airline pilots he remained forever vigilant. Fate could come knocking at any time.

More predictable was the hassle with passengers. Late arrivals, drunks, missing suitcases: these and other mishaps just before takeoff could ruin the day of a cockpit crew member. Not unknown was a last-minute disagreement between the pilot, keen for departure, and the purser, the crew member responsible for the passengers.

When everyone in the passenger section was seated, and everything had been checked and rechecked, and the plane was ready for takeoff, Jim Nichols heaved a deep sigh of relief.

After the passengers were seated and the doors closed, the next hurdle was obtaining permission to depart from LAX tower. Jim Nichols estimated a delay with that. Since radar systems cannot cover the entire Pacific Ocean, planes have to fly further apart from each other. No matter the immeasurable size of the Pacific, its air routes can become congested.

The delay was only fifteen minutes. On the asset side of the ledger, boarding the passengers had proceeded more smoothly than expected. At 8:57, Flight 582 called Ground Control for clearance.

'Oceans Airways 5-8-2, cleared to proceed on the outer 2-4 left,' a crisp voice from the Control Tower informed them. 'Number three for departure.'

'Oceans 5-8-2,' Greg confirmed.

Jim activated the anti-collision signal and the hydraulics for the operation of the brakes, rudders, and nose wheel. As he flicked on a switch, the first doses of high quality aviation fuel began flowing into the engines. After deactivating the air conditioning in order to redirect power to help start the main engines, he made radio contact with the man in the pushback truck located beneath the nose wheel.

'Ready to roll.'

'Release brakes,' the man on the ground responded.

As the truck pushed the aircraft back, Greg Huffstutter pushed the starter button to initiate the engine. Jim, meanwhile, reviewed the after-start checklist with Greg. Once the aircraft was pushed back, it was on its own. It would now have to make the balance of the long journey to Sydney under its own steam. Jim started taxiing from Delta to Echo 8 and stopped at holding position Victor 2-4 left.

The first plane in line, a United 737, turned right on to the active runway and took off with a roar of engines. When the second aircraft, an American Airlines 757, rolled into position at takeoff point for runway 24, Greg switched to tower frequency and clicked his mic button twice. As the 757 started its takeoff roll, the tower called in. 'Oceans 5-8-2 taxi into position and hold.'

'Oceans 5-8-2,' Greg acknowledged.

Moments later, the tower controller informed Oceans 582 that it was cleared for takeoff. 'Climb to 900 feet before you start your turn.'

'Oceans 5-8-2,' Greg repeated.

Suddenly Jim felt a wave of disease roil his intestines. He had felt that way earlier in the day, but this was the first time he had experienced such a sensation once inside the cockpit. He couldn't explain what it was or what had caused it. But of this he felt certain: for the first time in his aviation career he did not want to fly.

Acting on automatic, he pushed the thrust lever forward, and the plane picked up speed.

'V_1,' Jim said. 'Lift-off.'

The 747 accelerated and started its climb.

Despite a flawless takeoff, Jim was restless as he switched to climb power at 1,000 feet. Gradually he accelerated to 250 knots, the maximum speed below 10,000 feet. At that level he increased speed to 375 knots, the most economical climb rate. Subsequently, he increased the speed with the same power to compensate for the lower density of air molecules higher up in the increasingly thin air. His airspeed indicator read 260 knots, but the true ground speed of the 747 had by now increased to 400 knots. Sixty miles into their 7,500-mile journey to Sydney they were flying at their final cruise speed: Mach 0.84.

The *Princess of the Pacific,* the pride of Oceans Airways, flew steadily away from the west coast of the United States on a south-westward course across the vast and often tempestuous Pacific Ocean, bound for the east coast of Australia.

FIVE
Airborne

From the crew's perspective, the bulk of what needed to be done aboard the *Princess of the Pacific* had been done by the start of the flight. And after the passengers were served dinner and their trays were collected, members of the crew had time to relax a little. While the cabin crew tidied up the main galley, where Sharlene was stationed, tongues were wagging.

Alexandra Goldmacher started it. A friend of hers had planned to get married in a few weeks, but when her husband-to-be confessed to having an affair with another woman, the wedding was summarily cancelled.

'She had everything ready,' Alexandra explained to her female colleagues hanging on her every word. 'Her wedding dress, the rings, *everything*.' What Alexandra said, of course, spawned further dialogue about the fickleness of men.

Sharlene kept her distance until Alexandra made a show of telling Sharlene that *she* at least seemed to have found her soulmate in Aaron. Alexandra had been single for a year now, and until recently had been casting lustful eyes at the purser. Aaron could easily have fallen for her because Alexandra, who bore a sharp resemblance to the singer Shakira, was an attractive representative of the gentler sex.

'I hope so,' Sharlene said evasively. 'I've had my fill of cheating boyfriends.'

Yeah, sure! Alexandra's jealous eyes said.

But Sharlene was not exaggerating.

Todd Bower had been a monster. He hadn't seemed a bad sort at first, but then at first men like that rarely do. Sharlene had been attracted to Todd and had seriously considered him the love of her life. One morning he left early for work at a small transport company he owned. It was a one-man business, and his pride and joy was his brand new Ram Van 2.5 High Roof. That morning, while Sharlene was still in her nightgown in his apartment, the doorbell rang.

She opened the door to find a pretty girl on the doorstep who introduced herself as Kristin. The girl had fiery-red hair, a perky freckled nose, cloud-white teeth, and a look that suggested she could take on the world and any man in it.

But she was not alone. In the crook of her arm she held a small female child. That cute little bundle of joy turned out to be Todd's daughter.

Kristin had no qualms about telling Sharlene about her affair with Todd. What it boiled down to, she claimed, was that Todd was an unholy bastard who had run out on her and their daughter Tina and refused to give them a dime in child support. She had been keeping an eye on her ex-lover, and it had not escaped her notice that he had found a new girlfriend. Kristin's intention was not to drive them apart, she insisted. She wanted no part of the son of a bitch. She just wanted Sharlene to know what kind of reprobate she was sleeping with.

When Todd returned home that evening, Sharlene told him about Kristin's visit. Todd responded with a dismissive wave of his hand. His ex was his ex, he scoffed. It was over and that was all he had to say on the subject. Sharlene, however, had more to say. She informed him in no uncertain terms that this was something they *needed* to talk about. How could she trust him if he kept secrets like this from her?

He, in turn, insisted there was no need for her to keep nagging about it, because for him Kristin was history.

But what about Tina, your daughter? she had cried out. *You can't in good conscience abandon your own child. Do you even have a conscience?*

That got his dander up. He yelled at her that it was none of her damn business, it was all in the past, and he didn't want to open old sores.

Fuming, Sharlene snatched her car keys from the kitchen counter and yelled back that if *he* wouldn't talk, *she* would walk. She would go to see Kristin to ask her what kind of a man Todd Bower really was. She had intended to use her threat as a crowbar, to force him to open up to her. The fact that he had a child might be an unpleasant surprise, but it need not cause a break-up if he pledged to be honest with her from then on. She still loved him, or so she thought.

What happened next forced a sudden change of heart. Todd

ordered her to stay put and shut up. When she replied that he had no business speaking to her in that manner or telling her what to do, he hit her – a lashing violent whack across her face.

After Sharlene had been beaten by her father, she had vowed that no man would ever hit her again. Without another word, she left the house and drove away, forever, from Todd Bower.

But he had not accepted her decision. He called her at all hours of the day and night to say he was sorry. Sometimes he appeared on her doorstep in the middle of the night and rang the doorbell over and over again. That was when her nightmares started.

And then everything had gone terribly wrong.

That was six years ago. Sharlene had been nineteen, still a girl. That was how she regarded herself at that time: a girl who had been forced to walk through hell and back. But what she had experienced so far was but a prelude to Todd's final act of vengeance.

This night, however, she saw no purpose in expanding on her story. Let Alexandra go on thinking she was exaggerating. Sharlene didn't care.

After six hours in flight, Aaron Drake was still busily occupied in Business Class. Passengers kept pressing the crew alert button, summoning him to fetch them another beer, or a glass of wine or water.

Aaron was working the shift alone, waiting for Mara to relieve him so he could snatch a few hours of shut-eye before it was time to serve breakfast. He walked over to the passenger who had just paged him, a short man in a brown suit sitting in seat 78A.

'How may I help you, sir?' he asked the passenger politely.

The man picked up the little wine bottle from his tray table and wrinkled his nose, 'This Chardonnay is stale,' he groused.

Aaron fought an urge to take the bottle and sniff the wine. He restrained himself, however, because the customer was always right – a principle of salesmanship that his training had drummed into him. He looked down on the balding pate of the passenger and was reminded of another diminutive screen-hothead, the actor Danny DeVito.

Some people claimed Aaron had a woman's job. Others said he was basically a high-end waiter. The former claim was untrue, the latter absurd. Safety is the first priority for any member of the cabin crew. If any member of a flight crew failed an intense safety exam administered each year, his or her career was over. No exceptions.

Aaron, who had launched his own career on a 737, had moved on to a 767 and had been purser on that type of plane for more than a year. He took his job seriously, and those who flew with him respected him for his professional demeanor.

This Danny DeVito look-alike obviously saw him as nothing more than a dumb waiter.

'I'll get you a new bottle,' Aaron assured him.

'You do that,' the short man snorted. 'Drinking sour wine is unacceptable.'

'Yes, sir,' Aaron said obligingly.

'And while I'm at it,' the man ranted on, 'I've had far better meals on board airplanes. Obviously, Oceans is not doing so well. Other airlines still know the meaning of service.'

Although Aaron was getting annoyed, he realized the man had a point. Oceans Airways was not a luxury airline, and was in danger of being further minimized by the bigger players. The airways were filling up, and Aaron would not be surprised if Oceans ended up crushed in the throng or being sold.

'Shall I take this bottle away?' he asked.

'Good plan, my boy.'

Flight 582 had started out as a routine flight. At two o'clock in the morning only the dimmed cabin lights were left on. Passengers who were still awake amused themselves with a book or with programs on the entertainment screens secured in the backrests of the seats in front of them. They watched movies; someone was playing a game of blackjack against the computer; a bearded man with a thick chain around his neck was engrossed in a religious book. The wide-shouldered man and his fair-haired wife talked about what they were going to do in Sydney. He wanted to see the sights, whereas she was more interested in the beaches. The Asian father patiently answered a barrage of questions from his youngest son, who could not seem to sleep and wanted to know everything about planes and how they stayed up in the sky. To the crew members servicing these people, it seemed a flight like any other.

Sharlene Thier was in a bed in the crew bunk, a section in the back of the plane that served as a rest area for staff. The gray canvas over her head, with its zipper closure, created the illusion that she was inside a small tent. The section held eight beds, and all of them were occupied. It also held a few seats with entertainment screens like the ones afforded the passengers. Until the final two hours before landing, the crew had little to do. Sharlene called this phase of a long, intercontinental flight 'the dead hours.' Her sleeping bag was no luxury, but it did offer a degree of privacy. Beside her on the blanket, always within reach like a child's teddy bear, was her small black flashlight, spreading an aura of protective light. Feeling safe and tucked in, at least for the moment, Sharlene yawned and folded her hands behind her neck.

Sleep did not come easily, however. She was fretting. *Why*, she could not determine; but she knew it was precisely what she should *not* be doing.

In her perception of things, as a child Sharlene had been a caterpillar. Now, finally, she had become a young butterfly, hesitantly testing her wings to fly, occasionally crashing back down to earth. That had happened again just before she and Aaron left her house, when the heel of her shoe came undone. Then, on the plane, Alexandra had started going on about men and why they could not be trusted. She and Sharlene had never gotten along, and tonight Alex had managed to reawaken memories of Todd. The memories had stirred up dust clouds of toxic misery. After that, the dreaded fretting and stewing had settled over her. Sharlene tried to push the negativity away by focusing her mind on the positive things that had happened to her in recent years. She had applied for a job at Oceans Airways and, lo and behold, they had hired her. Today she was succeeding in ways she could only have dreamed about just a few years ago. She had climbed the career ladder with surprising speed. At the still young age of twenty-five, she was already an assistant purser on a 747. Outside work her life could still be fairly chaotic, she realized only too well. Aaron, too, had noticed her penchant for turmoil on the home front. But once on board an aircraft, a professional with a job to do, she deliberately set herself apart from the other flight attendants, some of whom were scornfully referred to as 'schoolgirls' by the pilots.

Aaron had proven himself immune to Alexandra's temptations. For months he had bombarded Sharlene with phone calls and text messages, and he had done everything in his power to make their shifts coincide whenever possible.

His attentions had flattered her, of course, but she had not let him sweep her off her feet. Every time she felt her heart succumbing to his charms, her brain reminded her of Todd Bower and the misery he had brought to her life. And there were other obstacles in the way of a serious relationship. On the outside there seemed to be nothing wrong with her. But beneath the surface swam dark memories, including the day when, like a bolt from the blue, she had lost her mother.

But two months ago, after she and Aaron had celebrated his thirtieth birthday in a bar in Tokyo, she had gone with him to his hotel room. That night her conviction that she was not yet ready for a new relationship vanished like dust in the wind. Suddenly it had seemed silly to put her life on hold. He was so handsome and kind, and he smelled so wonderful. His intoxicating Armani scent had sabotaged the last bolts on her internal brake system.

Standing before him, she had unabashedly unbuttoned her shirt and removed her bra. Smiling at his stupefaction and obvious appreciation, she had continued her striptease, opening the buttons on her jeans one by one and letting her fingers slide beneath her white panties.

'Do something, Aaron,' she had murmured. 'For God's sake, *do* something.'

He did, with a frenzy and need and passion that had surprised them both.

Since then, their love affair had been stormy and wonderful. She prayed it would never lose its allure. If only it could always stay the way it was now, she sighed, as she glanced around her cramped quarters on the 747.

On the other side of the canvas, beyond the glow of her flashlight, it was dark. Darkness was bad. Darkness could hurt people.

Sharlene felt for the crucifix on her necklace, and once she found it clasped it firmly.

Quiet imbued the cockpit after Jim signed off from the LAX air-traffic control tower twenty minutes after takeoff and had made initial contact with Oakland Center. They had reached their cruising altitude and speed, and *Princess* was flying on autopilot.

What Jim had told Ben Wright, and only him, was that he was about to quit his job. No more long flights for him, he said. Instead, he would find a different kind of job closer to home – in order to save his marriage. Jim had also told Ben that he had made his decision a year ago. But he hadn't acted on it yet because that decision would signal a drastic change in his life. Jim, Ben was aware, did not handle change very well. In that respect he was like Greg. Especially when it involved change that would turn his life upside down.

He needed time to sort out the implications for himself, he had told Ben. If he gave up his career, Jody and the children would not leave him. But the downside was equally clear in his mind. He loved his job – it was as simple as that.

These two sides of him had continuously crossed swords with each other, and it was damned exhausting. It ate at him constantly.

In his mind, quitting this job was the moral equivalent of giving up. Not only did he enjoy flying more than anything else he did, he would also be forsaking everything he had worked so hard for. At one time he had been Oceans Airways' youngest 747 captain. His father had beamed with pride. In his golden years, Larry Nichols had been the epitome of competition. He had set up a supermarket chain of forty stores in California and Arizona. He had called his livelihood 'Nice', and his motto was 'Nice Prices, Nice to Shop'. When Larry opened his first small grocery store in Los Angeles in 1974, he had given the name and slogan three seconds of deliberation. *The only thing I needed to do was add one letter behind the first three letters of my last name*, Jim had heard his father telling people countless times. His first store expanded, soon to be followed by a second outlet, then two more, and then four. His was a classic success story. 'Nice Prices, Nice to Shop' became a household slogan in Los Angeles, San Francisco, and Phoenix.

Larry had accepted early on that his son Jim needed to find his own way – Jim's brothers Steve and Jack had succeeded their father in his business – but he would never accept Jim telling him, in effect, that he was about to cut his own throat. Jim loved his father, and he never doubted he was the source of his own competitive spirit.

So why cut his own throat? Why quit? *He* didn't want to. It was only because Jody insisted.

Did he love her enough to give up his career? At first he could not ask himself that question without a keen sense of shame. Shouldn't it be self-evident for his family to take precedence over his job?

But as time went on, he had felt less ashamed.

Would his fights with Jody truly end when he had an office job and came home for dinner every evening? Was the source of their problems his being away from home so often for his job?

No. If he were honest with himself, he would admit that this was no longer about Jody.

Of greater importance were his daughters, Cara and Natalie. He did not want to lose his children. That, to him, was his top priority no matter what everyone said, including his father.

Jim had told Ben Wright about these worries during a recent flight to Asia. Should he continue down the road he was on, or change direction? He needed to make a decision. But his doubts kept nagging at him. In recent months he had been sleeping poorly, his mind plagued by stress.

Yesterday, the situation had taken a turn for the worse. That was something he hadn't told Ben yet.

The situation had taken a turn for the worse. That was one way of putting it, Jim thought to himself. Another way to put it was to say he had lost everything.

Two days ago he had thought the situation could not possibly get worse. Yesterday had proven him wrong. Things *could* get worse. A lot worse.

SIX

Behind the Door

She was inside the Tupperware room. Shelving along the walls held multiple rows of brightly colored bowls, pots, and pans. The only furnishings in the dimly lit room were a table and a few chairs. In front of the only window, a curtain was drawn.

Suddenly the floor and walls started shaking as though the building had been beset by an earthquake. Tupperware bowls and containers started tumbling down from the shelves around her. Feeling herself fall, she searched frantically for a pathway to salvation.

What was happening? Her brain demanded answers, but her body had frozen. Panic surged within her. Then she saw the door and heard a hollow pounding against it from the outside.

It seemed as if a bull on the other side was repeatedly charging the door and butting it with his massive head.

The room shook and trembled, Tupperware was strewn everywhere, bouncing around in all directions. But worse was that the door was being thrashed with inhuman violence. She shuffled backwards, wanting nothing more than to curl up in a fetal position.

After one last horrific bash, the lock gave way and the door flew open.

Behind it, she saw black darkness.

Nothing else. No person, no beast, no physical force of any kind. Nothing that she could see.

But she immediately sensed that she was not alone anymore.

They're here, she realized. And the thought paralyzed her. She started shivering violently.

A scream tore from her throat before it dawned on her she was not in that room. She was somewhere else.

She was lying supine in bed on board the *Princess of the Pacific*. A sweaty sheen prickled her brow as she blinked up at her surroundings. *Did I actually scream?* she asked herself. She thought she had. Her throat felt sore.

She was still shaking, but so was the airplane. They had apparently reached the area of heavy turbulence. She heard other people crying out and then noises that resembled minor explosions. *What the hell is going on?* she wondered.

Sharlene gripped the bedrail with one hand and unzipped the canvas with the other. She found her small black flashlight. Cautiously she poked her head out into the companionway and saw her fellow crew members, who had also been rudely awakened by the turbulence and were wondering the same thing. Nicky and Alexandra gave her a worried look.

Sharlene glanced down and saw the top of Ray Jacobstein's head. Had he heard her scream? Apparently not, since he was not looking up at her.

'Good God, it's so bumpy!' Nicky said, the concern in her voice evident. 'I've never seen it this bad.'

Sharlene nodded. Her main concern was simply to hang on tight to avoid being hurled out of her bunk.

Jim Nichols' voice came on the public-address system.

'Ladies and gentlemen, this is your captain speaking. We have entered an area of strong turbulence. We should be out of it shortly. I apologize for the inconvenience. For your safety and for the safety of those around you, please remain in your seats until further notice and keep your seat belts securely fastened.'

With that, he signed off.

'Let's hope he's right,' Nicky said. 'The part about being out of this soon.'

Sharlene thought of Aaron. She didn't see him in his bunk. Was he still at work?

She glanced around the area. 'I'm going to check on the passengers,' she said to her colleagues.

'I'd wait until it smooths out a bit, if I were you,' Nicky cautioned. She was a sweet girl, still happy with her childhood sweetheart, Raoul, whose name brought to mind a dark-haired stud with bronzed skin. Nicky was modest and, unlike Alexandra, she didn't talk much about anything, including Raoul. So Sharlene could only imagine what he looked like. She admired Nicky simply because the young woman was discreet, considerate, graceful, and never caused any problems. Sharlene had often thought what she would give to claim those traits for herself.

She had to admit that Nicky's suggestion made sense. But this severe turbulence, coupled with that wretched nightmare, made her bunk feel every bit as constricting as her small attic space at home. She felt hemmed in by the dark, trapped by it. She *needed* to get out.

'Perhaps,' she said. 'But I'm going to go check anyway.'

Sharlene switched off her flashlight, wriggled into her uniform jacket, and slid from the bunk on to the floor. Carefully balancing herself, she fought her way down the steps between the bunks and the cabin, and then paused at the rear of the Tourist Class section.

She heard the murmur of voices and wondered which passengers needed reassurance. Surely some did. Few veteran fliers would have experienced this degree of turbulence; she couldn't imagine what novice fliers must be thinking. She heard a baby crying, but to her amazement the passengers seemed quite calm. Maybe they were on autopilot, she mused, too frightened to call out.

Sharlene decided to look for Aaron despite the incessant bumping and shaking impeding her progress. Stoically, she pulled herself forward by grasping the headrests of passenger seats.

The aircraft groaned from the pounding it was taking. She kept hearing rolling noises, like the echoes of distant gunfire.

It was dark inside the cabin, *too* dark. The passengers were shadows. Most of the entertainment-system screens were blank.

Her fear of the dark – what her therapist, Dr Noel Richardson, had referred to as *nyctophobia* – threatened to overwhelm her. Her fears were irrational, she realized, but that mattered naught. As Dr Richardson had explained, hers was a mental condition that affected both children and adults, and it wasn't so much the darkness she feared as what the darkness might conceal.

His diagnosis was spot on, Sharlene realized. After all these years, she still couldn't sleep in an unlit room. And she couldn't sleep at all without her flashlight. It had taken Aaron some getting used to. But what he could never imagine, even after nine weeks of sleeping together, was the depth of her fear of the dark and the mental images it conjured up.

What was it about the dark that threatened her? he must be wondering. What upset her so much? The only answer that would make sense to Aaron was the horror of what Todd Bower had done to her. Dr Richardson had drawn the same conclusion. But that relationship had ended years ago.

Aaron had tried his best to be sympathetic. Their love was new – they were in a kind of honeymoon period when a partner's short-comings are easily overlooked. But how much longer could he continue to act so benignly toward a fear that deep down he considered to be childish? When would the reproaches begin?

He didn't yet know about the other horrors she had had to endure, beyond those from her father and former boyfriend. If she came clean about *that*, it might mean the end of their budding relationship. For her part, she knew Aaron well enough to guess how he would react if she told him the whole truth, and she didn't want to destroy the joy they had found together.

So she had been quiet about her fears to the extent possible. She had never told him what *she* feared was the source of her nyctophobia.

Fierce turbulence kept torturing the plane, causing it to lurch and tremble as if it were fighting for its life. That Sharlene was not cowering in a corner, terrified that they were going to crash, was another character trait she owed to Noel Richardson. 'Dare to live again' had been his motto for her and the basis of his treatment plan. In the end, this was what had made her apply for a job as a flight attendant, following in her mother's footsteps, something she had at one time believed she did not have the courage to do.

Sharlene took a deep breath and slowly exhaled. Breathing exercises. One of the fruits of her therapy sessions.

Don't overthink things, nothing is real, it's all groundless anxiety.

It may be another of the doctor's old wives' sayings, but it did help ease her mind at times such as these.

She walked deliberately forward until she reached the seat of the girl who had touched her during boarding and mumbled something to her. The child's eyes were riveted on her. She was *staring*.

Sharlene hesitated, expecting the girl to say something.

But her pale lips remained pressed together in determined silence.

Sharlene nodded at her and continued on, stumbling forward through the bucking and lurching aircraft.

SEVEN

Anxieties

Until 2:15 the Boeing had been like a fish swimming through calm water, but their smooth ride had suddenly unraveled when the aircraft flew into an area of extreme turbulence. A passenger who happened to be in the lavatory was shoved forward against the bulkhead then backward against the door, causing him to temporarily black out. Passengers who were asleep were rudely awakened. Some passengers, dazed, stared around with a blank look. Others gripped the arms of their chair so hard their knuckles turned white. Not a few fought to stave off abject terror.

Emilio Cabrera, sitting in seat number 59H, was one of those flirting with panic. Sharlene shuffled past him, unaware that he could lay claim to his own unique brand of anxiety.

Emilio hated flying. He felt extreme trepidation before any flight, but he had never experienced such dread as before this flight. That dread was worse, to him, than what awaited him in Sydney.

His problem with planes was simple: the damn things could go down. It was an undeniable fact, since he had experienced it first-hand.

Three years ago he had been on board a Learjet 45 leased by his employer. Something had gone terribly awry during the landing. Suddenly Emilio had felt a jarring impact. Flames had raged through the cabin. He had tried crawling toward an exit, but the blinding, suffocating smoke from the fire had overwhelmed him.

He had come to in hospital, where a doctor informed him that he had survived – unlike two other passengers, customers of his employer – because a rescue worker had dragged him from the burning wreckage seconds before the Learjet exploded. Emilio realized how incredibly lucky he had been. That day, for the first time in years, he prayed to God, to thank Him for his survival.

Ever since then he had suffered from recurring nightmares, in which he was surrounded by a thick, oppressive darkness unlike anything he had experienced. Emilio could not shake the conviction that the dreams were a memory from the crash and that the darkness represented the Hereafter, which he had actually visited for a brief period.

After his miraculous rescue Emilio had developed not only a fear of flying, but also a keen interest in plane crashes. His research confirmed that although there were many reasons why a plane might crash, human error was by far the biggest contributing factor. The technology was fairly reliable; bad things often happened because people handled the technology incorrectly. A botched repair job by a mechanic or an error in pilot judgment – the cause of the worst plane crash in history, on the island of Tenerife in the 1970s – or some other type of momentary inattention to a critical detail could sow the seeds of tragedy and cause untold human suffering.

Emilio had survived takeoff, the first of two critical phases during every flight, by nervously chewing on his fingernails. The second critical phase, landing, was still some six hours away.

But there was another reason for his crushing sense of dread: the tribunal awaiting him once he arrived in Sydney. If his enemies convicted him, he would be carrion for the vultures.

That image, he realized, was slightly exaggerated, but it was how he felt. In Australia he would stand trial. And when the trial was over, he would, at best, be wiped out financially. His entire existence would be shattered. But he was convinced he was innocent and by God he would prove it. He deserved none of this.

He was headed to the Almar Corporation's main office in Sydney, his first time traveling in Tourist Class, a step down from his normal Business Class ticket. But that's how it was for him these days. The only thing he had done wrong – the crime of which he was accused – was to siphon some money from a corporate account into his own bank account. Just because he was a bit short on cash. All he had wanted to do was solve a *problem*, nothing more, nothing less. A *temporary* problem, a passing predicament of a financial nature. It had always been his intention to repay the money as soon as he had put some meat back on his bones, so to speak.

For the life of him, he could not understand why the corporate accountant had given him such a hard time about this small loan. Apparently he had done something horrendous, and Emilio had the niggling suspicion that he had not been summoned to Sydney simply to be brought to account. He might well lose his job because of this presumed misdeed.

He couldn't imagine why this loan – which, granted, may not have been entirely legitimate – should have had such far-reaching consequences. He had worked his ass off for the Almar Corporation for years, and the company had done very well from him. The only thing he had asked in return was a little understanding now that he found himself in financial straits.

Besides, a little sympathy wasn't much to ask, considering that he had almost sacrificed his life for the company when the Learjet crashed.

What if he ended up unemployed? What then? At the ripe age of fifty-two he was accustomed to a comfortable lifestyle, as was his wife. He doubted that many companies out there would be eager to hire a financial director who had been booted out of his former company on fraud charges. He was too old to start a new gig and, if convicted, his reputation would be too tarnished. He would be passé, a man on his way down, a corporate pariah.

For Emilio, the turbulence made him feel as though he was on a rollercoaster ride in a cart that had flown off its tracks. His armpits were wet with perspiration and he could smell his own rank body odor.

He was convinced the plane was going down – and *that* would make the decision of the tribunal in Sydney a moot point.

Well, he thought with sardonic humor, at least it would mean one less thing to worry about.

Sharlene walked past seat 39K, occupied by the woman she had helped stow her cabin luggage at the start of the flight. The woman, who appeared to Sharlene to be either a nun or an aging Goth, was named Mrs Ramagan. People seldom addressed her by her first name because most people did not know her first name. She was, however, a well-known figure in Santa Ana, a community in Orange County, California. She always dressed in black. Another one of her fixtures was a pair of black Ray-Bans – her current pair had almost worn out – because she was hypersensitive to light. She depended on them because, according to the eye specialists she had consulted, she had an aggressive form of actinic conjunctivitis, an inflammation of the eye caused by prolonged exposure to ultraviolet rays. There had been quite a few specialists over the years, and they had tried a variety of ointments, liniments, and other remedies on her. But none of these so-called remedies had improved the redness and swelling around her eyes. She had finally decided to try to live with her condition, and she and her Ray-Bans had become inseparable.

Mrs Ramagan was stout in build and less than five feet tall. She weighed 128 pounds, which would not have been excessive had she not been so compact. As with many woman her age, her weight was concentrated around her waistline and hips, making her look inelegant in the extreme.

Citizens in her community thought she led a lonely life in her spartan home filled with crucifixes, depictions of the Virgin Mary, and stately votive candles. But that's not how she saw it. She had her virtues, her Bible, and a deep spiritual connection with Jesus Christ. In every facet of her life Mrs Ramagan felt blessed, especially in her volunteer work for the disabled at an assisted-living home.

People loved her there, because her prayers produced results for them. Sick people got better – thanks to her faith in Jesus Christ. Even her sister, Esther, had become suddenly free of the rheumatism that had plagued her life for decades.

Unfortunately, despite the blessing of a pain-free life, her sister did not share her deep faith. Esther had a college degree. She had always been the smart one. She had such a highly developed brain, in fact, that she couldn't ever explain to Mrs Ramagan *what* she had studied without resorting to extremely complicated terms and convoluted sentences. That it had something to do with economics was all Mrs Ramagan could glean from their discussions.

She and Esther had engaged in many heated debates about religion. Esther refused to believe that the Lord could work miracles. Time and again Mrs Ramagan summed up the miracles she had witnessed in person, including the greatest of them all when the Lord had saved her life. At the age of twenty-four, Mrs Ramagan had fallen seriously ill with a rare type of virus. She had lapsed into a coma, and had found out later that her doctors had essentially given up on her. To their great surprise, however, she had awakened and recovered, remembering nothing from the coma except for a luminescent figure who had appeared before her and emitted a warm, healing brilliance. It had to have been a divine intervention. After her miraculous recovery she had become very devout. The Lord had saved her life for a purpose: so that she could devote herself to Him.

Esther had told her it was a wonderful story, but she insisted it was nothing more than a coincidence. She attributed *all* good things that happened to coincidence, even the cure of her rheumatism. Mrs Ramagan felt her sister was being rather ungrateful, but she didn't want to press the issue and have a falling-out with her.

No matter how smart she was, Esther knew nothing about theology. She had been an atheist her entire life. Mrs Ramagan regretted that she would never share God's love and redemption with the only person in the world she truly loved.

Actually, not the only person.

Not anymore.

Mrs Ramagan had sinned. She had let herself be tempted by someone other than the Lord.

The man's name was Bob Fletcher, and he had been a patient at the home where she volunteered. Bob was restricted to a wheelchair and was a few years older than she. The first time she met this dear man, she had invested considerable time chatting with him and had enjoyed every minute of it. Since that first day, she and Bob had gotten along famously.

They had been seeing each other for six months when something happened that Mrs Ramagan could not have imagined even in her most secret dreams. That night, when she was inside his room to tend to him, he had locked the door. Then he started to undress her.

Mrs Ramagan had been utterly confused. He had done things to her that she had only seen in the magazines and television shows she tried so religiously to avoid. If she happened to stumble on a lurid or even suggestive scene, she would quickly turn the page or change the channel. She had always thought that such intimacies – were they ever to happen to her, God forbid – would be reprehensible and highly unpleasant. But the truth turned out to be surprisingly different.

The naked truth was that she had had sex. Afterwards, she hadn't slept for days and she had studiously avoided Bob. He kept calling her until she finally relented. She agreed to see him one more time, but just to tell him that they had made a terrible mistake and that there was no future for them.

But their visit ended in another round of passionate sex, and when Mrs Ramagan returned home that night she realized even more acutely, and with great abhorrence, that she had very much enjoyed the experience. Never before had she felt anything like it. Her brain had crossed swords with her heart. Horrified by her lustful desires, she swore on all that was holy that she would be faithful to God, who had blessed her so bountifully all her life. And she prayed more frequently and with more emotion, begging the Lord to forgive her sins of the flesh.

On one occasion she had discussed her dilemma with Esther, who promptly applauded her and gushed how *wonderful* this was. Her sister, with a man? Apparently miracles *did* happen, she had avowed, smiling broadly.

'Esther, don't say that,' Mrs Ramagan had said worriedly. 'This is not right at all.'

But instead of helping her back on to the straight and narrow, Esther wanted to hear more about Bob. What kind of a man was he? What did he look like? Was he good to her? And was he good in bed?

Mrs Ramagan had blushed furiously and had not deigned to

answer any of these questions. She had gone to see Bob one final time, firmly resolved to bring an end to her sinning, but that third encounter had predictably spun out of control. She had lain in Bob's bed again, completely disrobed, abandoning herself to girlish pleasures and passions. The worst of it was that the harder she tried to push him away, the more loving Bob became and the faster her heart beat for him. He suggested that they move in together, that with her help he would no longer be confined to the nursing home. His legs might not be in the best of shape, but his other body parts would work just fine for years to come, he assured her with a smile.

After she returned home that time, she decided that she needed to be ever more rigorous in her faith if she were to redeem herself in the eyes of the Lord. That she had fallen in love with Bob she regarded as an act of weakness and sin.

So to her mind it was no coincidence when a few days later she noticed an advertisement in the *Los Angeles Times* for a position as a missionary in Australia working with the aboriginals. Mrs Ramagan had immediately applied for the job and she had been accepted. Devastated, she had said goodbye to her patients and to Bob – who had shaken his head and cried, unable to understand why she would do such a thing.

Today, on the *Princess of the Pacific*, she was on her way to her new job. She hoped that a few months in Australia would cleanse her heart and mind of impure thoughts and convince God to forgive her.

But despite her constant prayer, she saw signs everywhere that the Lord remained disappointed in her. This turbulence the airplane was experiencing seemed to be one such sign. It was as if He had taken the aircraft in His grip and was shaking it, to remind her once again that, verily, her sins had been great.

She leaned toward the right, removed her sunglasses, and peered out the window. Despite the darkness, the glow of a nearly full moon highlighted, in stark detail, the wing shaking severely.

And she saw someone standing on top of it.

Mrs Ramagan leaned sideways until her nose bumped the small window pane.

She clearly saw a black figure, ramrod straight. He did not seem the least bit hampered by the streaming wind or the buckling wing.

Mrs Ramagan crossed herself: once, twice, three times.

The plane gave another fierce shudder, causing her nose to rub painfully against the window pane. She closed her eyes for a moment, and when she opened them again the figure was gone.

Mrs Ramagan kept her gaze riveted on the wing. Was what she had supposedly seen another symptom of her eye problems?

Sharlene made it into the galley on the upper deck, staggering and lurching as though she were drunk. Braced against the bulkhead to keep from falling, Aaron reached out his arms, caught her, and brought her to him in an awkward embrace.

'It's pretty fierce,' he said.

'You can say that again,' she agreed.

'It's pretty fierce,' he repeated with a grin.

'Jesus,' she admonished, holding on to him. 'We have a comedian on board. How can you joke around at a time like this?'

'For the joy of seeing you,' he said, and then kissed her quickly in the turbulence. 'It'll be over soon. Are you OK?'

'Not really,' she said, clasping hold of her necklace, her symbol of strength. The necklace had belonged to her mother, Claudia Thier, who had worn it on every flight except the one that killed her. Her mother had been given the necklace by *her* mother – Sharlene's grandmother, Beth – and so the heirloom, the only physical remembrance Sharlene had of her mother, had been in their family for three generations.

'My shift is almost over,' he said. 'Wasn't this supposed to be your break?'

She nodded. 'Yes, but I couldn't stay in bed any longer. Who's coming to relieve you?'

'Mara. She's probably waiting for the turbulence to settle. I hope so. There's not much any of us can do for the moment.'

The plane sank into another air pocket, and as he grasped Sharlene more firmly he caught a whiff of her lilac perfume. His hands slid down to her buttocks and he kissed her neck.

She felt cold to his touch. Her entire body was tense.

'You're not liking this at all, are you?'

It was an inane question, she thought: the answer was so obvious. He too was having trouble standing upright.

Perhaps there was no need to worry, but she was worried anyway.

'I'm sure it'll be over soon,' Aaron repeated over the clatter of trolleys and dishes in the galley. He hoped his voice sounded reassuring.

'Sure,' she mumbled, listless.

He frowned. 'Sharlene?'

She averted her eyes. 'It's nothing. I just had that nightmare again.'

'About the door?'

'Yes, that one.' She'd had this same dream several times since they started seeing each other. It was always the same. She dreamed she was in a room, and someone was pounding and kicking down the door. But when it finally crashed open, there was nothing behind it, just darkness.

Every time he asked what she thought it meant, she turned evasive.

The trolleys kept rattling and the turbulence showed no sign of abating.

He hugged her again. 'Everything is going to be fine, trust me,' he whispered in her ear.

Although she offered no reply, he sensed how nervous she was by the way she kept clasping and unclasping her hands. And the way she kept glancing around, as if frightened of what she might see.

A few minutes later, the jolting and bumping and throbbing of the aircraft finally began to ease. They both breathed a sigh of relief.

'See? It's over,' he enthused. 'In a few hours we'll be in Sydney. Then we'll take a few days off to enjoy ourselves.'

Several moments later Mara Trujillo joined them in the galley.

'How are things here?' she asked as she entered, as cheerful as ever.

The stewardess was a tad overweight, but not unattractive and always jolly. That brief description summed up Mara.

'Fine,' Aaron said with a smile.

At last it was his turn to crawl into a bunk and get some sleep. He hoped that Sharlene would start feeling better now that the aircraft had reached calmer air.

EIGHT
Cat

A t the first indications of heavy turbulence Jim, in the cockpit, switched on the passenger seat-belt sign. He had returned to his seat ninety minutes earlier. After takeoff, Ben had taken over the controls from him for four hours. Now that the relief pilot was asleep on a makeshift bunk in the back of the cockpit, Jim had joined Greg for the last stretch of the flight.

'I didn't see that coming,' Jim said. 'Nothing that strong, at least.'

'Me, neither,' Greg concurred.

Jim studied the instruments. 'I don't see anything on radar.'

'Clear-air turbulence?' his copilot suggested.

'Look at the temperature outside!' Jim cried out.

Greg followed his gaze and frowned.

Heavy turbulence, he knew from long experience, could arise in a violent collision between warm and cold air. Apparently that was what had happened, because the Outside Air Temperature gauge suddenly read −94°, a sudden plunge of 15°. Such extreme cold normally was recorded only in the Polar Regions.

'Check the weather chart again,' Jim fairly shouted. 'Did we overlook something? Christ, this turbulence is bad!'

'I don't think we overlooked anything,' Greg responded. 'But I'll check again.'

He opened the flight schedule as Jim stared in disbelief at the OAT. The 747 was shaking as if it were the plaything of a divine power.

'No particulars reported from London,' Greg said. He was referring to the World Area Forecast Center, which was responsible for the weather charts in their flight plan.

'But those temperatures can't be right,' Jim said.

'I think a malfunctioning sensor is more likely,' Greg agreed.

'I have to tell the passengers something,' Jim resolved. 'It's getting pretty rough.'

He picked up his microphone and pressed the PA button. 'Ladies and gentlemen,' he announced, 'this is your captain speaking. We have entered an area of strong turbulence. We should be out of it shortly. I apologize for the inconvenience. For your safety and for the safety of those around you, please remain in your seats until further notice and keep your seat belts securely fastened.'

As he switched off the PA, he heard someone move behind him. Ben was out of his bunk, hanging on to his chair with both hands.

'What the hell is going on?' he demanded to know.

'Clear-air turbulence, most likely,' Jim replied. 'We're passing through a layer of cold air.'

Ben whistled between his teeth, glancing at the Outside Air Temperature gauge while the *Princess* was pounded unmercifully.

'Contact Tokyo,' Jim suggested. 'See what they know.'

Greg pressed the transmit button on the high-frequency radio, which had worldwide reach and was the only way for the pilots to communicate with air-traffic control. The pilot responsible for monitoring the plane's progress was obligated to report their position once every hour to the closest of the three region points into which the Pacific had been divided: Tokyo in the west, Anchorage in the north, and Oakland in the east. When Greg tried to tune the high-frequency radio and make contact, he received in response a burst of static that exploded through the flight deck.

Greg tried using the squelch to get rid of the static. Unsuccessful in that attempt, he first tried searching for a higher frequency, then a lower one, to obtain a clear link. The bucking plane made his job difficult, but finally the static cleared and Greg hailed air-traffic control.

'Tokyo, Tokyo, Tokyo, this is Oceans 5-8-2.'

No response. Greg waited a few seconds before repeating his call. 'Tokyo, Tokyo, Tokyo, this is Oceans 5-8-2. Come in, please.'

His request was met with silence.

'Nothing,' Jim said.

Greg shook his head. 'There must be too much interference. The HF is a primitive device. I'll try to find another frequency.'

He tried several others but was unable to establish contact. It was something Jim had witnessed many times before, so he wasn't overly concerned. The high-frequency equipment *was* primitive, as Greg had pointed out, and as a copilot he had often become frustrated by its quirks.

The turbulence had started without warning, and it ended just as abruptly at 2:30 in the morning. One moment it felt as though they were aboard a ship in a hurricane-whipped sea, the next moment the storm had subsided and the *Princess* was continuing on her way calm and steady.

As she did so, the OAT started rising.

'Well, that's that,' Ben sighed in relief.

'Yes,' Greg concurred. 'But this is another one of those CATs that make no sense to me.'

'Try the HF again,' Jim urged. 'Let's see if we can get through this time.'

Greg once again hailed Tokyo. Apart from white noise, they heard nothing but silence. But the copilot had communicated with air-traffic control just half an hour ago.

'HF is still not working,' Greg reported.

'Transmit our position and try the shortwave,' Jim said.

Greg nodded in acknowledgement and placed the microphone close to his mouth.

'This is Oceans 5-8-2, transmitting blind,' he stated. 'Our position, roughly, is 14 north, 160 west. Zulu time is GMT minus twelve hours.'

'Zulu time' is a term of endearment for Universal Time Code, corresponding with Greenwich Mean Time, used routinely by airline pilots.

'We've just crossed an area with clear-air turbulence, and we are currently experiencing a malfunction in our high-frequency.' He stared ahead pensively for a moment and then continued. 'Possibly atmospheric in nature. We'll use VHF to try and contact another plane in the vicinity, and we'll try using ACARS. We have no satellite phone on board.' A pause, then, 'Oceans 5-8-2 out.'

Greg released the transmit button and switched off the HF as a new burst of static clogged the airwaves. 'I don't know if anybody heard that transmission, but I agree it was worth a shot.'

'Let's hope so,' Jim said.

One by one, Greg tried the three VHF radios – one used for communication with air-traffic control, the second for backup, and the third always tuned to an emergency frequency. But each attempt failed. He could not make contact with another plane or with a ground station on one of the islands in the Pacific beneath them. Nor was there a response on the emergency frequency.

'Without VHF, ACARS won't work either,' Jim observed.

Silence ensued, as each pilot weighed in his own mind the significance of what Jim had just said.

To Jim, silence sometimes spoke louder than words. He and his wife Jody had become increasingly reticent in each other's company, and that summed up their relationship these days. The only words they still openly expressed to each other involved recriminations. If their marriage was a candle, it had guttered and could not be re-ignited. That was the conclusion he had reached during the final hours before boarding the *Princess*.

He wished that *those* hours had never happened.

Suddenly Greg leaned forward, his eyes intent on something.

Jim followed his gaze and saw what Greg had seen. His jaw dropped.

Interlude 1

A friendly young woman with a pleasant smile invited her inside. She rose from her chair in the waiting area and smoothed her blouse and mid-length skirt. The young woman opened a door and she entered, walking toward a man named Gerald Pierce who was sitting behind his desk.

Except for thin wisps of white hair on the sides and back of his head, Pierce was a totally bald man with striking blue eyes. As he rose to greet her, another thing that impressed her about him was his six-foot height. She estimated that Gerald Pierce weighed more than 200 pounds and he seemed to be an excellent physical specimen for a man of his age and stature. He was not a man to be overlooked in a crowd.

'Have a seat,' he said in a deep, jovial tone of voice that seemed to suit him.

Sharlene sat down.

Pierce had her CV laid out neatly in front of him. 'Thank you for coming,' he said.

'Thank you for seeing me,' Sharlene countered politely.

'You're welcome,' Gerald continued. 'Now would you mind telling me a bit about yourself?'

'Of course.'

Sharlene started talking about her studies, her summer jobs, her first real job, and her hobbies. She was proud of her achievements as a long-distance runner, which she felt confirmed her self-image as a go-getter. She did not, however, tell him why she had taken up running in the first place. Initially it had been a release from her troubles at home. Only gradually had she started to enjoy it. Slowly, deliberately, Sharlene worked her way toward telling Pierce about her motivation for applying for the job.

'Actually, it all started with my mother.'

Gerald Pierce interrupted her. 'Yes, I understand that your mother . . . um . . . met with a tragic end. I can imagine . . .' He groped *for appropriate words.* 'Let me be blunt, Sharlene. I would expect this to be the last job someone in your . . . circumstances would apply for.'

Sharlene nodded. She had expected him to say that.

'My mother used to tell me stories about her work. She loved it, and I always enjoyed her stories. I've wanted to be a flight attendant since I can remember. She instilled a lot of enthusiasm in me, and it's thanks to her that I'm here today, with you.'

'But still, your mother . . .' Pierce did not finish his sentence. He didn't need to.

'It was a terrible thing,' Sharlene agreed. 'But I don't want her fate to control my life. The fact that my mother died in a plane crash doesn't mean that the same thing will happen to me. I just don't believe that. It was an accident, the same way anyone can die in an automobile accident because some other driver isn't paying attention.'

Gerald nodded. 'I admire that about you. You're not letting this beat you.'

'That's right,' Sharlene avowed.

Unlike her father. But she didn't say that out loud. It was fine with her if Pierce knew that her mother's death had not stopped Sharlene from following in her footsteps. What it had done to her father was something that no one else needed to know about. Or what Dean Thier had done to her, as a result. That, too, was a private matter, a family secret, just like the nightmare that went by the name of Todd Bower.

Gerald asked a few more questions, but Sharlene had the distinct impression that he had already made up his mind.

When a week later she received a call from Oceans Airways informing her that she had been hired as a flight attendant, the first thing she did was make a phone call. A familiar voice answered the phone.

'I did it,' she said. 'I got the job. I just heard.'

'That's wonderful!' Noel Richardson cheered. 'Good girl! I'm so proud of you!'

II

2:36 A.M. — 3:52 A.M.

NINE
Cacophony

When Sharlene and Aaron left the galley on the upper deck, a passenger in a brown suit seated a few rows down turned to look at Sharlene. As their eyes met, she thought he was trying to draw her attention. But when she started walking toward him, he turned his head back around and faced forward.

She followed behind Aaron as he made his way aft toward the crew's quarters. She had stabbing pains in her sides, as she often did when she couldn't control her nerves. And she couldn't hold a single thought – another symptom of stress she knew all too well.

In the Tourist Class section on the main deck, the girl with the ponytail gave her another sharp glare. Sharlene stopped beside her while Aaron continued on.

The girl's sky-blue eyes bore into her.

'What?' Sharlene said quietly. 'What is it?'

The girl did not respond.

Sharlene crouched down to eye-level with the girl. The mother looked askance at Sharlene and noticed that her daughter was staring.

'Cassie, stop doing that,' she scolded. In reply, the girl turned front and center. But she clenched her fists and her face twisted in an odd grimace, as though she was flummoxed by something she could not utter aloud.

'Cassie? Is that her name?' Sharlene asked the mother. 'I thought she wanted to say something to me.'

'Oh, hardly,' the mother answered, not unkindly and without the least hesitation.

'How can you be so sure?' Sharlene asked, mystified.

'Believe me, I know,' the mother said, her erstwhile friendly tone replaced by one of open hostility. Sharlene observed them both with uncertainty. But the girl kept looking ahead with that tortured look on her face as her mother waited for Sharlene to leave.

Sharlene decided not to press the issue.

In the crew's quarters, Aaron did not ask her what had delayed her. As he slid on to one of the beds, he said, 'What say you and I snuggle for a while in this bunk? No one's about and we can be discreet.'

'Get some sleep, Romeo,' she chided him with a slight grin. 'We both need our rest before we get to Australia. I'm not planning on either of us getting much sleep there, if you catch my drift.'

'Roger that, Juliet,' Aaron said as he turned on his side. 'Pleasant dreams.'

Sharlene shook her head, more in disbelief than humor. Her dreams, she knew, would not be pleasant, assuming she was able to doze off at all. Hopefully, she thought, she would feel better after the plane landed safely in Sydney and this night was behind her.

Sabrina Labaton was a twenty-seven-year-old woman with long, wiry hair and hazel eyes. When she smiled – in her own slightly cocky way – she was radiantly beautiful. She did not smile often enough, however, or so her friends told her. Every bird has its song, but she had quite a few birds inside her mind. And they would fly up in fright at the least provocation, besieging her with groundless insecurities and doubts.

It had not escaped Sabrina's attention how the ponytailed girl two seats away from her had stared at the attractive blonde flight attendant. She had also overheard the brief exchange between the mother and the stewardess, in which the name Cassie was mentioned. After the flight attendant left, Cassie had kept staring ahead. Her mother waited a few minutes, then turned with a sorrowful sigh toward Sabrina seated to her right.

'My daughter carries something of a burden,' she said apologetically.

Sabrina noted that these were the first words that the portly lady had said to her since boarding the flight. But then Sabrina had not said anything to her, either. She smiled briefly and shrugged, as if to say that what she had just witnessed was none of her business.

'That sure was some turbulence, wasn't it?' she said, steering the conversation toward a different topic. 'People say flying is so safe, but then people say a lot of things.'

'They sure do,' the woman concurred.

The turbulence had in fact made Sabrina seriously nauseous. In her overactive imagination, the bucking of the plane could have torn the aircraft to pieces. She had dug her fingers into her thighs so hard she had probably bruised them.

'What are your plans in Sydney?' Sabrina asked pleasantly.

'We're going to a minerals fair,' the mother answered. 'My husband sells gems. But he hasn't been feeling well recently, so I'm going in his place. With Cassie.'

'Sounds like fun,' Sabrina said.

'My name's Evelyn,' the woman said, finally introducing herself.

'Pleased to meet you. I'm Sabrina.'

Her look moved from Evelyn to Cassie.

'I'm trying to protect my daughter,' Evelyn said, her tone again apologetic. 'She's a bit of an outsider for several reasons. She's not my blood daughter, you understand. My husband and I adopted her.'

'Oh,' Sabrina said, wondering if this was an invitation for her to ask what those reasons were. But with the snappy answer Evelyn had just given the flight attendant, it seemed unlikely. And did she even want to know?

Cassie sat motionless, staring grimly ahead and pretending not to hear her mother. The girl *was* strange, Sabrina mused. Very strange.

But it wasn't Sabrina's problem. She had enough troubles of her own.

The only thing she wanted was to get to Sydney to be with her sister Susan and her sister's husband and their children.

Sabrina, however, was not someone who could easily switch off her mind. She had been nervous about the trip, worried she would miss her flight. Before she left for the airport, she had scheduled a number of sessions with clients who claimed they needed to see her before she left. If these meetings were to run late, she would have to hurry – and of course those sessions *would* run late because they almost always did. So she had decided to pack her suitcase two nights earlier, but then took so long to pack – she needed much more time to pack than most people did because she worried that she would forget things – that she had overslept and had to reschedule her first meeting for later in the day. When that last meeting was finally over, she had given the airport taxi driver fits by forcing him to drive as fast as he could in order to get to the airport with ample time to catch her flight.

That was Sabrina Labaton, noted psychologist.

Like others of her acquaintance in her field, she had chosen her

profession for the wrong reasons. One reason was to better understand herself. Thus far, she couldn't claim to have realized that goal,
but still she found her career rewarding.

She had started her job only a year earlier, when she was hired
as an assistant to Dr Pritchart, a man thirty years her senior. He
was exactly the kind of boss she needed. He was a father figure she
could look up to, someone who supported her and gave her peace
of mind, but also someone who was quick to reprimand her when
she said things he considered baseless.

Before this flight to Sydney, she had resolved to get as much
sleep as possible on the plane, both to pass the time and to keep
from fretting. In essence, she lacked faith in herself. Despite her
professional credentials she often felt insecure when interacting with
other people. She had blown too many fuses during her career,
including the one with Curtis Fausset, the primary inspiration for
her making this trip. There was no definitive reason for her bouts
of low self-esteem – that was the key message she had heard repeatedly from Martin Pritchart. But it was for sure no confidence-booster
when Curtis, her erstwhile boyfriend, ran out on her screaming
'You're fucking crazy!' after she hit him in the face with a
blow-dryer.

Sabrina had suspected him of cheating on her with Isabel
Stromeyer, her best friend. Isabel had suddenly stopped calling
Sabrina and returning her phone calls; as for Curtis, he was spending
less time at home, claiming he needed to work late. Even when
they were home together, their sex life had fizzled to a few quickly
doused sparks. Curtis had vehemently denied being involved with
Isabel. Although Sabrina had meticulously searched for evidence,
she had found none. No frilly underwear between the sheets, no
suspicious stains, and no confessions. A week earlier, when trying
to wrest a confession from Curtis, she had come unhinged. The
confrontation had led to a broken blow-dryer, a smashed mirror,
and the final words between them.

Her younger sister Susan had always been her closest friend and
advisor. Susan had moved to Australia in 2008 with her husband
Jerry, whom she had married when she was nineteen years old.
Despite having no personal career ambitions – or perhaps because
she had none – Susan was happy. Jerry brought home the bacon
while Susan stayed home and took care of their two toddlers, Josh
and Christopher. Detesting any form of showing off, she dealt with

problems by adhering to mottos such as 'A day without laughter is a day wasted'. A simple psychology, to be sure, but the sentiment sprang from her heart, and it seemed to work.

Susan was the opposite of Sabrina and Sabrina envied her sister's breezy outlook. She hoped that her vacation in Sydney would give her an opportunity to sit back and take stock of her life and learn the life lessons that her sister would surely try to instill in her.

She couldn't wait to cross the Pacific.

Joe Tremain's crotch itched. It did that sometimes, and he fought the urge to scratch it. But that was the least of his discomforts.

Since the turbulence erupted, he had been bothered much more by his *knowing*.

It had been a tumultuous few minutes, but nothing he hadn't experienced before. It was hardly his first time on a plane. The violence of the turbulence had left him with a throbbing headache, however, and he was acutely aware of what *that* meant.

Joe thought there was something going on behind his back. He glanced around, but it was only a flight attendant with long blonde hair, accompanied by that idiot steward who could not distinguish fine wine from slop you'd feed to pigs.

Whenever something was not right, Joe *felt* it. Some people claimed they could sense approaching calamity in their bones. In Joe's case it came in the form of migraine headaches above his right eye. From long experience he knew that aspirin would be useless, even if he could reach a bottle stashed in his suitcase in the cargo hold.

Joe had possessed this keen sense of *knowing* ever since the car accident.

Twelve years ago he had crashed his burgundy Chevrolet against a fallen cedar tree. During that December night, Southern California had been hit by the worst storm in two decades. He had not seen the uprooted tree blocking the road until too late and had awakened thirty-six hours later in hospital. According to the doctors treating him, he had returned from the dead.

Several days later, Joe suffered his first attack of serious migraine. When others followed, he saw these attacks as the price he had to pay for his survival. In time, however, he came to see the migraines as heralding a dramatic shift in his fortunes, since they gave him the guts to plant a fist in the face of the Frankenstein monster.

Boris Ferrell had been Joe's boss at the time. In private Joe called him Boris Karloff, because he bore an uncanny resemblance to the actor in tallness of height, plumpness of girth, and shallowness of brain. From the start, he and Joe had disagreed on nearly every subject. One day, however, Boris turned out to be anything but stupid. He proved himself to be an immoral asshole.

The matter at issue concerned a proposed takeover of a rival company. In the middle of the meeting, as they were analyzing the projected cash-flow figures, Joe got one of his splitting headaches above his right eye. The pain could have been inspired by the muddle of accounting numbers, but Joe suspected a different reason.

Joe knew the numbers made no sense. And true to his nature, he spoke his mind.

'If these figures represent the company's net annual cash flows for the next five years,' he stated emphatically to the group huddled around the table, 'then we're offering too much money for the company. I may not understand present value analysis and the other financial mumbo jumbo you're throwing around here today, but I can see with my own two eyes that we're about to grossly overpay what the company is worth.'

Karloff made a dismissive gesture, as if brushing off a bothersome fly. 'What would *you* know about that?' he sneered, his contempt for Joe's financial analytic abilities evident to all present.

Joe was unfazed. He realized Karloff had a point. Joe was no CPA or financial analyst, so it was natural to assume he was arguing simply for argument's sake.

But Joe was convinced he smelled something as rotten as a fish carcass left out in the sun. And there was something else he knew.

Karloff was not as stupid as he looked. He was hiding something, and he was trying to pull a fast one on them.

'Our offer is over the top,' Joe insisted stubbornly. But he was talking to deaf ears. Not one of the other managers at the table supported him. He was on his own.

Karloff heaved a sigh, indicating he wanted the meeting concluded. But as Karloff was about to call for adjournment, Joe, headache and all, shoved his chair back, strode purposely over to where Karloff was sitting at the head of the table, and punched him squarely in the face.

Karloff's chair toppled over with the impact and he collapsed on to the ground, blood oozing from his nose and upper lip. The others present were too stunned to lift a finger. They just sat there, slack-jawed.

'Fuck him,' Joe threw over his shoulder as he stormed out of the room. He then went home to await a letter of dismissal that never came.

A week later another man who had attended the meeting appeared on Joe's doorstep. He informed Joe that Karloff's figures had been re-examined by the board of directors. During its investigation, the board discovered that Karloff had cut a deal with the management of the targeted company. If the proposed transaction had been consummated, a substantial portion of the proceeds would have landed in Boris's bank account. Joe had saved the company's shareholders a bundle, and he had gone from goat to hero. After that incident, his life had improved dramatically. Today he managed his own business empire with 238 people in his employ. He could now afford to drink the best wines and order the best foods, so all in all his car accident had benefited him greatly. He had built his empire and his fortune on his *knowing*. Every time he suffered a migraine, such as on this flight to Sydney, it was a premonition to him that something was seriously amiss and to be on his guard. Sitting in his seat on the plane, he felt a fierce stab of pain lance his skull and he groaned. He felt as though he was in the belfry of a church spire, stuck between two enormous tolling bells.

Joe peered outside through his window. The black of night covered the ocean like a cloak.

He decided to switch on his entertainment screen. He hadn't touched it thus far during the flight. He hated television, for the same reason he had eventually started hating everything that emitted radiation. Cell phones were the worst horror, but he had to carry one around with him. Some people considered him paranoid, but he knew better. Not too long ago he had read *Cell*, a novel by Stephen King. Joe hadn't read many of King's books because he found them too disturbing. But he had selected this one because of its title, and to his mind it cogently explained why he hated the damn things.

Joe pushed a few buttons on the touch screen, searching for some flight information. He couldn't find anything useful, although he did stumble upon one channel whose screen was entirely black.

When he did, something clicked inside his tortured mind.

He squeezed his eyes shut, to let whatever it was reveal itself, and suddenly he understood what was bothering him.

We're going somewhere we're not supposed to be going.

He again peered into the nocturnal darkness outside, again observing nothing unusual. That was an illusion. He knew what was wrong now. He suffered no doubts.

He had to *do* something. But Joe had no authority on board the aircraft. He was only a passenger. The pilot would never listen to him, for the same reason the managers in the meeting with Boris Karloff had not listened to him – at first.

Nor would he get an opportunity to punch the pilot in the nose, to get his attention.

What on earth could he do?

TEN
Squawking

Greg Huffstutter had his eyes glued on the instrument panel; beside him, Jim contemplated the ruins of his marriage. But when his copilot suddenly hunched forward, Jim saw what Greg was gaping at. The navigation display was empty. The screen was blank!

Familiar locations – airports, beacons, waypoints – had all disappeared. It was as if a map on a car's navigation system had suddenly lost the names of roads and cities. Only the vast Pacific Ocean was displayed on the screen, dotted here and there with islands. The coast of California was visible on one edge, and the coasts of Queensland and New South Wales on the other. Even the miniature plane representing the *Princess* was gone.

Greg shook his head in disbelief. 'Malfunction in the database memory?' he ventured dubiously.

He was referring to the database memory that contains location points. But EICAS, a device that detects failures, had nothing to report. Worse, the navigation instruments no longer displayed either the plane's departure airport, LAX, or their destination city, SYD. A nondescript straight line on the screen suggested the system had no clue where they were heading, since there was no data and therefore no course it could calculate.

'No,' Ben muttered. 'If that were the problem we would still be seeing wind directions. There must be something wrong with the GPS or IRS. But I can't imagine *what*, unless our government has declared war on someone and switched off the GPS system.'

Jim was about to add a comment when a harsh beeping sound permeated the cockpit.

'She's using her wings,' he said, meaning that the 747 was now flying straight ahead, following its nose, because the autopilot was no longer functional.

This was not only indicated by the harsh beeping. Jim noted with his own eyes that they were deviating from their initial heading: a bright star that had been dead ahead had shifted slightly to the right.

'I'll adapt heading select,' he announced, as he entered a change into the autopilot to adjust the plane's direction. After he'd done that, the star shifted back to its original position, the straight line in the navigation system disappeared, and the beeping ceased. An eerie silence settled over the flight deck.

All three pilots on that deck understood that a manual change in the autopilot represented a stopgap measure only. Without computer data, Jim no longer had accurate bearings.

'OK,' he said. 'What the hell *is* going on?'

'The IRS is empty, as well,' Greg reported.

Jim quickly confirmed that report. The last time he had checked the inertial navigation display, it had indicated their position in degrees and coordinates in glowing bright-green characters. Now there was nothing. That screen, too, had gone blank.

'This can't be happening,' Jim mumbled.

Again he glanced at EICAS. It detected no equipment failures; thus it indicated that all systems were functioning properly.

Problem was, they weren't.

Ben cleared his throat, but said nothing. Greg, too, was silent. What was happening went beyond their collective professional experience.

'What about the mechanical compass?' Jim mused, unable to recall when the last time was he had even thought of this device. But now he found himself consulting the primitive, magnetic little sphere, inside a glass case filled with liquid fastened to the bar between two windscreens, right in front of him. A legacy from the pioneering days of aviation, in a modern-day cockpit this compass was the sole navigational aid not connected to computers.

'It's pointing north,' he said with disgust. 'But we're flying southwest. Damn it to hell, even this damn thing is nuts!'

'Magnetic interference,' Greg suggested.

Jim considered that. 'Could be,' he said. 'I haven't got a better answer. Have you, Ben?'

'No,' Ben said grimly.

Around them, stars bathed the world in a pale-yellow light. The vast ocean below remained hidden beneath a thick blanket of clouds. Everything seemed normal.

'What heading are you following now?' Ben asked.

Jim pointed straight ahead. 'That star over there. You see it?'

Ben peered his eyes. 'Yes.'

Jim bit his lower lip, trying to ease the roiling in his intestines. He had not felt that sort of ominous prickling since combat training as a Navy pilot. 'For the moment, at least,' he said tightly, 'we're continuing pretty close on our initial course. Nothing like having to rely on visual navigation,' he added with a sardonic chuckle.

'But what is all this nonsense?' Ben groused. 'What are we dealing with here?'

Jim shrugged. 'If this was some glitch in the computers or in the GPS, then the mechanical compass would still be working. Maybe Greg is right. Maybe it is magnetic interference.'

'Possibly,' Ben said in a faraway voice. 'So what are we going to do?'

'What choice do we have?' Jim replied. 'We're going to keep flying. We haven't enough fuel to turn around and go back to LAX. And I can't land anywhere because I can't determine where airports are located. Let's hope and pray you contact someone soon, Greg. Anyone will do.'

During the next few minutes, Greg sent out transmissions on all frequencies. None was answered.

The roiling in Jim's stomach intensified.

'Use the transponder,' he said. 'Let's start squawking.'

'Roger that,' Greg said. Betraying, Jim felt, his nervousness by using this old-fashioned slang.

The copilot entered code 7600, which informed anyone who happened to be listening that the cockpit crew of Flight 582 had lost all communications. The electronic radar signal they now broadcasted – or squawked, in pilot parlance – should be acknow-ledged by all ground stations and planes within a 250-mile radius. That distance computed to half an hour of flying, about as far as Jim would see at this altitude in daytime.

'The transponder should be picked up momentarily,' Jim said. 'Keep sending out radio messages every five minutes, as well. That's all we can do.'

Greg nodded and added, his voice calm and yet barely concealing his unease, 'I doubt it's a coincidence that we've been experiencing these malfunctions from the first moment that turbulence hit us.'

The copilot was a man of few words, but when he spoke, espe-cially at a time like this, he normally had something important to say.

'Yes,' Jim agreed. 'That's when they started.'

He threw another glance toward the navigation display and the IRS. The fact that they had received no immediate response on their transponder code could mean only one thing: the only other people within a range of 250 miles from their current position were the passengers and crew with them on board the *Princess of the Pacific*.

ELEVEN
Pursued

Sharlene had finally fallen asleep for a brief period. When she awoke, her wristwatch read 3:20, an hour before her next shift started. She couldn't determine if Aaron was asleep, but she assumed he was. It seemed that whenever his head touched a pillow, he fell asleep instantly, and it took a bucket of water in the face or a cannon firing to wake him. She envied that gift.

For her, rest had ended the moment she opened her eyes. Uncontrollable nervousness continued to rage within her body. Usually she managed to find some way to control her nerves. But not tonight.

'Might as well get up,' she mumbled to herself as she slid out of her bunk and tiptoed away from the crew's rest area.

Inside the cabin, the murk and dark threw elongated shadows.

Passengers were slouching or lying prostrate or sitting in their seats in every position imaginable. Some of them were snoring with their mouths open, while others were sitting up straight staring at their flickering entertainment screens. Whatever alarm and chaos had been generated by the fierce turbulence had apparently already been forgotten. Sharlene found Gloria Rodriguez and Ray Jacobstein at work in the main galley.

'We're having trouble with MEG,' Gloria said in greeting to Sharlene, using the acronym for Movies, Entertainment and Games, the onboard entertainment system.

Gloria was a svelte woman with short sandy-brown hair. As she normally did, she had applied a bright red lipstick, an adornment that Ray Jacobstein – the only other male flight attendant on board besides Aaron and Devin Felix – believed looked good on her. He had once confessed to Sharlene that he was very impressed with Gloria and found her attractive. And that was fine with Sharlene. Ray was single, as was Gloria, and she was not a woman to shy away from male attention.

'Trouble?' Sharlene said. 'What sort of trouble?'

'The flight map channel isn't working,' Gloria informed her. 'It's the same with the big screens.'

'All we're getting is black screen,' Ray put in. 'A few passengers have complained about it. I tried to reset the system, but that didn't help. So I decided to turn the large screens off. Do you think Aaron would want to know?'

'When did the channel go blank?'

'About half an hour ago, I think,' Gloria said. 'Maybe an hour, I'm not sure.'

'There's always something,' Sharlene said, shaking her head. 'Aaron had a busy shift. He's asleep now, and I suggest we leave him be. I'll tell the captain.'

She left the galley, this time choosing the right-hand aisle, so as not to pass the ponytailed girl who kept staring awkwardly at her.

When she walked past her row, however, she chanced a glance at the girl, four seats away. But Cassie paid her no mind, nor did either her mother or the brunette woman sitting beside her.

Sharlene glanced at the television monitors mounted against the ceiling. They had been switched off, as Ray had indicated. No one commented to her about it, so apparently the passengers didn't care. That would probably change at dawn, she speculated,

as they made their approach to Sydney and passengers began
waking up. Then everyone would want to know how much longer
until touchdown.

In the galley on the upper deck, she found Mara leaning against
the counter and looking bored. Her eyebrows lifted in surprise when
she noticed Sharlene approaching her.

'Hey, what are you doing here?' she asked cheerfully.

'I couldn't sleep,' Sharlene said evasively. 'How are things here?'

'Aaron said he'd had a pretty hectic night, but for me it's been
just the opposite. I'm bored silly, to tell you the truth.'

Sharlene smiled. 'Enjoy it while you can.'

Mara returned the smile. She then launched into details of the
diet she wanted to try – or rather, the diet she wanted to try next.
Every previous effort to shed excess pounds had ended in frustration
and failure, and a resolve to try some other plan.

'I envy you,' Mara said, with an admiring glance at Sharlene's
waistline. But while Sharlene did not have to exert herself to maintain a size-four dress, she didn't require the services of Sherlock
Holmes to discern why Mara's outfits were several sizes larger. On
the counter next to her were opened bags of chocolates, potato chips,
and fudge brownies.

'I'm heading to the cockpit,' Sharlene said, adding as she left,
'We're having problems with the entertainment screens.'

At the cockpit door, she rang the bell by pressing 1 on the code
lock. When the door unlocked with a loud click, she pushed it open.
All three pilots turned to look at her.

If everything had been normal, one of the three would have been
asleep and the other two on duty would have had little or nothing
to do. Sydney was still a long way off, and there wasn't much that
needed to be done on the flight deck. Usually during the dead hours
the pilots appreciated a visit by a crew member. Besides supplying
a happy diversion, he or she might be coaxed into getting them
some coffee or food.

But the look Jim gave her was far from happy or relaxed. He
appeared angry, as if she was an unwelcome intruder. The same
held true for Greg Huffstutter and Ben Wright.

'Can I bring you guys anything?' she asked when none of them
uttered a word.

'I'm fine, thank you,' Jim said.

Greg and Ben also declined.

'Is everything all right?' she inquired tentatively. The tension on the flight deck was palpable.

Jim had turned back to his instruments. With her question, he stared ahead into space. Sharlene waited, her body becoming increasingly tense. This was not the same affable man she had come to know that night in the bar of the Intercontinental Hotel in Singapore.

I'll get you home safely, Sharlene, and I always will.

He had made that promise to her after she confessed her fears and insecurities to him. She had needed a shoulder to lean on, and Jim had kindly taken her under his wing. She hadn't met Aaron yet.

Since then she had felt safe flying with Jim, and he had always treated her courteously, more like a daughter than an underling.

Tonight Jim seemed as fearful and insecure as Sharlene had been that night in Singapore. His expression was tight, his face pale, and the skin beneath his eyes was darker and puffier than before the flight, when she had noticed how tired he looked. What was going on?

'We're experiencing some problems,' he said to her. 'It's . . .'

He fell silent, weighing his words.

'We're not sure what it is,' he went on, 'but we're trying to deal with it. Don't worry. It can't be anything terribly serious.'

Sharlene took a step back, feeling as if something heavy had been thrust against her chest. Jim recognized the fright in her eyes. Was he remembering that night in Singapore as well? He *knew* her. And he knew her fears.

'Sharlene . . .' he said quietly. 'Sometimes things don't go as we would like. We're experiencing a few setbacks, that's all.'

Keep calm, she thought, *steady yourself, be professional.*

'Is there anything I can do?'

Jim didn't say anything. He didn't have to. Sharlene turned to depart.

'Oh,' she said, remembering herself, 'I almost forgot what I came in here for. We're having a problem with the flight-map channel on MEG. It's blank, and resetting doesn't help. I just thought I'd report it. I don't know if . . .'

She paused. Something in Jim's expression advised her to stop.

'It's no big deal,' Ben commented. 'What you could do is ask passengers to turn off all electrical devices. That might help. We'll have to see.'

Sharlene nodded curtly. 'I'm on it.'

'I'll keep you posted,' Jim said with a smile that Sharlene assumed was false.

When she stepped off the flight deck and closed the door behind her, she felt the same sort of headache she got from a hangover. Jim, she knew, had not told her the whole truth.

She walked back into the main cabin. The passenger in the brown suit, who had been looking at her as she made her way downstairs with Aaron, caught her eye again. Now that she saw him up close for the first time, she noticed his small stature. She was a good head taller than he. And yet she cringed.

It was his eyes.

She had heard it said that a man's eyes are windows into his soul. This man's glare reminded her of Hannibal Lecter, the cannibal in the horror movie *Silence of the Lambs*. As he raised his right hand to rub his forehead, the fierce look he gave her assumed a tortured quality.

He seemed to be suffering from a headache much nastier than the one she was battling.

'Apparently they're having some problems,' Sharlene informed Mara when she returned to the upper-deck galley. 'Jim wants us to ask everyone to switch off their cell phones and laptops.'

Mara opened her mouth in question.

'No, I don't know why,' Sharlene answered the implied question. 'Jim didn't tell me. But it's nothing serious, he said. Probably something to do with the plane's computers.'

'Oh,' Mara responded. 'Maybe that's what's causing the malfunction in MEG.'

'Yes, I think so,' Sharlene said, sounding more positive than she felt. 'I haven't seen anyone on the upper deck toying with devices, so you needn't do anything. I'm going down to give them a heads-up.'

Downstairs, she approached Michelle Hennessy, a stewardess assigned to First Class; she then informed her colleagues in the main galley. They promised to make the announcement and to make sure that everyone complied with the request. Sharlene's next stop would be the crew rest area. Should she wake up Aaron? she wondered. Possibly not, as the cockpit crew had assured her that the problems were nothing more than computer glitches. If she believed that explanation, which she didn't.

She decided to wake him. *If I'm being childish*, she reasoned, *he'll be sure to tell me that I am.*

Her attention was suddenly drawn to a lady in black sitting ramrod straight in her seat; the same woman Sharlene had helped with her cabin luggage. She was still wearing her silly oversized sunglasses. The way she sat so stiffly gave the impression that she was in some sort of pain.

Sharlene walked up to her. 'Are you all right, madam?'

She could not help but wonder what the lady's coal-black lenses were hiding. Was her eye color brown, blue, or green?

'I'm not sure,' the woman in black said, her voice so low Sharlene had to lean in close to hear what she was saying. 'I think he's here with us. I've seen him. Have you seen him, too?'

The woman's voice was filled with awe.

'He's here, with us,' she whispered vacantly, yet insistently.

What the hell was the woman talking about? Sharlene wondered. It could be simple ramblings or some sort of hallucination. But Sharlene was convinced it wasn't. The woman's words had stirred something deep within her. A shiver ran down her spine, as if from an injection of ice water.

Although she had not been a flight attendant for very long, Sharlene had met her fair share of odd passengers. She found it was usually best to humor them.

'Yes, madam, I have seen him,' she said, hoping that was the desired response. 'And everything else is all right? Can I get you anything?'

The woman did not move. The sunglasses remained trained on her. 'No, thank you. I need to pray.'

Sharlene nodded politely and stepped back. It was not her place to come between this woman and her God. Quickly she moved on toward the bunks, but before she reached them she stopped in her tracks. She sensed someone coming up fast behind her.

She whirled around.

No one was there. The aisle was empty. No one was in sight save for Gloria, halfway down the aisle, facing in the opposite direction.

She had been mistaken. It had only been an unpleasant feeling. A *familiar* unpleasant feeling.

Somehow it brought back more memories of Todd Bower.

Every night after she had broken up with him, she had worried that he would come back. She envisioned him breaking a window in her apartment, sneaking in like a thief in the night, and doing things to her she dared not imagine. She had slept uneasily, waking up at even the smallest noise, convinced that there *would* come a night when he would be standing there at her bedside, poised to have his sick way with her.

Which, of course, was exactly what had happened.

Now she was on board a plane full of people, Todd was thousands of miles away, and there was no reason on earth for her to be afraid of him.

What *did* scare her, then?

Suddenly there came a spark of inspiration and she knew.

'Oh God, no,' she whispered to herself, aghast.

TWELVE
Jerrod

Jerrod Kirby was sitting in seat number 28A, jammed uncomfortably between the window and his wife, Phyllis. The flabby meat of her arms drooped across his armrest and that of her neighbor on the other side, a long-haired young man dressed in jeans and an indigo-blue shirt. Few words had passed among them. The only time Phyllis had said anything during the flight was to complain about the meager portions of lousy food she had received. That every passenger had received the same food and the same portions did not dissuade her. Jerrod had voiced his agreement, as he was wont to do, even though he hadn't found anything to complain about. She should be perfectly content, he thought. There was no fridge to raid on the plane, and she was on a mini-diet for which a trained dietitian would have charged her dearly.

Jerrod understood better than anyone that his wife's appetite was substantial and insatiable. He had once, in a stab at spirituality, read up on Buddhism, an Eastern philosophy which claims that desire is the root cause of human suffering. Because Buddhists are enlightened, they forsake their cravings for undue earthly sustenance and therefore know no suffering.

Buddhism, Jerrod had often thought, would provide the perfect solution for Phyllis. No craving for food equaled losing a ton of weight, and she had about a ton to lose.

Early in the morning of this new day, Jerrod was himself in desperate need of enlightenment. He was experiencing even more suffering in his wretched existence than usual. The turbulence about an hour ago had shaken him and his fellow passengers awake. That was when he realized he desperately needed to relieve himself. When the bumping ceased, he debated whether or not he should leave his seat to go to one of the toilet stalls and empty his bladder.

The biggest challenge to following that course of action was the need to disturb his wife.

Hauling herself up from her seat to let him get out would require a Herculean effort on her part. He could easily imagine the toxic glare he would receive from her just for asking her to move for him. He would also need to shuffle past the young man, who had remained awake after the turbulence had eased with his usual open and friendly expression. Jerrod was sure the youngster would be more than happy to get up and let him out. That wasn't the issue. The only human barricade blocking his way to the bathroom was Phyllis.

The fluid that had filled his bladder was now becoming increasingly painful and he *had* to make his move.

When Jerrod glanced askance at his wife, he noted that she had closed her eyes and dozed off. That was not good. Now she would *really* be pissed off at him, and that was a turn of events he wished to avoid at all costs.

There was, of course, the added factor that he hated the insufferable tiny bathrooms afforded by airlines. His house in Santa Monica featured spacious rooms with as few doors as possible. He was the first to admit that he suffered from claustrophobia. Praise God, Phyllis seemed to accept his infirmity, and while she wasn't necessarily sympathetic to him at least she didn't constantly nag him about it.

Jerrod prepared for the challenge by trying to get up from his seat. He clenched the headrest of the seat in front of him with both hands, pulled himself up, and stood there, slumped over beneath the overhead bins.

A blonde flight attendant walked past. He turned and watched her as she disappeared into the galley behind the two toilet stalls.

Moments later she came back out and began walking toward the rear of the plane.

He noted, to his agony, that both toilet stalls were unoccupied. One of those tiny rooms held unspeakable relief for him. Thinking of that only increased his need and his pain, so he sat back down and tried to think of pleasant things such as his favorite pastime: fishing in one of Utah's pearly mountain lakes. He traveled there frequently with his friends, to escape his everyday worries and the drudgery of his life with Phyllis. These fishing trips were about the only pleasures she allowed him. Which is why they became his refuge, his salvation, from the miseries of his life.

Thinking of the rippling lakes of Utah made him think of water. And thinking of water aggravated the pain in his bladder.

He searched wildly through his mind for another diversion, but it was nigh impossible. His line of work didn't exactly stir the imagination – he had been promoted to head of accounting at Davison Electrical Systems, a title that sounded flashier than the job merited since the entire accounting department consisted of himself and a kid just out of high school who was incompetent but cheap and this quality was all that mattered to Jerrod's boss.

On top of everything else, Jerrod was hardly proud of the fruit of his loins. Last spring his eighteen-year-old son Zachary had told his parents that he was attracted to boys, something Jerrod found impossible to accept. Given the alternative, he could not for the life of him understand why any male would prefer the sexual ministrations of another man. He didn't care if that made him old-fashioned.

Except, perhaps, when a man was locked in marriage to a woman like Phyllis.

Still, he wasn't happy about it. Phyllis had been *very* under-standing when their son came out of the closet, but that was no surprise. Zachary had always been the apple of her eye and he was living proof that Phyllis was capable of love – of loving others, if not Jerrod.

The hardest time had been the day Zachary introduced his boyfriend Bobby to them. Bobby wore silver earrings, and Jerrod spotted a tattoo on the fellow's right arm that looked to be some kind of snake or dragon. Jerrod hadn't been entirely sure, but he *was* sure that the sight of it turned his stomach.

What have I done to deserve this? he had thought at the time.

Now, in his seat on board this plane, he was thinking more or less the same thing. It saddened him so much that he felt even more pressure on his bladder.

His musings were not getting him anywhere. Was there not *something* he could look back upon with more satisfaction?

Then an image of Mirabelle resurfaced. He had never forgotten her, nor would he ever want to. In recent years he had encountered her more and more often in the melancholy vault tucked away inside the mind where one stores one's most cherished images and memories.

More than two decades ago, when he was still a young and reasonably attractive man, he had dated two women. Mirabelle was beautiful, with warm, dreamy eyes and long, lanky legs, and he was madly in love with her. She loved him in return, but was perplexed and hurt by his seeming lack of commitment to her. One day she told him she was moving to Phoenix, and she gave him an ultimatum – either come with her or forget about her.

Jerrod had just landed his job at Davison Electrical Systems and was reluctant to follow his heart. His need for security outweighed his longing for love, or so he thought at the time. How could he have been so stupid? He had remained in Los Angeles, ending up married to his other girlfriend. And then, well, nothing much had changed, other than Phyllis expanding like a balloon and souring like milk left out for days on a kitchen table.

He was still working at Davison, and still living with Phyllis.

Had he made a different choice that day when Mirabelle asked him to come with her, his life surely would have turned out differently – and very much for the better.

What was her life like now? he wondered yet again. Who had she given her heart to? How was she doing? He didn't know, because he had never contacted her after she left Los Angeles.

But he thought of her often, and every time he did it made him sad.

By now, his bladder was starting to cramp up with pain he could no longer ignore.

Unaware of her husband's distress, Phyllis emitted a loud and offensive noise. The young man sitting next to her looked askance at her, met Jerrod's gaze, and then turned his face away in disgust. Jerrod shrugged. *Yes, that's what I'm married to*, his helpless gesture communicated to no one.

Phyllis unintentionally poked him in the ribs with her elbow. She snored loudly, like a gurgling machine, and then smacked her lips.

'Phyllis,' he hissed.

He *was* going to wake her up. He had thought he lacked the nerve to do so, but he had no choice. The pain was becoming unbearable. She grumbled something incoherent, but still didn't wake up. Jerrod's bladder was fit to burst. He *had* to go to the bathroom, no matter how Phyllis reacted.

'Honey?'

She remained asleep, oblivious. He poked her gently. She snorted and turned her triple chin toward him.

'Phyllis!' he said in a louder voice. The growling, lip-smacking, and rumbling ceased. She opened her eyes and gave him a glazed look.

'What is it?'

Jerrod was shocked to realize he didn't know what to say. Now that he had dredged her from sleep, he didn't know what to tell her. Phyllis's expression changed. Her eyebrows dipped and an angry glow emanated from her eyes. The longer he demurred, he knew, the angrier she would become. She stared at him like a rabid dog, primed to bite him.

'I have to get out,' Jerrod said at length.

'What for?'

'I need to use the bathroom.'

'Jesus!' she hissed venomously. 'Can't you hold it?'

Strike one.

'No. I've needed to go for quite some time now, actually.'

'You and your bladder.'

Strike two.

Her body odor bore an unpleasant resemblance to a rotten egg. Not for the first time Jerrod cherished the thought of a life without her. As he looked at her, he daydreamed about an emergency door opening behind her, sucking her out of the plane and out of his life. Sadly, that was not going to happen. But what mattered now was another door opening, the one to the toilet stall. Why did she have to torture him? Couldn't she see his pain?

Fleetingly he remembered reading about an aggressive type of spider. The female was much larger than the male and she killed him after mating; one sting and he was history. To Jerrod, it seemed a merciful ending.

Come to think of it, Phyllis almost *had* killed him. It had happened long ago when they were first married, about the time he was starting to curse himself for not going to Phoenix with Mirabelle. He and Phyllis had gone out to dinner to a Chinese restaurant – Jerrod would never forget its name, *Hae Chang BBQ* – and she had insisted they both order the clams. He had tried to make her understand that he didn't like clams, and in fact was allergic to them and had been warned by doctors never to eat them. She had told him to quit being such a baby. So he *had* ordered the clams, and consequently woke up in the middle of the night feeling nauseous. He had been short of breath and, oddly, his entire body itched terribly. Then everything had gone black. A nasty, sickly kind of black – for years, he had nightmares about it. When he awoke in the intensive-care unit, he heard that, as a consequence of severe anaphylactic shock, he had suffered an acute cardiac arrest. The medical team told him that for several minutes he had exhibited no pulse. He had been clinically dead for that short span of time, compliments of Phyllis.

To this day she had never apologized.

'Come on, get up,' he said, more forcefully. He knew he was asking for trouble assuming this tone of voice, but the acute need to relieve himself made him forgo his usual wariness.

Phyllis shot him a derisive look. After a grim silence of seconds that seemed to last for hours, she grudgingly began the evolutions of hoisting up her massive frame. Exhaling a loud rasping breath, she grabbed the headrest of the seat before her with so little finesse the passenger sitting in front of her uttered a startled yelp.

The young man next to Phyllis stared at her, fascinated. Then he jumped up limberly and stood beside his seat in the aisle.

Phyllis postured herself in front of the young man, who took several steps backward.

'Thanks, honey,' Jerrod said.

'Just hurry on up and get it done.'

Strike three and out.

Finally, the aisle was clear. Jerrod hurried toward the nearest toilet and disappeared inside. While opening his fly, he worried for a gruesome moment that he was too late, that there was no stopping the deluge.

He rolled his head back and heaved a sigh of relief when finally he discharged his load and the pain eased.

But then, from the corner of his right eye, he caught sight of an image in the mirror: a black figure behind him who was bigger and wider than Phyllis.

He spun around, his heart racing.

There was no one there. He was alone.

An icy shiver crawled up his spine, the origin of which he could not imagine.

Jerrod turned back to the mirror. He saw nothing there but his own pale, frightened face.

Urine remaining in his bladder momentarily blocked up, causing painful hot cramps in his lower abdomen. Gasping for breath, Jerrod finally managed to squeeze out the final streams.

Suddenly the temperature in the stall dropped precipitously. *I have to get out of here*, he thought.

He zipped up his fly and pushed against the folding door.

It didn't budge. Stupid! He had locked it, of course. He pulled the aluminum slider back and turned the latch. Still the door refused to budge.

Confused, he shoved the lock the other way and kept pushing against the door, rattling the latch. But it would not let him out.

Jerrod shivered in the cold. Was the air conditioner malfunctioning?

He was overcome by the ridiculous notion that this was Phyllis's way of getting rid of him – or at least of getting back at him for inconveniencing her. She would leave him to rot in an airplane toilet stall. But that, of course, was nonsense.

Just as stupid as his hallucination of the man in the mirror.

Except it hadn't *been* a man. It hadn't been *human*.

Warily, he peered around the small space.

In the mirror he saw only his befuddled expression staring back at him.

Jerrod pounded on the door, but he didn't have any strength left. His claustrophobia was beginning to paralyze him. He was locked in this little cubicle, and for him *that* was a nightmare in the extreme.

'Help me, I'm stuck!' he cried out, but his voice sounded more like a croak. Not a soul would hear him. He could not scream, his vocal chords had jammed along with the door.

'I'm stuck in here! Help! Please help me!'

But it was a hoarse whisper, a pitiful silent plea for help.

Although the stall seemed to be growing colder, Jerrod started to sweat. He couldn't breathe. It felt as if something or someone was squeezing his throat.

He was aware of something unimaginable happening. That door not opening was impossible. Utterly impossible. So was this frigid temperature. Impossible. It was as simple as that.

The 300 or more passengers on the plane were suddenly a long way away. Or could it be that everyone on the other side of this door was dead? It was another insane thought, but it seared through his brain, nonetheless.

Jerrod was having increasing difficulty breathing. He moaned and whimpered. Nothing happened and nobody came to help him.

Once more he glanced sideways at the mirror.

The enormous black form had appeared behind him again, leaning over him, almost *swallowing* him like a man-eating shark.

Jerrod again tried to shout, but his voice was reduced to a meaningless high-pitched gurgle, the same sort of strangling noise he'd made after eating the clams at *Hae Chang BBQ*.

THIRTEEN

Cassie

Evelyn Hooks was a surly woman who was not easily fazed. At home, in Sugar Creek, she could impose her will on just about anyone except Cassie – who alone could intimidate her.

That was in large part due to Evelyn's rather impressive figure. She had never been slim, but in recent years she had started piling on the weight and that made her even more daunting to anyone brazen enough to cross her.

Evelyn was respected by friends and enemies alike. Not that she had many enemies, apart from the local silly drunks who couldn't seem to get it through to their thick skulls that Sugar Creek was a *sober* city. If they wanted to get hammered, Evelyn often commented, they should move to Las Vegas, or Los Angeles. Plenty of sinful thinking there, but not in her town – or rather, John's town, since her husband was the one who had put Sugar Creek on the map.

Thirty years ago the town didn't exist. Today it was a prospering community of 3,000 people.

John had a nose for gold. Thirty years ago he had struck it rich by staking a claim in the Wah Wah Mountains. As Fate would have it, there was an old mine in the tiny plot of real estate that constituted his claim. In it John found a ripe harvest of beryls, precious gems that had made him rich overnight. He now owned six mines – seven until a few months ago, when he had sold one of them to an Australian trading company, clearing a cool 8 million dollars after expenses. Despite a healthy bank account – or rather, bank *accounts* – he saw no justification for changing his austere lifestyle. He still made regular trips to his mines, taking with him only his old Land Rover and a tent. Sometimes Evelyn accompanied him. She had married him, so she figured that half of what he owned belonged to her.

She wasn't greedy, and neither was John. Not anymore. He used to love money when he was younger and he had gone to merciless lengths to obtain it. But ever since his health had started to fail, he had come to realize that material possessions were only relative. They were by no means what truly mattered in this life.

Reminded on a daily basis of his own mortality, he began opening up to the prospect of marriage, something he had never anticipated or particularly desired. Evelyn could say the same thing. Always being on the road left little room for serious commitments, and she never would have believed that she would end up in the remote town of Sugar Creek.

Seven years ago Evelyn had needed some extra cash. She was broke, so she applied for a job at John's motel, where he was living by himself in a simple room. Although a wealthy man, he had never had much taste for luxury items. Evelyn and John were immediately attracted to each other, and in what seemed to them an amazingly short span of time, just a year after her job interview, they walked down the aisle together. Later, they adopted Cassie.

Evelyn and her daughter were now on their way to the Sydney Gem & Mineral Show. Several buyers who would be there had taken an interest in John's gems. That was reason enough to endure the long flight. In addition, for three years running John had skipped the Sydney exhibition, and it was about time he waved the family flag again. But two weeks ago he had taken ill with pneumonia. Although the worst was now behind him, his doctors had concluded that he had not recovered sufficiently to make such a strenuous trip. Evelyn had thereupon offered to go in his place. Her doing so raised the issue of what to do with Cassie. John suggested having Cassie stay with him, but Evelyn would not hear of it. She refused to be half a world away from Cassie, even if only for seven days. So they decided that Cassie would accompany Evelyn to Australia.

Evelyn prayed it would not prove to be a bad decision. Serious doubts had set in the day before departure, when Cassie had gone berserk.

Inside the plane, where it was quiet now, Evelyn was beset by memories. Yesterday, when she had returned to her home in the motel in Sugar Creek, she was not yet out of the car when she saw Ginette running out of the front door. Ginette and her husband also lived at John's motel. For many years the couple had managed the restaurant and bar, and taken care of the rooms.

When Ginette told her that Cassie was in a bad state, Evelyn ran inside the motel where she found Cassie in her bedroom fuming and growling, with a deep gash over her left eyebrow that was bleeding profusely. Evelyn's first thought was that Cassie had raked her fingernails across her face, causing the gash.

In her airplane seat located between her adopted daughter and the pretty brunette, Evelyn pursed her lips as the memory of yesterday's debacle assailed her. She raised her eyes to the ceiling of the plane to prevent Cassie and Sabrina from noticing her tears.

As she looked up, she spotted a scrawny man making his way hastily down the aisle. His seat appeared to be a few rows down where a rotund woman – Evelyn thought even she would look slim and sexy beside her – was blocking the aisle. The man stalked by, his eyes riveted dead ahead.

Evelyn's thoughts returned to yesterday's episode with Cassie. The girl had been furious for a reason Evelyn could not determine. She had formed a claw with her fingers and hissed at her mother like an angry cat. That same sort of thing had happened quite often during the first few weeks after Cassie came to live with them.

She had also trashed her room. Evelyn and John had seen this sort of destructive behavior before, when Cassie had broken mirrors and anything else that might reflect her image back to her. It was as though she could not stand to look at herself. She had also wrecked pieces of furniture and anything else she could get her hands on. But that wasn't the worst part of her tantrums. The worst part was her self-mutilation. Some nights Evelyn could not go to sleep out of fear that Cassie would cross a line and do serious damage to herself – perhaps even kill herself.

Yesterday Cassie had acted as though Evelyn and Ginette were out to get her. She didn't seem to recognize them. Evelyn had approached her carefully when Cassie began flailing her arms and uttering strange, incomprehensible sounds. By the time her anger had abated, she was exhausted and bathed in sweat.

As Evelyn and Ginette tended to Cassie, Evelyn repeatedly asked her daughter why she was so upset. Hadn't she been doing better recently? Why this horrible relapse?

Evelyn had received no answers, nor had she expected any.

By then their suitcases had been packed and their tickets were waiting for them at the airport. So Evelyn had stood by her decision to take along her daughter.

Now the only visible signs that anything untoward had happened yesterday were faint lines of scratches on Cassie's cheeks and a scab over her eyebrow. As if she sensed Evelyn's thoughts, Cassie started rocking back and forth in her seat. Then she leaned to the side and glanced over her shoulder down the aisle. She started whimpering like an animal in pain, sounds that Evelyn couldn't remember ever hearing before, although she *had* heard her daughter uttering strange noises over the years.

Evelyn turned her head and glanced behind them, to see what was upsetting her daughter this time. She saw nothing but passengers in various stages of sleep, plus the two toilet stalls at the rear of their section of seats. That was all. But Cassie continued making these strange whimpering sounds.

Sabrina Labaton noticed a colossal woman standing in the aisle a few rows in front of them, and wondered how anyone could let themselves go to that extent. The man darting away from her appeared to weigh a third as much as she did. Sabrina assumed they were married, judging by the peevish look the woman gave him. The man almost *ran* past Sabrina, and she didn't need a psychology degree to realize that he urgently needed to use the bathroom. She pitied him for a variety of reasons, but mostly for what undoubtedly awaited him upon his return to his seat.

Shortly thereafter, her neighbor again seemed to be having her hands full with her adopted daughter, who had not yet uttered a word during the flight. Cassie was leaning across the armrest of her seat, staring behind her and making strange small noises. Sabrina had once had a puppy who had his leg broken when he was hit by a car. The animal's pitiful cries had cut deep into her soul, and it was those same sort of whiney sounds that Cassie was making. The girl was staring at the skinny man who had hurried past them toward the toilet stalls.

Evelyn, who had followed Cassie's gaping, shook her head and settled back down. 'There's nothing going on,' she said to the girl. 'Don't be ridiculous.'

When Cassie paid no heed, Evelyn used her considerable strength to pull her daughter back into her seat. As she did so, Sabrina saw the pain in Cassie's eyes, although her mother apparently did not. She was breathing a sigh of relief that yet another crisis seemed to have been averted.

'She doesn't talk much, does she,' Sabrina said. It was not a question, and her voice conveyed a mixture of concern and worry.

Evelyn's eyes found hers, and she seemed hurt.

'I didn't mean to . . .' Sabrina started, although she didn't really see a need to apologize.

'Cassie hasn't spoken a word in two years,' Evelyn said as a matter of fact.

Sabrina's jaw dropped.

'Longer, even,' Evelyn went on. 'My husband and I adopted her two years ago. She had already lost her speech by then.' She rubbed tears from her eyes. 'She's going through another bad spell that started yesterday.'

All kinds of questions seared through Sabrina's mind, but the first one she came up with was 'Why did she stop talking?'

Evelyn shrugged. 'What difference does it make? She's a branded child.'

Sabrina frowned. 'A *what*?'

'A branded child,' Evelyn stated as though speaking of a well-rehearsed routine, 'What I mean is, Cassie witnessed her parents being murdered. Her biological parents. She barely escaped with her life. Had she been less fortunate, she wouldn't have survived.'

Sabrina's eyes went wide.

'It's wrong, but these things happen,' Evelyn went on in a quiet voice. 'The psychiatrists think that the terrible trauma she has suffered makes her retreat inside herself and causes her to become autistic.'

'I . . . I can imagine,' Sabrina said in a half-whisper.

For a moment neither of them spoke.

'I'm one myself, you know,' Sabrina suddenly said.

'What?' Evelyn asked, confused.

'I'm a psychologist,' Sabrina said in a more professional tone of voice. 'I graduated not long ago. I am now practicing in Los Angeles.'

Evelyn's eyebrows lifted. 'Would you like to treat Cassie?'

Sabrina shook her head. 'No, at least not here. There's not a lot I could do in a few hours on an airplane. But if you wouldn't mind telling me Cassie's story, I'd be interested to hear it. We'll see where we go from there.'

Evelyn hesitated and then nodded. 'All right,' she said. 'I'd like to do that. I need all the help I can get.'

Sabrina waited while Evelyn gathered her thoughts.

'It happened three years ago, while Cassie was living in Chicago,' Evelyn began, sounding relieved, as if the story was a burden she desperately needed to unload. 'After it happened – the murder of her parents, I mean – Cassie stayed in a city clinic for a year, where she was treated by doctors and psychologists. When they went in search of a new home for her, they picked us. I don't know why. Maybe it was because we seemed trustworthy and caring. Or maybe it was because we have some financial means. Or maybe because no one else stepped forward to take her. Children with severe traumatic experiences such as hers are not exactly hot items in the adoption market, as you can imagine.' Bitterness imbued her voice as she said that. 'John and I had made the decision to adopt a child and we had filled out the required paperwork. A foster child was the only option left to us. We couldn't have children of our own.'

'Didn't she have any relatives who could take her in?'

'No. At least no one the doctors deemed suitable. I haven't really looked into it. I don't need to know about Cassie's family.'

'Why not?' Sabrina asked.

'Because Cassie's uncle – her father's brother – was the prime suspect in the murders,' Evelyn said. 'Apparently the two started a fight and things got totally out of hand. I want nothing to do with people like that. I have Cassie now, I've become attached to her, and I want to do everything in my power to make her happy. I want her to grow up believing that she is loved and that violence solves nothing.'

Sabrina considered that. 'So Cassie saw everything . . .'

'Yes. She had been left for dead in the same room in which the bodies of her father and mother were discovered. They found the body of her uncle there as well. He had killed himself. At least, that's what the evidence points to. The only survivor of the assault was Cassie, despite a bullet fired into her abdomen. Had the police arrived even a few minutes later than they did, she would have bled to death.'

The drone of the plane's engines sounded muted to Sabrina. She stared ahead, her eyes focusing on nothing, her mind conjuring up images of three bloody corpses and a young girl in contortions, suffering horribly in the grip of panic and terror.

'What happened, exactly?' she asked at length. 'Why did her uncle do this?'

Evelyn shrugged. 'Apparently there had been strife in the family for a long time,' she replied. 'According to Cassie's friends at her old school, the strife made her very unhappy. She was talking normally before the shooting. But after she recovered physically from the bullet wound, she became emotionally withdrawn. No one knows exactly what happened in the house that day. When I look into her eyes, I see so much fear and pain it makes me feel we don't know half of what she saw, or what she went through.'

'I don't know what to say,' Sabrina said, as if in abject surrender to evil.

'There's not much you *can* say,' Evelyn comforted her. 'Yes, it's bad. I deliberated a long time before deciding to bring her with me on this trip. But I couldn't find it in my heart to leave her alone for a whole week, even though that might have been the wise decision. Cassie is going to have to pick her life back up sooner or later, I thought. But now I worry that I'm pushing her too hard too quickly. I hope I won't be sorry for bringing her.'

Another pause, and then Evelyn sighed. 'Why can't she feel safe? She's in a sheltered environment now. John and I love her. She must know that.'

'Traumas like that can stay with a person for a long time,' Sabrina commented.

'I know, and that's what I'm afraid of,' Evelyn said. 'What if this trauma haunts her for the rest of her life? My only wish is that she can leave it all behind and lead a normal life. I feel so badly for her. I want so much to help her. So does John.'

They sat in silence as the plane flew on into the night. Cassie was silent now. Perhaps she had finally fallen asleep.

'You said her uncle was the main suspect,' Sabrina suddenly interjected. 'Wasn't the evidence conclusive?'

'The evidence certainly pointed at him, as I indicated,' Evelyn said. 'But some doubt was cast because of what Cassie said after the murders, shortly before she stopped speaking altogether. She was terrified of a man who was hurting her, a man who wouldn't leave her alone. She wasn't referring to her uncle. She was referring to some other man she claimed had been inside the house.'

'*Another man?*' Sabrina queried.

'I realize it's all very confusing. The police didn't find a shred of evidence that anyone had been inside the house besides the victims and Cassie, and they conducted a very thorough investigation.'

Evelyn glanced up at the curved ceiling and covered her mouth with her hand. Her eyes shone with unshed tears. 'Well, that's it. That's the entire story. After she made that statement she stopped talking, almost overnight.'

When Evelyn said nothing for a while, Sabrina assumed she had indeed related the entire story. But the way Evelyn kept nibbling on her lower lip made Sabrina suspect there was more to come.

'Did something else happen, Evelyn?' she asked softly.

The older woman hesitated for a moment, then said, 'I don't know, I really don't. I sometimes think that Cassie *sees* things.'

'What sort of things?'

'Well,' Evelyn continued, 'there are times when I wonder . . .'

She was struggling to find the right words. Sabrina glanced at the girl, who sat quietly, seemingly unaware that the two women were talking about her.

Unwittingly, Sabrina started chewing her fingernails, a nervous habit of hers. '*What*, Evelyn?'

'Let me put it this way,' Evelyn said cautiously. 'One day John and I took Cassie to church with us in Sugar Creek. During the entire service she kept staring at Rosa McGraft, the town's teacher, who was sitting down from us in the same pew. Rosa was a few years older than me. The next day I heard Rosa had passed away during the night. It was very sudden. She had suffered a stroke.'

Sabrina said nothing.

'The same thing happened with the mailman, Larry Biffin. We saw him every day, but the last time he delivered our mail,

Cassie . . . *stared* after him. The next thing we heard was that Larry had died from a heart attack.'

Evelyn looked away, embarrassed. 'You must think I'm nuts.'

Before Sabrina could respond, Evelyn said, 'It's not just creepy things like that. I'll tell you something else. A while ago my knee was acting up. It got so bad that I had trouble walking. Our doctor couldn't figure out what was wrong with it. He was about to send me to a specialist in Salt Lake City when Cassie placed her hand on my knee. You may not believe this, but I swear it's true. The pain started to ease immediately and within an hour it was gone. And it has never come back. Our doctor was thunderstruck. He had never seen anything like it and had no rational explanation for it.'

There was still no indication that Cassie was listening to what they were saying about her. She just sat there staring dejectedly at her hands folded in her lap.

'So,' Sabrina whispered, 'you're saying that she's been seeing and doing these things ever since the tragedy with her parents?'

Evelyn nodded. 'I asked around a bit, of course. It seems she was always somewhat eccentric, even before the murders. But as far as I could tell she had never done such, well . . .'

'Such strange and inexplicable things,' Sabrina finished for her.

'Exactly,' Evelyn said. 'What troubles me most, however, is that she still won't talk. She does mumble to herself sometimes. I call it babbling. And sometimes she makes louder noises. Throaty sounds . . . they give me the creeps. I can't stand listening to them.'

'Yes,' Sabrina acknowledged. Evelyn's story had stirred up memories of her mother, Patricia Labaton. The cacophony inside her mind started up anew.

Phyllis Ruth Kirby watched her husband hurry toward the bathroom. He waddled a little, like a duck, swinging his head. She had never found these traits very attractive. Or anything else related to his fragile body, for that matter.

Not that outward appearances mattered to Phyllis. She knew she was no pick of the litter, either. That would be Roberta, her only sister, a stunning beauty by anyone's standards.

Roberta was thirty-four years old, still blessed with the svelte, sexy waistline of her youth. Even today she could easily pass for a seductive woman in her mid-twenties.

She had fallen for a man named Lupe Wolfe, a Brad Pitt look-alike.

Life had been good for them until a police SWAT team, four men armed to the teeth, had stormed their house on a cold November morning before sunrise. The police had dragged Lupe from his bed and slapped handcuffs on him. Roberta had gone rigid with shock, so overwhelmed that she hadn't uttered a word. The police carted Lupe off in a squad car while she stayed behind, alone, with her child.

When Lupe appeared in court, Roberta found out what a low-life bastard she had taken up with. Wolfe was convicted for perpetrating three armed robberies. One robbery had spun out of control when he stabbed a bank employee who'd tried to call the cops. Although the victim survived, he had been scarred for life. Now Lupe resided in the Desert Valley State Prison in Big Bear Lake, a place he would call home for many more years.

Roberta had never recovered from the trauma of that night. She no longer trusted men, she had trouble sleeping, and she was on antidepressants. Landing a decent job was out of the question. She would be unable to keep it, and there was no one to look after her child if she did go to work. Her life of luxury had ended abruptly. Now she was at home with a young son, penniless, and she had become the black sheep of the family.

Phyllis, ten years older, had often warned her sister about Lupe, but her words of caution had fallen on deaf ears. Even when she first met him, Phyllis had sensed that Lupe was untrustworthy. She saw something in his eyes that to Roberta conveyed fierceness and courage, but to Phyllis emanated pure evil. Lupe was interested only in himself. Everybody else, as far as he was concerned, could go screw themselves. And that included Roberta, whom he was screwing unmercifully.

Phyllis did not possess her sister's physical beauty – quite the opposite, in fact – but she was smart *and* she commanded respect. Jerrod would never overstep his bounds with her. That's why she was so clear-cut with him, maybe even a bit harsh. But such behavior got results. She knew where she stood with Jerrod and he knew where he stood with her. She would tolerate no unpleasant surprises.

Jerrod disappeared into the toilet stall and closed the door behind him. She waited for him to come back out, but her patience soon ran dry. She remembered that he had complained about constipation recently; and knowing her husband as she did, she realized this could take some time.

Phyllis decided to return to her seat. With a sigh she squeezed past the young man and plopped down on the cushion, her ample derrière consuming the entire space. She closed her eyes, waiting impatiently. She had no intention of falling asleep – she would have to get back up when Jerrod returned to his seat – but her eyelids seemed so heavy.

Phyllis dozed off, trying to return to the dream her husband had intruded upon so rudely. That dream of course had nothing to do with him.

FOURTEEN
Pamela

Aaron Drake rarely remembered the details of his dreams. Often, moments before he awoke images appeared in his mind's eye, as clear and sharp as a movie. This morning these images slipped away from him – as they usually did – when he opened his eyes and saw Sharlene standing over him in the dim light of the crew bunk.

'What is it?' he mumbled, still half-asleep. 'Are you looking for a hot body? I'm ready if you are.'

'Stow it, Aaron,' she said forthrightly. 'Would you please get up?'

The strict tone in her voice brought him fully awake. He slid from the bed and put on his uniform jacket.

Sharlene waited for him by the steps leading down into the cabin. He followed her down the steps and they paused behind the last row of passenger seats.

'Well, what is it?'

'I was just in the cockpit,' Sharlene informed him. 'Apparently they're experiencing some trouble with the computers. Jim wants all electronic devices switched off. We've made the announcement and Michelle, Gloria, and Ray are making the rounds to make sure everyone complies. And the flight map in MEG isn't working, either.'

'Hmm. What's the matter with the computers?'

'I don't know. Jim wasn't specific. I'm not sure he knows.'

'Well,' Aaron said, 'these things happen. That's all?'

Sharlene looked away and bit her lip.

'Was it really necessary to wake me to tell me this?' he persisted.

'I just thought I should let you know,' she said.

Small issues were not uncommon; flights without glitches of any kind were rare. As long as the crew had the situation under control, there was no need to involve the purser. Let alone wake him up. Something else was going on, he intuited. Sharlene looked haggard, as if she hadn't slept in days. He took her hands and wrapped them in his own.

'Come on, Sharlene, out with it. What's the matter?'

She stared at her feet and took a deep breath. He sensed she was about to tell him something important.

But, unexpectedly, she shook her head. 'Why should I always have to tell you everything about me?' she snapped.

The reproach in her voice rendered him momentarily speechless. He hadn't seen this coming. 'What's that supposed to mean?' he asked after a moment.

But there was no need for her to explain. Aaron realized she had a point. He *was* overprotective, and he could imagine that at times she felt suffocated by his controlling nature. He was aware that the reason for his concern and propensity for overprotectiveness was grounded in Sharlene's tumultuous past. He feared that it might trouble her for a long time to come.

His own past played a role, as well. Pamela had never really let him go. She had carved a scar into his soul. He saw her again now, in his mind. More than once she had confessed to him that he was the kind of man she could have fallen for, were he not her brother. He was dependable, charming, and attractive, she told him.

'And you have a brain,' she added with a grin.

Aaron had insisted that she should be looking for a different kind of man. Her praise was flattering – and he wouldn't contest it – but in the long run she would find a man like him too boring. Pamela craved excitement, the thrill of the unexpected and the unknown. His life was much too predictable. In the end, she had to admit he was right.

Aaron knew he was attractive to women, but Pamela had truly been one of Mother Nature's gems. Her long ebony hair, symmetrical face, and soft, smooth skin could turn a normal man's eye anywhere, at any time. Her radiant smile alone would have taken her places.

She was a regular male-magnet and the envy of legions of other women. Pamela had everything – beauty, intelligence, charm – yet lacked one attribute, which was invisible on the outside but manifested itself in what she did. Or rather, what she *didn't* do.

After what happened to her – when it was too late – Aaron had developed an internal radar system to detect similar issues in other people.

Such as Sharlene.

In the nine weeks he and Sharlene had been a couple, she had had several anxiety attacks. Her main problem was darkness. What was she afraid of? He assumed it was post-traumatic stress. Although her father had passed away and Todd Bower was in jail, her mental scars had not yet healed. The worst was her recurring nightmare, which she apparently had had again this night. He suspected the dream was related to the terrible sufferings she'd been forced to endure. He prayed that Sharlene would someday come to terms with her past.

As long as she doesn't decide to take the car out and drive it into a lake.

Aaron wished he could grab that thought and crush it beneath his heel.

Just like Pamela, Sharlene seemed to have everything going for her. And just like Pamela, inside she was as vulnerable as a newborn babe.

'So stop pestering me!' Sharlene woke him from his reverie.

Yes, with that tone of voice she sounded depressingly like Pamela.

When she was twenty-four, Pamela – who was three years his junior – had fallen in love with a man twice her age with four children from two previous marriages. His name was Borislav, and he hailed from Lithuania. Aaron was convinced his sister must have suffered one of her fits of madness to be attracted to a man so unworthy of her.

Everything went along fine for a few months, a long span of time by Pamela's standards. Her relationships with men rarely lasted more than six weeks before they turned sour. One day she came to Aaron in tears, to announce she was pregnant. *That* was something entirely new. Aaron was stunned.

Borislav, she said, wanted to marry her, but how would she break the news to their parents? They would disown her if she married someone so abominable in their eyes. In the end, Aaron had stood by his sister, although he would have preferred to see Pamela have an abortion and be rid of the son of a bitch forever.

Their father and mother were devastated when they heard the news. But they could see no way out. In their views on sex and marriage, Donald and Clarice Drake were traditional parents. An abortion was something they would never condone. If their daughter was pregnant, she had to wed the father. It was as simple as that.

Aaron tried to prevent the marriage, but in vain. It might have worked if Pamela had spoken up and refused to utter her vows. But she hadn't, which was typical of her.

She never stood up for herself. Not when it mattered.

And she had been afraid of Borislav's friends. Even now Aaron was convinced he knew only a fraction of what the man and his shady pals had done to her.

The wedding took place, as scheduled. For Aaron and his parents, it had been a day they wanted to forget as soon as possible.

But then other things had gone wrong.

Aaron felt a lump form in his throat. The memories were still as vivid and as painful as the actual events had been.

'I'm not trying to pester you, Sharlene, believe me,' he said.

Tonight was a world away from the hours they had spent alone on the beach together before the flight, just the two of them and the roaring surf and the love they had shared upon the soft white sand.

She looked away from him and folded her arms across her chest. When she looked back, he saw tears welling in her eyes.

'I can't . . .' she whispered.

Maybe she was finally going to open up to him. Aaron held his breath and waited.

'What is it?' he urged when she refused to continue. 'What can't you do? Please, Sharlene, tell me.'

'I can't, I can't tell you,' she said tearfully.

His eyes posed questions at her. 'I don't know what you're referring to, Sharlene,' he said quietly, 'but please let me help you.'

Despair was clearly etched on her face. He saw an unspeakable hurt there, as if she had taken off a mask and he was only now seeing the real Sharlene. There was something hidden inside her that he didn't understand and couldn't uncover.

'Sharlene,' he persisted. 'You have *me*. What's the matter? You trust me, don't you? You know I love you.'

She stared at him as though he had just claimed to have found the solution for bringing peace on earth.

But then she shook her head. 'No, you wouldn't understand. *No one* understands.'

He felt more confused than ever.

'Come, we have work to do,' she said before he could respond. With that, she turned and walked into the cabin.

He wanted to stop her. On the beach, everything had been so idyllic. But something had happened between then and now. What was it? *What* had happened?

First the scare in her attic at home, then the turbulence, and the nightmare on board the plane. What connected the dots? What in the world was going on, he wanted to cry out in despair.

You wouldn't understand.

Pamela had said basically the same thing to him after her miscarriage. And after her fights with Borislav, after she had told her husband she wanted a divorce, and he had reacted with all the fury and vengeance of a madman. And after her bouts with depression, just before in a final act of despair she drove her car into a lake.

The police had called Aaron first. He had identified Pamela's body, to spare his parents the ordeal. Later, he had fallen sick, suffering from feverish nightmares in which Pamela kept returning. In them, she was as pale as a corpse and soaking wet. But an accusing glint shimmered in her eyes, as if she blamed him for her death.

Aaron had agonized over the reason why his sister had wanted to kill herself. What more could he, *should* he, have done? The longer he tormented himself, the more he became convinced that Borislav had not been the cause of her misery, but rather a symptom of it.

Harsh as it might be to accept, Pamela had done it to *herself*. But why? Was it a character flaw? Was it a lack of self-esteem? Someone who lacked it, or lost it, was defenseless and could be dragged kicking and screaming into the depths of mental anguish.

Aaron would do anything not to end up in the same state of utter despair. Depression, he knew, often ran in families. Despite what had happened to Pamela, he had kept his back straight, however hard it was to barricade himself from his grief. But he had never let on – or at least he had tried his damnedest not to let on.

Aaron had told Pamela's story to Sharlene, whose self-esteem had also been shattered, first by her father and then by that bastard Todd. The death of her mother had been the seed of her misery.

How deep did her misery go? What was she still keeping from him? No matter what it was or how complicated it might be, he had resolved to protect her better than he had Pamela.

It was almost 3:50 in the morning when he followed Sharlene into the cabin.

Gloria informed him that they had finished their rounds checking for electronic devices. Two laptops and a handful of cell phones had been switched off.

'I'll go tell the cockpit crew,' Aaron announced. He could just phone it in, but he was curious about the computer glitches that Jim seemed to be having.

FIFTEEN
Anomaly

Seventy-five minutes had elapsed since the pilots received their last radio contact or navigational signal. During that time they had received no response to their squawking, either. Such universal silence ran contrary to everything Jim Nichols deemed possible.

When Sharlene had stepped into the cockpit a few minutes earlier, he'd decided not to confide in her. She was just beginning to feel at home as a member of the Oceans Airways family. Although she'd admirably climbed the promotional ladder, he questioned if she was sufficiently experienced to weather a crisis.

Jim was at his wits' end as he concentrated on keeping the nose of the plane aimed at the star they'd been flying toward since before the turbulence.

'Another four hours and we're out of fuel,' he announced.

He consulted the totalizer, the gauge indicating how much fuel remained. According to the reading, they had about 122,000 pounds of J4 left to burn.

'We'll make it to Australia,' Ben said without a trace of doubt in his voice. Jim nodded and rubbed the weariness from his eyes.

If they were at the position of his dead reckoning, they should be able to land safely at an Australian airport.

But he wasn't sure about much of anything anymore, including their current position.

In the last hour he and Ben had desperately tried to figure out what had gone wrong. Ben's suggestion to have the passengers switch off all electronic devices stemmed from the fact that, a few years earlier, a Qantas plane had deviated from its heading due to the use of laptops in the passenger cabin. Jim didn't think a simple laptop could interfere with so many onboard systems, but it couldn't hurt to shut them off.

'I remember hearing something about peculiar trouble on board a Martinair jet,' Ben had offered during the last hour. 'It was weird. Really weird.'

Jim frowned. 'Which sort of plane? And when was it?'

'A 767 from Amsterdam to Orlando, I think,' Ben replied. 'It happened about eight or maybe even ten years ago.'

'*What* happened?'

'As I recall, the plane suddenly had warning lights turning on and off and seat-belt lights blinking. And then the autopilot shut down and a few systems malfunctioned, including navigation.'

What Ben had described stirred something deep within Jim. 'Yes, I think I do remember hearing about that,' he mused. 'Do you recall how it ended?'

'The pilot had his hands full landing the plane in Boston,' Ben said. 'But all's well that ends well, right?'

'Did they ever find out what caused the problems?'

Ben shook his head. 'No, I'm pretty sure they didn't. I remember reading something about a faulty battery, but that was conjecture. It had all the earmarks of a Bermuda Triangle event.'

'Well, that's not our problem,' Jim stated categorically. 'The Bermuda Triangle is in the Atlantic. We're over the Pacific.'

He asked Greg to review the gripe sheet that contained information about earlier defects detected in the aircraft. It was generally used by mechanics when making repairs, and not by pilots trying to make a safe landing.

'Nothing special,' Greg reported after giving the report a quick once-over. 'After the previous flight, they changed a navigation light on the right wing. Earlier, one of the wheel brakes was acting up. That's about it.'

Jim kept searching for explanations, but none came to light. EICAS was no help; it still reported no malfunctions.

If EICAS was right, the fact that they had no radio and that no one had yet responded to their squawking meant that they were still too far out of reach of ground control or any other signal of civilization. But that was ridiculous. There were islands down there and there were people living on them. Jim estimated that they had left Polynesia behind and were now approaching the Kiribati Islands, or maybe the Solomons. These places all had airports, some of them large enough to accommodate a 747, so why the hell had no one from air-traffic control responded to their transponder code?

Mechanical reasons might account for the flight-management systems failing, but they would have been duly noted by EICAS. That even the mechanical compass was acting up smacked of something inexplicable.

Had it been an option, he would have landed at the first airport they encountered. But all airports had disappeared from the computer map. His thoughts raced, seemingly out of control.

The world has ceased to exist. But that's impossible, isn't it?

At 3:45 Greg transmitted yet another radio blast to any planes or air-traffic control towers within hailing distance. Jim's sense that the world no longer existed kept nagging at him, no matter how ludicrous such a Doomsday scenario seemed.

As he had pointed out to Ben, the Atlantic Ocean had the Bermuda Triangle, infamous because of the planes and ships that had mysteriously vanished within its confines. But the Pacific had its Devil's Sea, not far from Japan, where it was also claimed that ships and aircraft had disappeared without trace.

It was said by some that in the Bermuda Triangle all radio contact with planes had been normal before they suddenly vanished from the computer screen. Researchers reported strange phenomena in the area: heavy turbulences, magnetic disturbances, and compasses going haywire. Jim saw a disturbing resemblance between such phenomena and their current situation. He looked back at the navigation display, devoid of location points. It made no sense. No sense whatsoever.

What if we have disappeared from the world? Have we ceased to exist?

'Jim?' Ben ventured.

He turned around. 'Yes?'

'I asked what you're planning to do.'

Jim hadn't heard him. 'I don't know . . .' he started.

He would sell his soul to receive confirmation that he was still in the land of the living, in the world he knew. Peering down at the sea, he searched for lights on ships or islands. But he saw nothing in the darkness beneath them – thanks to the heavy cloud cover, he presumed.

Of course the world was still there. Yet still he prayed for confirmation.

His only option was to follow the stars – just like some ancient mariner or Peter Pan, he thought bitterly. *Second star to the right, and straight on till morning.* But at the moment a needle in a haystack would be easier to find than Kingsford Smith International Airport in Sydney.

He shook his head. 'I don't know, Ben. We can stay up here for a few more hours. We just have to wait until we establish radio contact with *someone*. We must assume that ground control is trying to find us just as hard as we're trying to find them.'

You've got that right, especially after what you did yesterday, Jody's voice whispered in his ear.

Her voice sounded so clear to him that he dismissed her words as a passing thought. It seemed as if she were standing right there beside him. He even caught a scent of her perfume, or so it seemed.

Jim Nichols suddenly felt a lot worse.

Someone rang the cockpit doorbell. He looked at the camera screen and saw Aaron Drake standing there. Jim pressed a button and the door opened.

Aaron stepped inside the flight deck. 'I just wanted to let you know that a couple of cell phones and laptops have been switched off,' he reported.

'Thanks,' Jim said. 'Anything else?'

Aaron hesitated. 'Sharlene told me we're experiencing some problems. Is there . . .' He hesitated again. 'Is there anything the crew should know? Anything we can do?'

Jim decided to lay it on the line. He could not leave the cabin crew dangling in the dark for much longer. He needed to bring them into his confidence, consequences be damned.

'OK, Aaron,' he said. 'As crazy as it sounds, here's what's going on, or not.'

Interlude II

'Good, very good,' Dr Richardson said, his bald head glistening in the sunlight filtering into his office. He was sitting across from her in a plush chair, and she was lying on the couch. It was December, eighteen months before she applied for her job at Oceans Airways, something that was inconceivable to her at this juncture in her life.

'You're doing a brave thing,' he continued in a soothing voice. 'Not many people in your position seek help.'

He tried to appear sympathetic, to win her trust, but she didn't need anyone to tell her: Noel Richardson was the last chance she had of getting her life back on track. She was standing on the brink of the same abyss into which she had once fallen.

During their first of many sessions, Richardson had asked her to start by telling her story. She had complied and the first thing she told him involved that unforgettable day during the summer a year after her mother's death.

It had been a scorching day in mid-July. Sharlene had recently turned sixteen and her life had changed dramatically since that fateful day in March of the previous year. She came home, tanned from the sun, sweating and itching to take a shower. When she stepped into the house and yelled out in greeting, she heard no response from the living room. For a moment she wondered whether her father had gone out. A quick glance at the kitchen counter, however, confirmed what she needed to know.

She removed her Los Angeles Dodgers cap and tiptoed into the house. No, her father was not in the living room. She walked up the stairs to the hobby room where she found him, as she often did, slouched in a chair. He had one elbow on the table and his hand was clenched into a fist under his right cheek. His other hand was on his legs, below the table top. Beside him was an opened can of beer. She had seen a number of empty ones downstairs on the kitchen counter.

When he glanced up and noticed her standing there, his eyes appeared red and puffy. He had considerably more gray hair than the year before and he had added a good twenty pounds to his girth. Sharlene could see he was drunk, but she could not determine how drunk.

'I'm not feeling so hot,' he mumbled. Sharlene understood what he meant: it had turned bad again.

'Why don't you lie down for a while?' she suggested, but he waved his hand dismissively.

After he slept, if only for a few hours, he wouldn't be so hammered and she might be able to have a conversation with him. In former days her father rarely drank liquor. No more than a few beers a week, and only occasionally. That routine, however, had changed. In the beginning she hadn't known how to handle his increasing use of alcohol. But gradually she had learned.

'Do you need some help?'

She bit her tongue as soon as she uttered that inane remark. Her father reacted as if he had been slapped across the face. 'I don't need any bloody help,' he slurred, 'least of all from my own daughter.'

Sharlene thought quickly. She needed to get her father into bed so he could sleep it off. He was too stubborn to go by himself even if he had been able to stand. During an earlier such encounter, Dean Thier had barely reached the landing before collapsing in a heap.

'Can I get you some coffee or water?'

She didn't have much hope he would accept her offer, but it was worth a shot.

Her father lifted his beer can. 'I'd rather you bring me another one of these,' he slurred.

That was the answer she had dreaded.

'I think we're all out.'

Her father pounded his fist on the table. 'The hell we are! Make yourself useful and go look in the fridge! There's plenty more in there.'

His voice was raw and thick and accusatory. Sharlene could deny it, pretend it wasn't so, but she knew better. No matter how far gone Dean Thier might be, when it came to his beer supply his memory was as lucid as a crystal-clear mountain lake.

'Come on,' she insisted. 'You're not feeling well. Go lie down.'

'I need a drink first, and you're going to get it for me,' Dean said as a matter of fact.

Sharlene crossed over to him and tried pulling him up by his arm. But then she heard herself say the worst thing she could have said to him at that moment. She wasn't sure why she said it. Maybe it was her keen frustration over the derelict her father had become, or maybe she was simply desperate. Or maybe it was the result of being exhausted from being outdoors for so long.

'You've had quite enough,' she stated in no uncertain terms.

His eyes bulging, her father stared at her.

'Where do you come off thinking that's your call, girl?' he fumed.

Instead of keeping her mouth shut, Sharlene took it one step further, realizing all too well that this would end badly. But she could not help herself.

'You have to stop doing this to yourself,' she screamed at him, a tone of voice she had never used in his presence. 'It makes no fucking sense.'

Dean Thier did not immediately respond. For a moment Sharlene thought she might have finally gotten through to him. For that one moment she thought she saw understanding in his eyes. But the moment proved to be fleeting.

'I found this in your room,' he hissed, his breath reeking of beer and his voice hoarse with rage.

Sharlene saw her father lift his other hand, the one he had resting in his lap. Dean opened his palm and showed her a toy airplane. A model of a Western Sky Boeing 737, the same type of airplane her mother had flown in. And died in.

'Weren't you supposed to throw this out?' he barked.

Sharlene shook her head, unable to speak.

Dean took his beer can in hand and crushed it. 'This is what happens to planes,' he said, his eyes boring into her. The can slipped from his hand and hit the floor with a muted thud. 'They go down, baby,' he added in an icy voice. 'They go down.'

Again Sharlene shook her head. 'No. Why are you doing this? You—'

She cringed when her father struck her hard on the side of the face.

'That thing should have been in the garbage!' Dean Thier roared.

Sharlene did not cry out. She didn't even get angry. She stood there, her pent-up rage boiling to the surface.

'Go to hell, you bastard!' she screamed at him. 'Damn your sorry

hide. You're not my problem anymore. I've had enough, do you hear me? I want nothing more to do with you!'

She ran from her father and locked herself in the one room he had not once entered since his wife had died: her Tupperware room.

It had become Sharlene's sanctuary. It was the only room where the pathetic excuse for a father never bothered her. Where Claudia's Tupperware, in every color imaginable, collected dust on the shelves.

She sat down on the floor, crossing her legs and folding her hands on top of them, and lowered her head, as if in prayer. She could no longer contain her tears. Her mother's gold crucifix on its silver chain dangled beneath her chin. She closed her hand around the necklace and brought it to her lips. 'Mother . . .'

That's when her father started kicking down the door of the Tupperware room.

'Sharlene!' Dean yelled in a drunken rage. 'Sharlene, you get out of there!'

She pursed her lips as he kicked again, harder this time. The door shook. Another fierce thud. And another. The lock broke.

The rest of it, she didn't want to remember.

Sharlene returned to Noel Richardson's office.

She glanced furtively at his door, silent in its frame.

No one was kicking it.

III

3:52 A.M. — 5:08 A.M.

.

SIXTEEN
Emilio and the Outlaw

Because Emilio Cabrera was terrified of flying, he had felt unspeakable relief when the turbulence ended. His euphoria, however, was short-lived. When the turbulence ebbed, his fears of the tribunal awaiting him in Sydney mounted. Perhaps, he thought, a movie might provide a welcome diversion. That, and a little liquid refreshment to calm his nerves. As a friendly flight attendant served him a mini-bottle of Johnnie Walker Red, he donned his headset and managed to calm his nerves by watching *The Invention of Lying*, a romantic comedy about a world in which little white lies were tolerated and even rewarded.

When the movie ended, he searched for another and found an action movie starring Bruce Willis. Too violent, he decided. Bad for the nerves. He channel-surfed to the next movie. An actress with ample breasts and cherry-red lips was kissing her co-star. That was certainly a reason to keep watching – but, oh dear God, was her co-star Nicolas Cage? Yes, it was. Emilio hated the man with a passion. He couldn't explain *why* he hated him. He just did.

On the next channel was a Western. Obviously an oldie, or what these days would be called a classic. John Wayne, wearing a white wide-brimmed hat on his head and a bandana around his neck, filled the small screen. This could be something worth watching, Emilio suspected. As a little boy, he had always enjoyed Westerns. So he slouched down in his seat, comfortable in his resolve to enjoy himself.

The storyline didn't amount to much. Wayne played the sheriff in a hick town of wizened cattle drivers. As with most John Wayne oaters, it would end with the inevitable shoot-out and Wayne emerging, yet again, as a hero of the Old West. He who wanted to pump Wayne full of lead was an outlaw named Phil Clark, a cagey desperado with an unshaven face and a few missing teeth, leading a gang of thugs. Phil swore revenge against Wayne, in his role as sheriff Jeffery Eastman, for icing one of his men. That would surely end badly for Phil, Emilio presumed, involuntarily comparing the movie script with his own unsettling state of affairs. He also noticed that his little bottle of Johnnie Walker was empty. He wanted another one, and he didn't have to wait long. A flight attendant was coming his way. He raised his hand.

After Aaron had left for the flight deck, Sharlene wished she had some downtime. She hated confrontations with Aaron, on any level. But personal time was impossible in the confines of an airline galley. Jessica Orrigo and Rosette Fiske had joined Gloria and Ray in the galley and the four of them were engaged in a lively conversation.

'I'm going to make another round,' Sharlene said to them. 'Stretch my legs a little.'

She walked away, seeking privacy. She wanted to empty her mind, to think of nothing. She headed toward the tail section of the plane, turned the corner in front of the aft toilets and the crew bunk, and started another round of walking on the opposite side of the plane.

One of the passengers raised his hand.

'Miss?'

The man, a Latino, emanated a pungent odor of sweat. His neighbor by the window seemed bothered by something, probably the stench. She was a sprightly young girl with short blonde hair, who was leaning her head against the bulkhead. The girl was either pretending to be asleep or trying to go to sleep, but Sharlene could tell by her dour facial expression that she was wide awake.

'Could you get me another Scotch, please?' the man asked politely.

Although her father's alcoholism had instilled in her a hatred for hard liquor, she only refused such requests from passengers who were well on their way to becoming blotto. This man might have a problem with body odor, but he was far from being drunk.

'Of course,' she promised. 'I'll be right back.'

She returned to the main galley. To her surprise, she found no one there. She wondered where Rosette, Gloria, Jessica, and Ray had gone.

Not that it mattered.

Sharlene squatted down, selected a mini-bottle of Johnnie Walker and placed it on the countertop, next to a plastic cup and a small tray.

Behind her, the galley curtain swished open.

'Where have you been?' she asked, without looking up to see who was there.

She assumed her co-workers had followed her example and taken a stroll through the aircraft. Apparently she had been so lost in thought that she hadn't spotted them inside the cabin. That was not unusual, however. A 747 was a much bigger airplane than most people thought.

A hand caressed her back. So, it was not her co-workers after all.

She stayed in the same position, still not looking up but enjoying the attention. 'What did Jim say?'

He didn't answer. She couldn't blame him. She had just snapped at him outside the crew's bunk. She had let herself go, and now she felt remorseful.

'Look, Aaron, I didn't mean what I said. I . . .'

She hung her head, considering what to say to bridge the gap. 'I don't know why I yelled at you. It was my fault, not yours.' She ran her tongue over her lower lip. 'After we land in Sydney, we'll talk about it. All right? I'll explain.'

Just when she had given up on love, she had finally found a man she could trust. She must now give him her trust in return. She knew their relationship could not keep going on the way it was, stuck in neutral. She had to listen to her heart and move it forward.

Even if he can't handle it and it ends with him breaking it off, at least we will have been honest with each other. At least I will know I have been honest with him.

Aaron still had said nothing. But his hand kept caressing her back.

Sharlene closed her eyes and remembered the last time she had seen the sun, on Venice Beach. No one there but the two of them, just like now. The roaring surf and the shade of the overhanging rock, a secluded area just big enough for them to crawl into and cuddle. She had wanted time to stand still that afternoon, but the minutes had ticked by much too quickly.

Aaron drew closer as his hands moved around her, cupping her breasts and gently stroking them. She sighed with pleasure when he tweaked her nipples.

'Stop it, Aaron!' she whispered, despite the ripples of pleasure coursing through her. 'Someone might come in!'

In reply, he pinched her hard.

'*Stop* that!' she said more forcefully.

What has gotten into him? she wondered. He shouldn't be doing this. How embarrassing would it be for someone to walk in and catch the purser feeling up a stewardess! But Aaron still did not release her. He kept squeezing her breasts and massaging her nipples until they grew hard despite herself. Then she heard a dull thud close by.

Sharlene opened her eyes. In front of her, on the floor, was the small bottle of Scotch whisky, the one she had put on the countertop for the man with the foul body odor. How did that happen? she wondered. She couldn't have knocked it over, and they hadn't experienced any turbulence.

Suddenly she felt a severe chill, as if she had stepped into a frigid storage locker. She looked back over her shoulder.

There was no one behind her.

She stared at nothing, shivering and rubbing her arms.

Then the galley's curtain was swished aside.

Gloria and Jessica were back.

Jessica frowned. 'Is everything all right, Sharlene?'

'I . . .' Sharlene looked away and picked up the whisky bottle. 'I dropped this.'

'Are you really OK?' Jessica persisted. 'You look like you've seen a ghost.'

Sharlene's hands were shaking so badly she was having trouble holding on to the little whisky bottle.

I have to get out of here. Now!

She clenched the little bottle between both hands, left the tray on the counter, and stormed out of the galley.

It was only when she handed the whisky to the Latino that she noticed she had forgotten the cup. Fortunately he had another one jammed into the seat pocket in front of him.

'Here you go,' she said.

'Thank you.'

'You're welcome.'

Sharlene walked off and then stopped beside an exit, facing the door. Had she been at home now, she would have crawled into bed with a pillow over her head. But there was nowhere to be alone in this plane.

Until what had just happened in the galley, she would have

believed that her anxieties had returned, and that was all. She had had that nightmare, and then the feeling she was being pursued. Illusions. They were all just illusions.

But if those were just illusions, what the hell had *this* been? She could still feel the warmth of the hands on her breasts.

As she struggled to compose herself, another bizarre event happened. A woman somewhere behind her started yelling in a loud voice. She was an enormous lady who came waddling down the aisle toward Sharlene, calling out to someone named Jerrod.

Emilio gratefully accepted the bottle of Scotch. He adjusted his headphones, poured a measure of the golden liquid into his cup, and turned his attention back to the movie.

Phil Clark was hiding behind an old barrel on the porch outside the saloon. Gun in hand, John Wayne, alias sheriff Jeff Eastman, was crouching behind the doorframe of a building on the other side of the street. The two men were separated by a few yards of sand and dust. Tumbleweeds rolled past, propelled by a hot desert breeze.

The camera zoomed in on Eastman's pinched eyes set beneath the brim of his grayish white hat. He was chewing on something that could have been a piece of gum. Next in view came a close-up of Clark's grim unshaven face. With his black hat and the long dark coat he was wearing, he cast a menacing glare as he squatted behind the barrel, a shotgun resting on his knee.

'Come on out and I'll spare this town!' Clark shouted at Eastman. 'My men are on their way. There's nowhere for you to run.'

The camera zoomed in on Eastman again. He didn't answer, but you could see his mind working. The outlaw was right. He was trapped.

Another close-up of Clark, whose face filled the screen. His beady, heavy-lidded eyes fearsome beneath the black hat. He grinned mockingly.

'What are you doing this for, Jeffery?' he shouted out to the lawman. 'Don't you see what's going on here? Cabrera is pulling a fast one on you. He stole from the boss. Hand him over to us!'

Emilio's eyes went wide. He reached up and pressed the headphones down more firmly over his ears.

'I'm telling you, the gringo is a thief!' Clark rasped. 'We want him, Jeffery. This time he won't escape. *Hand him over!*'

Emilio pulled off his headphones and, with trembling fingers, started pushing the touch screen at random. Phil Clark's face remained on the screen a moment longer, and then Emilio's finger hit the off button. The screen went black.

Emilio sat there wide-eyed.

Then he heard a commotion and looked up. Ahead, down near the lavatories, something was going on. Something bad.

SEVENTEEN
Occupied

It was 4:10. Although Sabrina Labaton had not exchanged a word with Evelyn in twenty minutes, she kept rewinding Cassie's story in her mind. At the moment, Evelyn was holding Cassie's hand. Both mother and daughter appeared lost in thought. In the main cabin all was quiet. Only the flight attendants were moving about.

Sabrina decided to stretch her legs. She got up and started ambling through the aisle. Her thoughts returned to her mother, Patricia Labaton, who had been confined to an institution for years. Sabrina's sister Susan had accepted the fact that their mother would never be able to leave the institution. But Sabrina could not accept that dire fate. It was, in part, why she had majored in psychology.

On a hot summer day that was otherwise quite ordinary, Patricia Labaton was struck by a car while crossing the street. She had recovered physically from the accident, but not emotionally. Her mind remained permanently damaged, according to her primary physician. Since then, she had heard voices inside her head. The voices made her do things that heretofore were totally out of character. What was strange, though, was that in earlier years, long before the accident, their mother sometimes talked about things she had no way of knowing. If Sabrina lost something, her mother often told her where to find it. And she always seemed to know when Sabrina would call her. Patricia had also predicted that Susan would move to Australia long before Susan had even considered the notion.

Sabrina had discussed all this with her mother's doctor, who in a derisive tone had summarily dismissed it as irrelevant. But when Sabrina had decided to read up on alternative psychological disciplines, a new world had opened up to her. She was reminded of this after what Evelyn had told her.

Sabrina glanced around furtively, as if fearful that other people could sense her musings about her mother. Her eyes locked with those of a balding man in his forties who was studying her intently. Was he entertaining sexual fantasies about her? She detested men like that. Then she saw, across from her in the opposite aisle, a heavy-set woman shuffling past. Sabrina had noticed her before. The obese woman was glancing around, clearly agitated.

'Jerrod! Jerrod!' she started shouting in a voice so loud she immediately got everyone's attention.

When the blonde flight attendant walked toward the woman, she started gesturing wildly. A glint of a distant memory dawned in Sabrina's mind. At first she failed to understand its meaning. Then it blossomed into full sunlight.

She set off to talk to the big woman. The closest path across to the other aisle was straight through the main galley, which is where she went. As she approached the woman, she was already joined by two more flight attendants.

'Yes, I'm serious!' the portly woman bellowed to the blonde stewardess. 'Of course I'm serious! What do you think, that I'm an idiot? *He's been gone for half an hour, for Christ's sake!*'

'Is Jerrod . . . the skinny man?' Sabrina blurted out.

The woman swiveled toward her. 'Yes, he is. Where is he? Do you know?'

'He went to the bathroom, I think.'

As the woman stared at her, Sabrina thought back. She had noticed a skinny man hurry past her in the direction of the bathrooms. Everything about him bespoke an urgent need to urinate. That was when she had noticed the fat lady for the first time.

And it was also when Cassie had started making strange noises as she leaned across the armrest of her seat and stared at the man's back. Afterward the girl with the ponytail had been curiously downcast. Without Cassie, Sabrina would not have noticed Jerrod. She was not in the habit of keeping track of complete strangers on a plane, especially those on the way to the lavatory. Sabrina couldn't recall seeing the skinny man emerge from the toilet stall. But why would she recall such a thing?

Except, for a reason she could not explain, it seemed evident that Jerrod had not returned to his seat.

'*Which one?*' his wife thundered.

'What?' Sabrina replied. 'I'm sorry, I don't understand.'

'*Which stall!*'

'Um . . .'

Sabrina thought hard. 'One of these two, I think.'

She pointed toward the toilet stalls, feeling uncomfortable being the center of attention for this large, demanding woman and three flight attendants. Everywhere she looked, passengers were craning their necks to get a better view.

On the stall to the left, the green indicator beneath the door handle read UNOCCUPIED. For a reason Sabrina did not understand, the fat lady yanked the door open. Did she think her husband was hiding in there?

Then the woman started pounding on the other door, which displayed a red OCCUPIED indicator under the door handle. 'Jerrod!' she yelled shamelessly, making no effort to control her voice. '*Jerrod! It's me! Phyllis! Open up!*'

Sabrina was tempted to tell the woman she was behaving like a mad heifer, but she restrained herself.

No answer was heard from inside the occupied stall.

Phyllis threw another perplexed glance, first at Sabrina and then at the blonde flight attendant, who had said nothing since Sabrina came on the scene. She just stood there, watching. Before one of the other two flight attendants could interfere, the woman pounded the toilet door again. 'Jerrod! Are you in there? *Say* something!'

Nothing but silence greeted her entreaties.

Phyllis's eyes bore through the blonde flight attendant. 'Open it!' she demanded in the tone of an incensed drill sergeant. But the blonde stewardess did not salute or snap to attention. Nor did her two colleagues. They deferred to the blonde, who apparently had seniority.

'*Open it!*' Phyllis screamed.

Sabrina opened her mouth as if to say something, but whatever it was she swallowed her words.

Cassie had drawn her attention.

The girl had risen from her seat. The flight attendants followed Sabrina's gaze and saw Cassie as well. She stood in the aisle; her face was twisted into a grimace and her fists were clenched. For a fleeting moment she reminded Sabrina of her tomcat Toby, the pet her father had given her when she was a little girl. Toby had been a kindly animal, except when she took him to the vet. There he would hiss menacingly, arch his back and extend his claws, and there was no placating him.

Evelyn stood up, too. She was trying to coax Cassie back into her seat.

'*Open it!*' Phyllis bellowed yet again, drawing herself up to her full imposing height. With every eye in the cabin hard upon her, Sabrina looked back at the toilet door with its clear red shield that read: OCCUPIED. *Was* the skinny man in there?

If so, what had happened to him?

EIGHTEEN
Jody

'OK, Aaron,' Jim said. 'As crazy as it sounds, here's what's going on, or not.'

The pilot then told Aaron Drake what those in the cockpit were struggling to understand. He said that when the turbulence hit, some ninety minutes earlier, they had lost radio contact as well as their navigation systems. Jim tried to sound calm and professional, as if these were routine challenges for a seasoned pilot. He blamed the lack of radio traffic on bad frequencies, and the malfunctioning navigation on defects in the flight-management systems.

'We're on top of it,' he said, 'but I assume that's why the flight map in MEG has stopped working. Don't worry. The engines are fine and we'll land somewhere. The transponder is active, so I'm sure it'll be picked up by a ground station any moment now. After that, we'll see what happens.'

Aaron nodded. 'OK. We'll tell the passengers we're experiencing a slight malfunction and are working to restore it.'

'You do that,' Jim said. 'There's no cause for alarm.' *Not yet at least*, he thought to himself.

After the purser left the cockpit, Jim heaved a sigh. He believed he had given Aaron the right amount of information. Aaron could brief the cabin crew members, to set them at ease, and they in turn would calm those passengers who suspected that something might be amiss. At 4:17, Greg sent out another flurry of messages on all radio frequencies. None of them proved fruitful.

'Let's assume for a moment,' Jim conjectured, 'that we're unable to get our radio back. In that case we will be intercepted by Australian fighter planes as soon as we enter their airspace. We'll have to use hand signals to get them to help us land.'

'But what if we *don't* encounter any F16s?' Greg said.

'What do you mean?' Ben asked.

'Exactly what I just said,' Greg insisted.

'Jesus, Greg,' Ben countered. 'Australia is a big country, we can't miss it. Of course they'll intercept us. Do you think their air force is asleep down there? If we intrude on their airspace without proper identification, they're going to send up fighters. You can bet your life on it.'

Ben Wright was one of the most pragmatic people Jim knew. And that was a good thing. In the next few hours he would need a clear head in the cockpit.

Jim could only imagine what was going through Greg's mind. Was it possible that his copilot had been wondering the same thing he was? That maybe Flight 582 was about to turn into some kind of Bermuda Triangle mystery?

He remembered something his flying instructor had once told him. *Jim, there's only one thing missing in the cockpit and that's a crystal ball.*

Ben grumbled something and Greg decided not to press the issue. And Jim decided not to stoke up the fire.

'Let's keep our heads together, guys,' he said, with all the objectivity he could muster.

Jim had dealt with these kinds of issues before. Once, in another Boeing 747-400, two engines had stalled. On another occasion they had lost air pressure, causing oxygen masks to drop down in the passenger cabins. In both cases he, as captain, had kept his cool. That kind of professional behavior had been expected of him then and it was expected of him now.

The engines are fine. We'll land safely somewhere.

That was Jim's most devout hope and prayer. But something deep within him questioned whether that was true.

You're a murderer. Remember yesterday? Jody suddenly whispered into his ear. Again it seemed as though she was right there beside him.

A shiver assaulted him.

He understood, of course, that Jody's voice had emanated from his own mind. The phenomenon had started ever since he first realized that his marriage was heading for the rocks regardless of his decision to quit flying. He could remember the exact moment he had heard that voice for the first time.

It had been last year, on November 12th, the first day of his life he'd spent in a hospital. The previous night he had cruised the local bars on a serious drinking binge. As a result of his intoxication, twelve hours of his life had been permanently erased from his memory. He was told that he had consumed enough alcohol to knock out a normal human being and should thank God that he was still alive. After that near-death experience, Jim had controlled his liquor intake. He had to if he wanted to keep his job. He had taken a few weeks off to clear his head, and by the grace of God had managed to keep the 'incident' a secret from his superiors at Oceans Airways.

But ever since that awful night Jim had been having trouble staying asleep. He often had weird dreams. At times he would dream about a frightening darkness that hid something evil that wanted to hurt him. Sometimes he would wake up drenched in sweat. He also started having emotional problems: listlessness, hypersensitivity, mood swings, depression, and rage. At times his world seemed to turn surreal. Sounds became much more intrusive. Normal street noises or the crash of breaking glass sounded to him like a recycling bin being emptied a foot away. Everything pointed toward a mental breakdown. That worried him, but what worried him most was his anger. Sometimes he felt like he had awakened from a daze, unable to remember what he had done, or to whom.

He had felt that way only yesterday, in the hours preceding this flight.

'Jody' – the mysterious voice that had suddenly materialized during or right after the night he almost killed himself drinking – helped him remember. It was his subconscious, painstakingly reporting to him everything he had lost on a conscious level. Although likely a self-inflicted punishment rather than a coincidence, the voice in his ear sounded disturbingly like *her* voice.

He hadn't been himself in the final hours before this flight. He was sorry about that now, but it was too late. He had hit his wife in a fit of rage and frustration. He had lost it after another fierce argument, this one over Jim's visiting rights with their two daughters,

Cara and Natalie, once the divorce was finalized. Jody had talked about that as if it were already a *fait accompli*. She was claiming custody of their daughters and had every intention of keeping them from him. When she told him that, something inside him snapped and he hit her hard in the face.

All true. But he hadn't *killed* his wife, had he?

Jim rubbed his eyes and shook his head to clear the demons.

'Are you OK?' Ben asked.

'Yes,' he said, adding evasively, 'I was just thinking of something.'

His thoughts kept churning.

What if he *had* left Jody's dead body behind when he left the house yesterday? If that was true, she should have been found by now and the police would be arranging a reception committee for him at the airport when they arrived in Sydney.

Bearing that in mind, perhaps it wasn't so bad that the onboard radio had failed. Up here in the sky he might have his worries, but down there on *terra firma* hell could be awaiting him.

But it made no sense.

How could he have killed Jody without being aware of it?

He didn't want to imagine that. He couldn't.

Yet his imagination was running wild and he saw no possibility of reining it in.

How often had he hurried to the airport wondering if he had switched off the coffee maker? Or if he had locked the door properly? Yesterday had been no different. He may have swept out the door fuming like an angry bull, but certainly he was aware of where he was going.

You were too far gone, Jimmy, he thought to himself. *You weren't yourself yesterday.*

Although he had calmed down in the car on the way to LAX, he still couldn't remember much of what had happened before he left the house. Not whether the coffee maker had been switched off, or whether the door was locked, and whether or not he had hurt Jody more seriously than he had intended.

What if she had hit her head on a sharp edge of the kitchen table? What if he had attacked her with a knife – a long, sharp-edged carving knife?

A terrible image appeared in his mind: the head and arms of a corpse, not buried deep enough, revealed in a shallow grave after a heavy rainstorm. He only needed to dig a little deeper to see what had truly happened yesterday.

He didn't want that. *He really didn't want that.*

He started sweating and gasping for air. He couldn't afford to lose control, not tonight. He needed to keep a clear head. He glanced over his shoulder, worried that his evil thoughts and deeds were being scrutinized by his copilots. Ben frowned at him, but said nothing. Greg didn't seem to have noticed anything. He was speaking into the microphone again, appealing to anyone who could hear him to respond.

I didn't kill her.

He had to hold on to that.

But if he didn't kill her, then there was something inside him – his subconscious – trying to contradict what he believed to be true. And his subconscious usually knew better than his conscious mind.

'Jody' was silent, for now.

Tonight Jim had to get more than 350 people safely back on the ground.

Do your job. Put everything else out of your mind!

His gut instinct was to descend a few thousand feet, to see what lay beneath the clouds. But he didn't. If the plane descended, it would burn more fuel. If this flight were to last much longer, he would need every pint of kerosene he had in the tanks.

Outside, he saw only the limitless darkness of eternity.

You're going to kill them, Jody said.

'No!' he said aloud through gritted teeth. He had to put an end to this.

He hadn't killed anyone and he wasn't going to start now.

Oh, yes! Jody said in a dry voice. *You're going to kill them all.*

NINETEEN

Phyllis

When the plump woman named Phyllis ordered her to open the toilet door, Sharlene felt as if her throat were being squeezed, as Todd Bower had done to her.

'*Hurry up!*' Phyllis barked.

Sharlene's hands were sweaty, and she had a bad headache. The fat lady had clenched her fists. What did she intend to do? Hit her?

'Jerrod is in there! *Do something!*'

She just couldn't.

A mystery presence was with them on the plane. That presence had fondled her.

And now Phyllis was screaming at her and her co-workers were staring at her, as were the passengers, as was that young girl with the ponytail. Not able to retreat somewhere and put a pillow over her head, she felt like a doe frozen in a car's headlights.

When she saw Aaron hurrying up the aisle toward her, she softly exhaled a sigh of relief. 'What's going on here?' he asked when he reached her.

She took a deep breath before answering in a shaky voice. 'This lady', she said, indicating Phyllis, 'claims that her husband has been inside this stall for quite some time.'

'You're damn right!' Phyllis roared. 'He's been in there for half an hour. I pounded on the door, but he's not responding. And *she* won't open the damn door!'

'All right, calm down, we'll have a look,' Aaron said.

Sharlene stepped to the side. As Aaron overrode the door lock, she looked away from what might be revealed inside the stall.

The door opened, and she heard a shriek from Phyllis and a startled cry from Aaron. Despite herself she chanced a quick peek.

A slender man was down on the floor. One of his legs rested on the metal toilet seat, and the other was lying crookedly beside it. The man's eyes and mouth were open, and he was staring at them with a glazed, lifeless expression.

Phyllis dropped down beside him.

'Jerrod!' she croaked. '*Jerrod!*'

When she shook him, the man's head fell backward and his eyes rolled in their sockets.

Aaron tried to squeeze inside, but Phyllis's massive back and bulbous derrière blocked access. When he asked her to move out of the way, she acted as though she either didn't hear him or just didn't give a damn.

Just then, Ray Jacobstein stepped forward and grasped one of the woman's arms. As he struggled to heave her upright, she teetered, and for a moment Sharlene feared the woman would topple over backwards and crush Ray beneath her. Whimpering, the woman finally agreed to step back and make room for Aaron.

Aaron knelt down and felt for a pulse in Jerrod's neck. Sensing nothing in the carotid artery, he shook his head and turned toward Sharlene.

'See if there's a doctor on board,' he said grimly.

Sharlene had only seen a dead person once before in her life. Her father had stared at her the same way, with his eyes and mouth open, while slouched grotesquely on the living room sofa.

She nodded and grabbed the nearest public-address speaker.

'Ladies and gentlemen,' she said, unable to keep tremors from her voice. 'If there is a doctor, nurse, or paramedic on board, would you please identify yourself to one of the crew members.'

She repeated the message and replaced the speaker in its cradle. With over 300 passengers on board, the probability was high that there would be a physician among them.

With that announcement, Phyllis emerged from a trance-like state she had briefly entered.

'Jerrod!' she screamed. 'Get up! Get a hold of yourself and *get up!*'

It was heartbreaking. A blanket of sympathetic silence settled over the passengers seated nearby. Moments later Mara approached, followed by a balding, muscular man in his fifties. He was a good six feet tall.

'This gentleman is a doctor,' Mara announced.

'My name is James Shepherd,' the man said. 'I'm a surgeon. What's the problem?'

Aaron pointed to the stall and the doctor peered inside.

'This gentleman apparently collapsed,' Aaron said, as Shepherd leaned forward to examine the man. Nobody spoke while the surgeon did his work.

In short order he said softly, 'I'm sorry, but there's nothing I can do for him.'

With those words Phyllis lost it. She flung Ray away from her while making hysterical noises that combined the howling of a jackal with the grunts of a pig.

'This can't be happening!' she uttered more intelligibly, after the first wave of savage disbelief. 'Jerrod is healthy. There's nothing wrong with him. *This can't be happening!*'

Shepherd stepped back and Aaron took over. He seized Phyllis by the shoulders and spoke calmly and soothingly to her. At length, he managed to quell her fury.

The surgeon placed a hand on her shoulder. 'Madam, I'm truly sorry,' he said evenly and authoritatively, a tone of voice he had undoubtedly used to break bad news to countless people in the course of his career. Phyllis, tired and pale and lips twitching, stared back at him as if she were on the brink of a nervous breakdown.

'It's *impossible*,' Phyllis suddenly cried out. But her voice was weaker, as though the utter horror of it all was beginning to sink in and she had not the strength to fight it. 'There was nothing wrong with him,' she added as a plea. 'He's just pretending. That's what Jerrod does. Believe me, I know. I always need to watch him, he's such a baby. He *needs* me.'

Her cries of despair morphed into babbling sounds as she looked past Shepherd at her late husband lying motionless in the toilet stall. 'Jerrod,' she said, as though making a final assault on reality, 'for the *last* time, *stop* being ridiculous and get up!'

He did not stir.

'*Don't do this to me!*' Phyllis insisted woefully.

Sharlene stood there motionless. 'How?' a voice asked, and then she realized it was her own voice.

The surgeon looked at her, his eyebrows raised in question.

'How did he die?' she asked quietly.

Shepherd's answer was directed to both Sharlene and Phyllis. 'I really can't say. It looks like a heart attack. That would be my first guess.'

'He doesn't have a bad heart. Never had any problems,' Phyllis contradicted him. She was sounding more and more washed out, like a wind-up toy crippled by a broken spring.

The surgeon shrugged. 'That's just a guess. An autopsy will tell us more.'

Phyllis fainted. What Shepherd had just said may have been the last straw, Sharlene mused. Only a few hours ago Phyllis and Jerrod had boarded the plane to start a wonderful vacation. Now there was talk of cutting open his corpse to conduct an autopsy.

Aaron acted quickly, catching Phyllis before she collapsed and holding her even as he lost his balance from the sheer crush of her weight. Gradually he let her fall to the cabin floor without hurting herself.

Aaron beckoned Ray over, 'Let's put her in First Class for the time being. Sharlene, lock this door. Everyone, for God's sake, keep calm. We must attend to the passengers. You can imagine what they're thinking.'

'What do we do with . . . What do we do with *him*?' Sharlene asked, pointing inside the stall.

Aaron bit his lip. 'Leave him where he is. We have nowhere else to put him. Just lock the door and keep an eye on things here.'

He and Ray escorted Phyllis to the First Class cabin as though she were a member of the walking dead. Aaron could not recall seeing anyone acting so despondent.

'Tell the passengers someone has been taken ill,' Sharlene told her colleagues as they gathered around her. 'These things happen. They'll understand. I'm going after Aaron.'

'Is there anything else I can do?' Shepherd asked.

'No, I don't think so, Doctor. Thank you very much for your assistance.'

'I'm in Business Class, seat 72D, should you have further need of me,' Shepherd said, before turning away. Sharlene lingered a moment to watch as her colleagues informed the passengers that someone had been taken ill. Then, feeling strangely calm – or perhaps in a state of shock – she followed Aaron and Ray. When she joined them, they had settled Phyllis in an empty seat and were tending to her.

'He's making a fool of me,' Phyllis was saying, while rubbing her red-rimmed eyes. She sounded like she actually believed it. 'He doesn't know how to behave himself sometimes. He's lost without me.'

Aaron offered her some water and, when she refused that, offered her something stronger. Again she refused. Because Phyllis was busy reproaching her deceased husband, Sharlene had difficulty consoling her. The brutal reality of Jerrod's demise had not yet fully sunk in.

Phyllis *did* love Jerrod, Sharlene suspected, but in her own rather odd way. She talked about her husband as if he were some sort of a pet who required a firm hand and short leash, who otherwise would be unable to fend for himself.

As Aaron and Ray continued talk soothingly to her, Phyllis revealed that her last name was Kirby. Sharlene offered no comment.

A heart attack?

It was possible, of course.

But she didn't believe it.

At length, Phyllis became drowsy. A frontal assault of dismay, dizziness, and depression had taken its toll. She stopped reprimanding her dead husband and sat quietly.

Aaron made eye contact with Sharlene and Ray. 'I'm going to report this to Jim,' he declared.

'I'll come with you,' she said.

Aaron nodded. 'Ray, will you stay here with her?'

'Sure,' Ray said.

Aaron led the way to the cockpit.

Halfway up the stairs to the upper deck, Sharlene suddenly stopped.

Something was behind her. She knew it with an absolute certainty. A cold draft hit her, as it had earlier in the galley.

As if something dead was breathing on the back of her neck.

TWENTY
Where We're Not Going

Aaron had already disappeared around the corner upstairs, leaving Sharlene alone with whatever was behind her.

She was afraid to look. She couldn't move.

A scream formed inside her throat.

Just as she was about to scream, the chilly breath on her neck faded and was gone.

She stood there for a while longer, gathering her courage. Then she whirled around, to find no one behind her.

Not anymore.

But something or someone *had* been there. And it might come back.

Propelled into action, she ran up the last few steps and heaved a sigh of relief when she saw the Business Class passengers sitting upright or stretched out comfortably in their seats as if nothing untoward was going on – or had gone on.

Would she be brave enough to go back down those steps later on?

She saw Aaron, who had been held up by the short man in the brown suit, the one with the Hannibal Lecter eyes who seemed to have such a terrible headache earlier. The Danny DeVito look-alike had risen from his seat and was gesticulating urgently as he spoke quietly to Aaron.

Sharlene crossed over to them.

'Yes, I'm *sure*,' she heard the short man whisper. His eyes revealed barely controlled rage; he looked as though he was about to stamp his feet, or throw some other kind of hissy fit.

Aaron remained a paragon of sobriety despite the man's aggressive behavior. 'We're having some trouble with the flight map, yes, but there's no need for concern,' she heard him tell the man.

'We are *not* going to Sydney!' the short man whispered with as much conviction and righteousness as he could muster.

'Everything is all right,' Aaron deadpanned.

'The hell we are!' the man fumed, his temper rising with his voice. He started rubbing his temple, as Sharlene had seen him do before, and his face reddened. 'You're full of shit!'

Sharlene doubted that Aaron had ever been spoken to in such a rude manner by a passenger. This man, she speculated, was not only angry, he was also not used to being contradicted.

'Sir, please take your seat,' Aaron said, in a tone of authority.

The short man jerked his thumb toward the cockpit. 'In there they know about it. You're letting them fool you, but they won't fool *me*.'

'I'm telling you for the last time,' Aaron said, his voice laced with warning. 'Sit down and be quiet. You're upsetting the other passengers.' The man then saw Sharlene and cast her a menacing look. There was no avoiding those piercing eyes.

His mouth went slack, and Sharlene had the unsettling feeling that he was looking straight through her, into her soul. He shoved Aaron out of his way and stepped toward her, his eyes looming.

Suddenly his hand shot forward, and he clenched her wrist so tightly it hurt.

'You, too?' he asked, in a surprisingly quiet voice.

'What?' she mumbled.

Aaron pulled the man's hand away from her and positioned himself between them. Passengers seated nearby became keenly interested in the drama unfolding before them.

'I've had just about enough of this,' Aaron said tightly. 'Take your seat, sir, or I will *make* you take your seat.'

The man clenched his fists and held them out in a boxer's stance. But then he dropped his hands and shook his head. 'You'll come to believe me, but by then it will be too late.'

He peered at Sharlene a final time, as if searching for an answer of some kind. 'Don't let it get that far, you hear me? *We're not supposed to be here.*'

It sounded more like a plea than a demand. The man's suddenly soft voice betrayed a level of fear that seemed entirely out of character. That overt expression of fear terrified Sharlene.

The man did as he was bidden. He sat down and stared at his feet.

'Call Mara and ask her to come back here right away,' Aaron told Sharlene. 'And have her bring Ray. They'll need to keep an eye on this gentleman.'

Despite Sharlene's complex emotions, she had to comply with Aaron's request. She walked back to the galley, but not before throwing a glance toward the stairway. Seeing no one there, she drew aside the galley curtain.

She paged Gloria on the phone and informed her that Mara and Ray were needed on the upper deck because one of the passengers there was causing problems. As she talked to Gloria, she cast furtive glances over her shoulder.

'I'll send them up,' Gloria assured her.

When Sharlene returned the phone to its cradle, the words of that irate passenger in the upper deck echoed within her.

We're not supposed to be here.

Then she left the galley and waited on the other side of the curtain.

She heard footsteps coming up the stairs, Mara and Ray. She noted that Mara no longer had dimples in her cheeks. Her eyes were grim and sober from witnessing the death of a passenger.

'Go on,' Sharlene directed them. 'Aaron's there.'

He had posted himself beside the man in the brown suit who, at least for now, was obediently remaining in his seat. Did he realize he would only make things worse for himself if he kept creating a ruckus? Sharlene mused. Or was he truly frightened?

Sharlene crossed her arms and watched while Aaron explained the situation to Mara and Ray. Then he walked back to her.

'Are you all right?'

Sharlene bit her lower lip.

No, I'm not all right, Aaron.

Irritably, Aaron ran a hand through his hair. 'That little guy really got on my nerves. Ray's promised to keep a close eye on him. If necessary, well . . .' He sighed. 'Let's just hope he keeps his cool.

I've got enough to worry about. By the way, Nicky took over from Ray downstairs. She's staying with that woman, Mrs Kirby.'

Sharlene barely heard him. She had to say something, but what?

'Didn't you hear what he said?' she blurted out suddenly.

Aaron gave her a puzzled look. 'No. What did he say?'

'That we won't make it to Sydney . . .'

'Oh, that. Don't worry. The man's deranged,' Aaron stated angrily. 'What did he say when he grabbed your wrist?'

Her heart was beating hard as she considered his question.

'I don't know. It was very strange.'

It was not that Sharlene truly did not know what the man had said. It was that she couldn't comprehend it.

She thought for a moment longer before reaching a decision.

'You go on and speak to Jim,' she said, her mind made up. 'I'm going to . . .' She searched for words. 'I have something else I need to do.'

'What?' he asked. '*What* did he say?'

'Nothing, just go on ahead,' she insisted.

He thought to object, but changed his mind. With a shrug, he turned around and walked off toward the flight deck.

A small part of her was surprised that Aaron had not questioned her more intently. He had so quickly dropped the subject, and that was unlike him.

Was he hiding something, too?

At 4:35, Aaron Drake stepped inside the cockpit for the second time that hour. There he duly informed the captain that one of the passengers had died from an apparent heart attack and his body was being kept temporarily in a locked toilet stall.

Jim Nichols was startled by the report, as were his two copilots. As he was talking, Aaron recalled that Jim – or was it Greg? – had experienced death on a flight before. The cause of that death had been thrombosis, an obstruction inside a blood vessel caused by sitting motionless for an extended period of time. This so-called 'economy-class syndrome' was not uncommon during long-haul flights.

'You did the right thing,' Jim said. 'It's unfortunate you had to leave the body inside the stall, but at least it's out of sight of the other passengers. And I wouldn't know where else to put it. Please be sure we are doing everything we can for the man's wife.'

'We're doing that,' Aaron averred. 'Is there anything else I can do?'
Jim shook his head. 'Not at the moment.'

'I haven't had time to brief the cabin crew about our difficulties yet,' Aaron confessed. 'When I came downstairs, that passenger had died and we had our hands full. Is the situation still the same as before?'

Aaron was more worried now than he had been forty-five minutes ago. He'd assumed then that the basic problem was a technical glitch that could be fixed in relatively short order. Now he wasn't so sure.

And it ate at him that that Danny DeVito had been correct. The *Princess* was not headed toward Sydney – at least, would not be until the glitches had been resolved. How could the man possibly have known that? Just because there was no flight map data available on MEG?

Aaron was so puzzled and put off by events that he still had not told Sharlene about the problems on the flight deck, even after the storm surrounding Danny DeVito had calmed. She was nervous enough as it was.

'We're doing everything we can, Aaron,' Jim said calmly.

How much fuel did they have left? And how much longer could they remain flying? That was what crossed Aaron's mind at a full gallop, but he bit his lip and said nothing. The pilots knew precisely what was afoot.

'OK,' he said. 'Let me know if there is anything I can do. In the meantime, we'll do our best to keep the passengers quiet.'

He left the cockpit and passed Dr Shepherd, who smiled politely.

'Danny' was a few rows down, sitting in his seat just as he had been ordered to do. He had stopped making a fuss, but there was no ignoring the rigidity and bleakness of his facial expression.

'Everything appears to be all right,' Aaron said to him in passing. He didn't stop, because he did not want to give the man an opening to launch into another tirade.

You're letting them fool you. You'll come to believe me yet, but by then it will be too late.

Mara and Ray were poised outside the upper-deck galley.

'I'm going to go check downstairs,' Aaron said. 'How is Mrs Kirby doing?'

'Not so good, but at least she seemed calmer when I left her,' Ray said.

Aaron walked down the steps. He was starting to worry a lot, and that was not like him. 'A steady hand on the wheel' was how people who knew him described him.

Would everything be all right? He was startled to realize that he was actually wondering if he would ever see Sydney again.

Or any other place, for that matter.

TWENTY-ONE
'They'

While Aaron made his way forward to the cockpit, Sharlene paused before the steps leading down into the half-light. She tried to collect herself and gather courage. Whatever was haunting her tonight could re-emerge on the stairs. Still, she couldn't just stand there; she had a job to do and people who depended on her. She took a deep breath, clenched her jaw, and then, before her doubts and fears could assail her, stepped quickly down the steps.

A few rapid heartbeats later she was on the main deck, and nothing had happened. No chills this time, no presence of an invisible fiend.

She kept going, straight through into Tourist Class.

The passengers nearest the toilet stall with Jerrod Kirby inside were awake but seemingly unruffled. The other lavatory was available, although no one was using it. Maybe people were afraid to come near a dead body, Sharlene speculated. Or maybe they were spooked by what had happened to Jerrod and didn't want whatever it was to happen to them. Devin, Alexandra and Joyce were patrolling the aisles, but nothing demanded their immediate attention.

Sharlene saw Cassie and crouched down beside her. The girl gave her but a brief glance in response. Her mother, however, inquired after Mrs Kirby.

'Several of the crew are keeping an eye on her,' Sharlene informed her. 'They tell me she is doing as well as can be expected.'

The brunette sitting next to the mother listened in on the conversation.

'Dreadful business,' the mother said, shaking her head.

'Yes,' Sharlene confirmed quietly. She hesitated, then: 'Would you mind if I speak to Cassie for a moment?'

The mother's expression changed instantly from one of sympathy to one of infinite sadness. 'I'm afraid not,' she said.

'Why?' Sharlene asked. 'I don't mean to be rude, but . . .'

The mother shook her head dejectedly. 'You aren't being rude. You just *can't*.'

Sharlene didn't understand, and the look she gave the woman conveyed her confusion.

'Cassie is severely autistic,' the mother explained. 'She hasn't spoken a word in two years.'

Sharlene went slack-jawed.

'I told Sabrina the entire story,' the mother said, nodding toward the brown-haired woman sitting next to her. 'I'm Evelyn, by the way.'

Sharlene was at a loss for words. 'I'm sorry, Evelyn. I didn't know,' she managed at length.

'That's OK,' Evelyn said. 'I certainly understand. So what were you going to ask her?'

Sharlene chose her words carefully. It felt strange talking about Cassie as if the girl were somewhere far away and not sitting right in front of her.

'When you first came on board this flight, Evelyn, and you were standing in the aisle, Cassie was between us. She looked at me and . . .' Sharlene leaned in closer. 'And she *said* something. Very quietly, not so I could hear the words. But I swear to you that she spoke to me.'

Cassie's shoulders quivered. She was looking forward, but the motion suggested that she was listening. And understanding what was being said.

Evelyn shrugged. 'I'm not surprised. She was probably babbling. She can express herself, but it's not really *talking*.'

She shook her head. 'It wasn't babbling, Evelyn. She was talking. I'm sure of it.'

Sharlene had no idea how Evelyn was interpreting what she was saying, but in that very brief moment when Evelyn and her daughter had come on board all of Cassie's senses had been keen and alert, and her mumblings could not be discounted as some kind of gibberish. She had uttered *real* words.

But Evelyn hadn't heard Cassie at that moment, so she couldn't imagine it and didn't believe it. Sharlene sighed. She had wanted to ask the girl what she had said, and why. Not least because on several occasions Cassie had stared at her so intensely, just as the short man on the upper deck had done.

Cassie *was* able to speak, Sharlene was convinced of that, regardless of what Evelyn claimed. But why wouldn't Cassie repeat what she had said to her? Sharlene wished Cassie could give her some signal of recognition or understanding – a nod or a hand motion – to convince her mother that she was capable of more than babbling incoherently.

'Evelyn,' the brunette then said, 'I did see Cassie staring at this stewardess . . .'

She leaned slightly forward and peered with eyes half-closed at Sharlene's breasts.

'. . . Staring at Sharlene,' she continued, and Sharlene realized she had been looking at her name tag.

'I remember thinking how peculiar it was,' the brunette went on. 'And I noticed Cassie staring at that man when he walked past us toward the bathrooms. When the door opened and they found him in there, she was standing in the aisle. Most children would never do such a thing. They would cringe and cower, maybe even cry.'

Evelyn sighed audibly. 'And what's your point, Sabrina?'

Something in Evelyn's tone, Sharlene mused, suggested that she understood perfectly well what the point was – but did not want to hear it, or talk about it.

Sabrina tucked a strand of hair behind her ear. 'My point, Evelyn, is that while Cassie may be locked inside herself, she *can* hear and see. You told me so yourself. And maybe she sees more than we do.'

Sabrina nodded at Sharlene. 'I'm a psychologist,' she explained. 'I also know a thing or two about parapsychology, because my mother . . .'

She paused as a dark cloud passed over her face. 'Well, because of my mother,' she finished, and left it at that.

Sharlene did not respond. Cassie continued to stare ahead.

'Can I tell her the story you told me?' Sabrina asked Evelyn.

Evelyn threw up her hands. *I'd rather you didn't, but if you insist, go ahead*, the gesture implied.

'All right.'

Do what you must.

Sabrina told Sharlene how the girl's parents had been brutally slaughtered. Cassie had barely escaped with her life. After that, she had become autistic and had been adopted by Evelyn and her husband.

Sharlene was shocked. This was worse than even her own background. A *lot* worse.

That was not all. Sabrina also told her that after her parents' death Cassie had seemed to develop a gift of clairvoyance. She apparently could tell when people were close to death – it was as if she could *see* it coming.

'You know,' Sabrina continued in a near whisper, 'I can't help wondering . . . Did she perceive that the man on his way to the bathroom was . . . Was going to his death?'

Silence followed that question. Then Cassie's hands started shaking, and the corners of her mouth twitched although her lips remained pressed together. She looked as though she was about to have an epileptic seizure and was doing everything in her power to control it.

She *had* heard what was being said about her, Sharlene was convinced.

'I think so,' Sabrina said, also convinced. 'I believe she *saw* that he would not be coming back out alive.'

Evelyn's facial expression was unreadable. Sharlene looked at Cassie, who was becoming increasingly agitated, like a rumbling, bubbling volcano in the moments before erupting.

Sabrina waited for Evelyn or Sharlene to say something. To say *anything.*

When a draft caressed Sharlene's back, she glanced over her shoulder. All the passengers were in their seats, and none of her co-workers were in the vicinity. To her surprise, no one seemed to be paying any attention to the extraordinary conversation taking place just a few feet away from them. Despite their soft tones, their conversation must have been overheard, she speculated, and *that* she didn't want.

When she turned back, she saw that Cassie was suddenly staring at her again – or so she thought at first, before she realized that the girl's sky-blue eyes were not focused on her, but on something *behind* her.

Sharlene's eyes went wide.

My God, she can see it. There is something behind me, and she can see it!

'Cassie,' she said, her voice trembling, 'what is it? What do you see? Please tell me. I need to know. Please, I beg of you.'

The girl did not respond. She kept staring over Sharlene's shoulder.

'*What?*' Sharlene whispered in desperation. '*What is it?*'

Then a word passed the girl's lips.

'They . . .'

It sounded like a sigh, but it wasn't. Evelyn had heard her as well. Her jaw dropped and she put her hand on the girl's shoulder.

'. . . want . . .'

Cassie's voice was very low, like a whisper in the wind. Her large eyes remained glued on the same spot. Sharlene stared intently at Cassie, not daring to look back, afraid of who – or what – might be there. She understood better what that something might be after the girl spoke the last word she uttered. It was a small word, but to Sharlene it conveyed a doomsday warning from hell.

'. . . *us.*'

TWENTY-TWO
In the Dark

Cassie's body, coiled like a spring suddenly disengaged. Her chin dropped, her eyelids grew heavy, and her arms fell to her sides.

'What was *that?*' Sabrina gasped. 'Who on earth was she referring to?'

'Beats me,' Evelyn murmured. 'Cassie? Honey?'

Sharlene couldn't speak. Her throat was clogged.

'Cassie?' Evelyn pressed. But the girl had reverted to pretending she didn't hear anything.

The cold behind Sharlene faded to nothing, just as it had on the stairs and again in the galley.

Sabrina leaned across Evelyn, closer to Sharlene. 'What was that about? Do you have any sense at all?'

The suspicion that she was being pursued by some inexplicable force was intensifying. But could she say anything about it out loud?

If she did, who would believe her? Aaron would likely get mad at her and ridicule her.

Sharlene decided to keep her cards close to her chest. She rose to her feet and held out her hands as if to say I have no idea.

'*Why did she talk to you*?' Sabrina persisted.

Sharlene shrugged. 'I haven't a clue.'

'According to Evelyn, she hasn't said a word in two years,' Sabrina pressed on. 'And now, all of a sudden, she starts talking, to *you*. But she doesn't know you. Am I to believe there is no rhyme or reason to any of this?'

Yes, that is exactly what you are to believe, Sharlene thought. *Cassie didn't know Jerrod Kirby either. She stared at him and now he's dead.*

'I have to go,' she said, unable to mask the tremor in her voice.

Before Sabrina could add anything further, Sharlene quickly walked back to the emergency exit in section C, opposite the toilet stall where Jerrod Kirby lay dead inside.

Cassie had just confirmed, in her own unique way, that intruders had come aboard. But what sort of intruders? Where had they come from? Most importantly, who did 'they' refer to?

Sharlene felt her head spinning. *Dear God,* she thought, *what will happen next?*

Then she remembered her necklace, her amulet. She clenched her fist around the crucifix, took a deep breath, and exhaled.

Passengers and colleagues were giving her worried looks and were whispering among themselves. Sharlene considered going into the galley to get away from it all, but that was no longer an option. If she found herself alone in there, the invisible presence could manifest itself and she might end up like Jerrod Kirby.

Aaron approached her. What had he and Jim discussed? Sharlene wondered. But he was detained for a moment by Devin Felix, who asked him a question Sharlene couldn't hear. Then Aaron continued on his way and came over to her. Even as he smiled, Sharlene saw worry in his eyes.

'Bad news?' she ventured.

He bit his lip and lightly gripped her elbow. 'Yes,' he said. 'I need to tell you something. Want to step into the galley?'

She nodded. 'OK.'

With him by her side, she felt safe, unafraid.

A few minutes before five o'clock she opened the galley curtain and saw Alexandra standing there. *Oh, no!* was Sharlene's first thought.

'Alexandra, could you please give us a minute?' Aaron inquired politely. 'I need to speak to Sharlene alone.'

'Well, if you must,' Alexandra sniffed, and left the galley.

After this night was over, assuming it ever ended, she would have her hands full with that woman, Sharlene thought. Alexandra was a mangy cat with sharp claws and a jealous mind.

'What is it?' she asked, turning to face Aaron.

Aaron told her that the trouble on the flight deck was more serious than he had initially imagined. They had no radio and, worse, no navigational systems that were functional. The passengers were not the only ones who couldn't determine where they were or where they were heading. The pilots were equally in the dark.

'I'm going to tell the others in a minute, but I wanted to tell you first,' Aaron concluded.

Sharlene nodded her understanding. 'Sounds like we're not going to make it to Sydney,' she concluded.

'Hard to say. I hope they can solve these issues, but it's not looking good at the moment. It's almost as if this flight . . .' He left the rest of his sentence hanging.

'What?' she asked quietly. 'What about this flight?'

It's almost as if this flight were cursed, is that it?

'This is the first time . . .' he started, but then shook his head. 'No, I don't want to be thinking like that. It's going to be fine. It might take some effort, but in the end everything always turns out fine, right? We'll just have to put our trust in that.'

Despite his comforting words, Aaron was entertaining his own set of doubts. Of that Sharlene was certain. Should she tell him what Cassie had said? Would he listen to her now? Would he believe her?

'I have to stay focused, and so do you and so do we all,' Aaron insisted. 'What matters is that Jim gets us back on the ground, if not in Sydney, then someplace else. I'm sure he'll be able to do that. There is no cause for alarm.'

A sinking feeling told her that Aaron did not need to hear about her own concerns. He had enough on his mind already.

'I'm going to inform the others,' Aaron said. 'We need to get everyone up to speed in case we have to land at some other airport.' He gave her a quick kiss. 'Let's just try and remain calm. This is all very much out of the ordinary, especially with that man dying;

but we *have* to remain professional. Our passengers have put their trust in us.'

He left the galley. She followed him, not wanting to stay behind, alone. Aaron stopped to talk to the cabin crew, the first of them Alexandra.

Sharlene walked in the opposite direction, her thoughts crossing swords with each other.

'Madam?' someone said in a voice she recognized.

It was the Latino man in seat 59H, he who had asked her to bring him a Scotch. He seemed to be sweating even more profusely than before.

'Yes, sir?'

'I'm almost afraid to ask, but could I please have another round?'

He flicked his eyes toward the mini-bottle of whisky, the one that had been knocked over earlier in the galley by an invisible force. It now stood empty on the tray table.

'I could really use another drink,' he said apologetically.

Sharlene vividly recalled what had happened the last time he had made that request, and she was none too eager to tempt Fate again.

The man noticed her hesitation.

'Please,' he insisted.

The young woman sitting next to him by the window was still leaning her head against it, pretending to be asleep. And her nose was still wrinkled. She *smelled* him, as Sharlene most assuredly did.

'I don't like flying,' the Latino said. 'I was in a crash once. Two people died. I was very lucky. I came very close to dying myself. I'm telling you, I've looked death in the eye . . .'

Sharlene held up her hand, signaling him to cease and desist. 'Please, sir, we don't need to be hearing this,' she said softly but firmly.

'Ever since then,' he said absently, as though he had not heard a word she had said, 'I fly only when I absolutely have to. A drink really helps. I think I need a bit more this time.' A shudder coursed through him. 'Ever since that crash I've been feeling that it's not over yet. It's like I'm destined to die on a plane. That it's going to happen *again*. Does that make any sense to you?'

'Sir, I have already asked you. Please stop talking like this.'

'This little box here . . .' He indicated the entertainment system in the backrest of the seat in front of him. The screen was black, he had switched off MEG. When he looked up at her, his eyes were moist. 'Oh, I'm just being foolish, aren't I? You probably think I've had enough.'

But he sounded stone-cold sober.

'*Could* you bring me another one?'

He wasn't asking. He was begging.

Sharlene decided to get the bottle of Scotch for him, but not before asking either Gloria or Rosette to accompany her to the galley.

'Yes, sir, coming right up,' she said. 'But what were you saying about the entertainment system?'

'Nothing,' he sighed, seemingly ashamed of the way he had acted. 'It's nothing. Never mind.'

Sharlene wanted an answer, but decided to wait for it until after she returned with his drink. 'I'll be right back.'

'Thank you,' the man said.

On her way back to the galley, her nerves twisted her stomach and intestines into painful cramps. Then she found herself beside the woman in black with the oversized sunglasses. She was still sitting in the same seemingly uncomfortable posture: ramrod straight, her hands folded in her lap, and those Ray-Bans looking like square black screens in front of her eyes. The woman had all three seats in the row to herself.

Acting on an impulse, Sharlene sat down beside her.

The woman glanced askance at her.

'You asked me a question earlier,' Sharlene heard herself say.

She felt like she was a mere spectator to her own intuition.

'Do you remember? You asked if I had seen *him*.'

The question had stirred something deep within her. It had been the first time this night that she had the distinct feeling something was pursuing her, and that something or someone was neither a passenger nor a member of the crew.

'Who were you referring to when you said that?' Sharlene asked.

The woman's facial expression remained rigid. Sharlene found it impossible to gauge her reaction or thought process. Those large black glasses hid more than just her eyes. They seemed to hide her soul.

She heard the woman's thin reedy voice.

'I thought that the Lord . . .'

Sharlene frowned. *The lord? What lord?*

'I had hoped that He had come, to . . .'

When the woman bowed her head and folded her hands as if in prayer, Sharlene understood that she was referring to God.

'. . . to grant me forgiveness,' she said timidly.

When the woman removed her Ray-Bans and looked at her, Sharlene noticed that her eyes were large and azure blue, a darker blue than Cassie's, and that a mixture of fear and sadness was embedded in them.

'I saw the Lord when He saved my life. He is light and love. He's not . . .'

She faltered, and the fear in her blue eyes intensified.

'He isn't what?' Sharlene asked.

'The Lord is not *dark*,' the woman answered.

'Dark?'

The woman nodded earnestly. 'The Lord is not dark,' she repeated. 'So it was not the Lord I saw. Whoever I saw was dark.'

'And you say he's *here*? On board?'

'He came in from outside,' the woman said, as if in some sort of trance. She pointed toward the window. 'He stood on the wing, in the wind. Then the plane started shaking and he was gone. I haven't seen him since. I don't know where he is now.'

Sharlene moved closer to her. 'What did he look like, besides being dark?'

The woman shrugged. 'I didn't see his face. I don't think he had one.'

Goose bumps sprouted on Sharlene's skin. She craned her neck, narrowed her eyes, and peered outside. She saw nothing.

'When the plane shook? During that turbulence. Did you see him while the plane was shaking earlier tonight?' Her voice had assumed a raspy quality.

'Yes,' the woman said, nodding. 'That's exactly when I saw him.'

'I see.' Sharlene felt beads of cold sweat breaking out on her forehead. She had one more question to ask the woman.

'If it wasn't the Lord you saw . . . who *do* you think it was?'

'Lucifer,' the woman said at once, without a trace of doubt in her voice. Her face contorted in revulsion.

Sharlene froze.

'You saw him, too,' the woman said quietly, not as a question.

'No, I didn't,' Sharlene said numbly, hardly aware of these words passing her lips. 'I just felt him.'

The plane tilted slightly. Outside, through the window Sharlene saw the wing turn up. But no dark shape was perched upon it.

Now what? Did Jim have navigation back, and was he adjusting their heading to reach the nearest airport?

She felt a glimmer of hope.

The wing turned down again, and that hope was dashed.

Of course, it could still be that Jim was altering their compass heading.

But what if he *wasn't*?

'We should pray,' the woman said, and immediately followed her own advice.

Sharlene closed her eyes, trying to sort through a storm of conflicting emotions.

It started during the turbulence. That's when I had the nightmare. We shouldn't be here. But where is *here?*

She opened her eyes.

The woman had told her that her life had been saved. The Latino had said he had come face to face with death. Just like Cassie.

We have all *been behind the door.*

Sharlene began to discern something. She grasped understanding, a terrible kind of understanding, worse than her darkest nightmare.

At the same time, the meaning of what the man in the brown suit had whispered sunk in, or so she believed.

You, too?

Yes, she too.

Sharlene peered beyond the lady in black, out the window and into the black of night. She imagined herself staring into the darkness of another world.

'If I'm back,' Sharlene mumbled to herself, 'then we're all back now.'

Interlude III

'When I woke up that night, it was pitch black,' she told Noel Richardson. 'That's when I knew something was wrong.'

She hesitated.

'Go on,' Richardson said calmly.

She knew something was terribly wrong because it was so dark in her bedroom. Since she had broken up with Todd, she always left a light on during the night.

She was sure the bedside light had been on before she fell asleep. But now it wasn't. Maybe the bulb had burned out, she thought fleetingly.

But when she reached for the light switch, she noticed an outline in a corner of the room. Or was it only her charcoal Anna Scott dress hanging on a coat hanger?

No, because a dress could not detach itself from the background, let alone move toward her, as it was now doing.

In the next instant, two coarse hands grabbed her wrists and she recognized Todd Bower.

'He had a knife,' she told Richardson, in a choked voice. 'A knife, rope, and tape. Before I could collect my senses, he had me tied to the bedposts, my arms forced above my head, and my legs spread wide. Do you really need to hear the rest?'

Before he could answer, she continued.

'He cut off my clothes. My shirt, my bra, and my panties.'

Lying on the therapist's couch, she let her tears flow freely.

'I lay there, naked, and I couldn't do anything. I couldn't even scream, because he had taped my mouth shut. He was taking his time. He was enjoying this and he had all the time in the world. It was the middle of the night. Who would rescue me?'

'You don't need to . . .' Richardson began, but she didn't let him finish.

'He raped me. I don't know how long it took, but when he was *finally done, it was starting to get light outside. He pressed his knife to my throat, grinning. I can still see that horrible grin. I thought I was going to die. I thought he was going to kill me. Part of me hoped he would.'*

With eyes blood-streaked and tearful from the horrible memory, she glanced at her therapist. 'Maybe that was his intention, or maybe he thought I was dead already. I don't know. What I do know is that I lost consciousness. When I came to it was daylight. I was still tied up, the tape was still across my mouth, and I was lying in a pool of my own blood. He had stabbed me in the abdomen with his knife.'

Noel Richardson folded his hands and observed her solemnly.

'Go on,' he bid her quietly.

'It took me most of the day to free myself. I lived in the apartment alone. Only my best friend, Nance Partington, had a key, but she didn't stop by that day. No one was coming to help me. That day was even worse than the night before. I thought I was going to bleed to death, slowly and painfully.'

She turned her head away from Richardson and looked out the window. 'I was so relieved when I finally got the ropes off, and even more relieved when Todd was later arrested. But my joy was short-lived. I was still alive, but at the same time I wasn't. Even though he had failed to kill me, he had succeeded in destroying me. I felt like human wreckage. I was afraid to go anywhere, so I stayed inside. I put extra locks on my door, and I had a security system installed. It wasn't something I could afford, really, but it gave me the confidence that if he ever came back I could alert the police from my bed, simply by pushing a button.'

'How did you arrive at your . . . decision?' Richardson asked at length.

She knew what he meant.

'I held out for a long time, isolating myself, but it wasn't something that could continue indefinitely. That was not possible. I was becoming morose, sinking into an abyss of depression. I was losing myself. To be honest, I don't remember a lot from that time. Some part of me must have decided I couldn't go on this way. I didn't want to live like that anymore, sick with misery and with the constant fear that Todd would someday return. I was sure he would, sooner or later. What I knew for certain was that I never wanted to see him again and never have him touch me again.'

She kept staring out the window. 'So there was only one thing I could do . . .'

'And you did,' Richardson said resignedly.

'Yes,' she confirmed. 'I committed murder.'

IV

5:08 A.M. — 5:47 A.M.

TWENTY-THREE
Silence

'It's so *quiet*,' the woman with the Ray-Bans said.

Sharlene pricked her ears. It was true, it had become deathly quiet inside the aircraft. But she had been so lost in thought she hadn't sensed the moment when the engines ceased operating.

Sharlene got up and hurried toward Aaron, who had returned to the main galley. Alexandra, Devin, Gloria, and Rosette were already there with him. Their faces radiated grave concern over the sudden eerie silence.

'This is not good,' Aaron said.

'What do we do now?' Devin asked.

'Everything possible to keep the passengers calm,' Aaron replied without pause. 'We wait until we hear from Jim. I'm not going to call him. There must be a crisis in the cockpit.'

'How is this *possible*?' Gloria cried out.

'Control yourself, Gloria,' Aaron snapped. When she nodded her understanding, he said, 'All I know is that more than one system has failed. We have no navigation, no radio. Jim didn't say anything about engine trouble, so this is probably as much of a surprise to him as it is to us.'

He looked at them each in turn.

'All right, let's get to work.'

They left the galley. Sharlene was about to follow her colleagues, but Aaron put his hand on her arm, holding her back.

'We *are* going to be OK, Sharlene,' he told her in no uncertain terms.

The stress clearly etched on his face seemed to belie his words. She knew that he had no real knowledge of the nature of their problems, let alone a solution to them. He had no more notion of where they were than did the pilots. What's more, he had no idea what or who was aboard the plane with them.

Which was just as well, Sharlene thought. He *couldn't* understand.

'We'll be back on the beach in no time, just like yesterday,' he said.

'May it be so,' she said wearily.

'Come on, we've got work to do.'

Outside the galley, the murmurs of passengers talking among themselves was growing louder. To Sharlene it felt as if they were seated in a sold-out movie theater just before the curtain was raised and the show began.

When one of the passengers demanded Aaron's attention, he told the man not to worry, it was simply a matter of technical difficulties. Sharlene wondered if she would be as adroit in withholding the truth from the passengers. She was afraid she wouldn't. So she stood motionless near the galley, as if frozen in place.

Suddenly the overhead lights started flickering.

It resembled a ghostly phenomenon in a haunted house, Sharlene observed with horror, except unseen intruders had now seemingly entered this Boeing 747-400.

Shrieks erupted in various sections of the cabin. A woman screamed. Aaron and the other members of the cabin crew tried their level best to keep everyone calm, but they all recognized that they wouldn't be able to maintain the charade much longer. Every soul on board sensed that something terrible was happening.

Inside her mind, Sharlene heard an old, familiar, frightening voice. *Planes go down, Sharlene, they go down!*

Lights started going out.

Dark settled in.

Sharlene could still discern the seats nearest to her, but her vision beyond those seats was negligible. She glanced toward Cassie's seat, but could not determine if the girl was trying to make eye contact with her. Aaron had disappeared. He had probably gone forward. More screams erupted among the passengers. Crew members strode through the dark aisles, trying whatever ruse they could to quell the rising tide of panic.

Why didn't Jim announce anything on the PA? Because, Sharlene answered her own question, he had more important things on his mind, as Aaron had assumed.

Or had he become incapacitated, not able to tell them anything? *They've taken over the cockpit too.*

Aaron needed to check on the pilots, to ensure they were all right – to see if they were still *alive.*

An hour earlier she could not have dreamed anything like this could happen. That was when she had assumed they were simply having problems with MEG and she was just being plagued by old anxieties. But a lot had changed since then.

She started moving forward and immediately felt a presence behind her. Slowly she turned halfway around and saw Devin Felix walking past in the opposite aisle. He glanced at her, then looked at something she would have seen too had she turned completely around.

He appeared shocked. His jaw went slack and he raised his arm, pointing at something behind her. At that moment a passenger, clearly upset, pulled on his other arm, forcing Devin to divert his attention.

Sharlene then did make the complete turnaround.

Devin must have pointed toward the toilet stall where the body of Jerrod Kirby was being stored. The door should have been locked. But now it wasn't.

It was wide open.

She was no more than three steps away from the small, dark space. Of the dead man she glimpsed, from where she stood, only an extended foot.

Something was with Jerrod inside the stall. She *sensed* it.

Devin must have seen what it was.

Something that shouldn't be here, Sharlene thought in horror.

TWENTY-FOUR
The Door

Aaron was having his hands full placating the passengers. Tension was increasing by the minute, on what was fast becoming a nightmare flight.

'Technical difficulties,' he announced. He kept to himself the brutal truth that if all the engines had failed – and that certainly seemed to be the case – their situation was worse than dire.

He was in the tail section of the aircraft when a number of ceiling lights started flickering. As some of them went out, he heard frightened cries surging around him like a covey of startled quail flushed from their nests.

Jesus, why was everything falling apart? What legions of hell had been unleashed on them? Aaron's first impulse was to run toward the switchbox, to at least try to repair the lights. On his way there he was accosted by two passengers. He kept a straight face when talking to them, and even managed to smile and assure them nothing was seriously wrong. Then, in front of him, a giant of a man rose from his seat.

'Please sit back down, sir,' Aaron advised him. 'We're having some difficulties . . .' The passenger ran a finger across his throat as if to say 'Shut the fuck up!'

'I don't hear the engines,' the man said with authority. 'And we're losing electrical power. I happen to be a pilot. I fly a Cessna. You can't fool me. This crate won't stay in the air for much longer. We're losing altitude and we'll have to land as soon as possible. Tell me this, *can* we make it to an airport?'

The man's booming voice commanded the attention of everyone around him. Aaron decided that arguing would be pointless. Better not to lie, to be honest with this man and appeal to his common sense.

He stepped close and lowered his voice. 'Listen,' he said, 'I know as much as you do, which I admit is not a lot. Believe me when I say the pilots are doing everything they possibly can. At the moment, my primary concern is the passengers. Please, may I ask for your help with this? You're a pilot; you should understand. A panic would make things infinitely worse.'

The man stared at him intensely, then nodded in resignation. 'OK, I get it. But I would have preferred a different answer.'

'I think we all would, sir,' Aaron said *sotto voce*.

Sitting near the man was a middle-aged couple, who started barraging him with questions. 'What did he say? What did he say?' Aaron heard them demand to know. When the man turned toward them and spoke in soothing tones, Aaron breathed a sigh of relief. One fire out, but the forest was still ablaze and out of control.

As Aaron remained in the tail section for a few more minutes speaking to passengers, something started to nag at him. He felt as if he had overlooked something important.

We're not going to Sydney, but you'll believe me only when it's too late.

He kept thinking of the Danny DeVito look-alike. What had that man whispered to Sharlene?

That was what had been bothering him. Aaron searched through the semi-darkness. Where was she, anyway?

She had to be close by, of course. They were on an airplane. But suddenly he felt concerned and longed to see her.

He saw Alexandra just down the aisle from him.

'Do you know where Sharlene is?' he asked her.

She gave him a look that seemed to say she couldn't imagine in her wildest dreams why *that* would matter, given their current predicament. Besides, she was jealous of Sharlene and hated her guts. She didn't say that to him, of course. She didn't need to. Aaron understood well enough and thanked God he had never fallen for the bitch.

He hurried forward. Despite all his worries about the *Princess*, he felt for some reason more worried about Sharlene, inexplicable as that was. He ran into Nicky, Jessica, and Joyce on the way and asked them if they had seen Sharlene. None of them had.

He threw to the wind the long list of things he should be attending to and went in search of his girlfriend, throughout the main cabin. Not finding her, he concluded that she must be on the upper deck in Business Class.

Then he met Devin in the aisle.

'Devin,' Aaron asked with some urgency, 'have you seen Sharlene?'

Devin nodded. 'She was just over by the toilet.'

'Which one?'

'*That* one,' Devin pointed. 'The one with the dead man inside. The door was open. That surprised me a lot.'

'*What?*'

They were near the stall Devin had indicated. Aaron looked over the heads of passengers toward it. He did not see Sharlene and the door was closed. Just as it had been a few moments ago, when he had walked past it in the gloom of the cabin.

'What are you talking about?' he asked. 'The door is closed, isn't it? So where's Sharlene now?'

Devin raised his hands, as if in surrender. 'I had a passenger who needed my attention. When I finished with him, she was gone. She must have closed the door.'

'Did you *see* her close the door?'

'Well . . . no. I assume . . .'

'When was this?'

'I'm not sure. A few minutes ago. Look, Aaron, shouldn't we . . .?'

Devin gestured impatiently toward passengers waving their hands in the air at him, like students trying to get a teacher's attention.

Aaron headed toward the toilet stall, ignoring a man who was writing something on the back of a menu. The morbid thought crossed Aaron's mind that this might be the first passenger on board to start writing a goodbye note.

As Aaron stood outside the toilet stall, he was suddenly assailed by the notion that Jerrod Kirby wasn't dead at all and was in fact *looking* at him. It was insane, utterly ridiculous, but—

Just at that moment the oxygen masks dropped down and dangled above the passenger seats. Now, it seemed, *everyone* was astir. Panic was bubbling up, as within the depths of a volcano, and threatening to erupt at any moment in a gush of shouts and screams and cries of woe.

His crew started assisting people with the masks. They must have come down because the cabin pressurization had failed. Aaron could feel the plane descending. He purposely yawned to relieve the pressure in his ears, and that helped a little.

Then he looked back at the toilet stall, the one Devin said had been opened.

Sharlene must be in there with Jerrod Kirby, Aaron thought.

She must be behind that door.

TWENTY-FIVE
Catastrophe

The challenges confronting Jim Nichols had gone from bad to worse, to insurmountable. At first he had worried about the mysterious defects in the cockpit computers. Then he had started worrying about his state of mind. He began imagining the weirdest things. Had the *Princess* disappeared from radar and vanished into the unknown? Would he be able to function properly as the captain tonight? Had he murdered his wife?

When Aaron Drake had come in half an hour earlier to report that one of the passengers had been found dead in one of the toilet stalls, he had done his utmost to stay as calm and collected as a highly trained and experienced airplane captain should.

But then, shortly after five o'clock he found he had much more to worry about. A shrill alert sounded through the cockpit – a loud jarring noise that cut to the quick of his very being.

Equally shaken, Greg stared at EICAS.

'Engine failure,' he reported. 'Flame-out. Engine two.'

Jim couldn't believe it until he saw the readings for himself:

ENG 2 FAIL

GEN 2 FAIL

'*What the bloody hell?*' he cried out, no longer able to mask his concern behind a professional mien.

Air speed and the temperatures of the engines were falling fast. When *Princess* rolled to the left, Jim stepped on the rudder with his right foot to stabilize the aircraft. Greg grabbed the checklists and searched for the FAIL ENGINE instructions.

'Turn autothrottle off and close the fuel valve,' he read out loud.

When Jim complied, engine two shut down.

'I thought we had plenty of fuel,' Ben said, confused.

'We do, according to the totalizer,' Greg said. He raised his hands French-fashion, as if to say he couldn't make sense of it either.

'Try a restart,' Jim said. 'We're at 30,000 feet, so we don't have to descend. We're good to go.'

'OK,' Greg said. He clicked the fuel valve, a switch beneath the gas regulator, to the up position to restart the engine. 'It's going to be two to three minutes before we know if it's going to ignite.'

'Have any of the fuses blown?' Ben asked.

Greg and Ben studied the overhead panel. If any of the fuses had become overloaded, it would have clicked out from the casing and could simply be pushed back in.

'Well?' Jim asked.

'I don't see anything,' Greg said.

'So we'll just have to wait and see if engine two will turn over,' he said grimly.

Jim realized that these failure readings confirmed what he had long suspected: EICAS was, in fact, functional. Nor were there malfunctions in the radios and flight-management systems.

If all that were true, the problems they were experiencing had come from some source outside the *Princess.*

Twenty seconds later his musings no longer mattered.

Suddenly the EICAS screen exploded with alerts. To Jim's amazement, engines three and four stalled at nearly the same moment. The aircraft rolled haphazardly to the right.

Just as his copilot switched off the stalled engines and Jim was again able to use the rudder to stabilize the plane, engine one also quit on them.

'We've lost all four engines within ninety seconds!' Greg cried out, visibly shaken. 'That's impossible!'

'Apparently it's not,' Jim said solemnly.

For him and for pilots like him trained as Navy pilots, danger actually increased a sense of calm and efficient decision-making. As the alarms went off in the *Princess,* it was as if a fog inside his mind had lifted. He was a pilot in his heart and in his soul, and for the first time in a long while he actually *felt* like one.

Jim focused on what needed to be done. He determined that the autopilot was still functioning, at least for the time being, and that was a good sign.

'Start the APU,' he said.

First order of business. Without engines, they had to rely on the plane's batteries for power and those batteries would drain within thirty minutes.

Greg turned the starter button of the auxiliary power unit toward the right and let it go, thus activating the small turbine engine in the tail of the aircraft. Several alerts disappeared from the EICAS screen.

'Now get the engines up and running again,' Jim said.

Greg went to work.

'How much altitude are we losing?' Jim asked.

'Normal descent without engines is about 2,000 feet per minute,' Ben answered.

Jim quickly did the math. That had to be right.

'OK, *what* happened?' he said, frustrated to his limit.

'Volcanic ash?' Ben suggested.

Jim shook his head. 'No, we would have noticed. We would have seen a kind of sparkling rain.'

'Saint Elmo's fire?' Greg put forth.

'That's it, yeah,' Jim said. 'And we would have smelled something strong. Like sulfur.'

'Hmm,' Ben mumbled. 'If we've remained more or less on course, we should be flying over the Ring right about now. You can't discount it.'

He was referring to the Ring of Fire, an area in the Pacific that was infamous for its volcanic activity.

Jim shrugged. 'Maybe. It could also be a fuel leak, or maybe the fuel is contaminated. Or it could be a problem with the fuel lead.' He rubbed his face and shook his head. 'I don't know.'

'Number two is not igniting,' Greg reported.

'Keep going. Start them up one by one,' Jim insisted.

He glanced at Greg, who had used the fuel valve to start engine three and was now waiting, biting his lower lip so hard Jim was sure it was bleeding.

Within a minute and a half, his aircraft had been transformed from a jumbo jet into a jumbo glider. If he didn't get engine power back, and soon, they would have about thirty minutes before he would have to perform an emergency landing.

That was the cold reality, and every pilot on the flight deck was keenly aware that it was.

'What do you want to do if we can't get the engines back on line?' Ben asked. 'Should we keep trying a manual restart, or are you going to try a general restart?'

Jim considered the options. If Greg's efforts to manually start the engines failed, he had one last resort: a general restart. He would have to increase air speed for that, by pointing the plane's nose down and allow air to flow through the engines. Then they would start all the engines simultaneously, hoping and praying that the maneuver would prove to be successful.

It was a Plan B. The downside to Plan B was that, if it failed, there was no Plan C.

'Too risky,' Jim said. 'It would be all or nothing. If it doesn't work, we'd be going down fast and there would be nothing more we could do.' He shook his head. 'No, we'll have to restart the engines manually, and if they don't respond we'll descend in a slow slide. Then I can try to land on the water at the lowest possible speed. So that's it, my friends – we either get things going again or we ditch.'

'I strongly disagree,' Ben said curtly. 'If we ditch, we're screwed. We *have* to risk it if there's no other choice.'

'Ditching a plane doesn't necessarily make the situation hopeless,' Jim said.

'It *is* hopeless, Jim,' Ben countered, anger in his voice. 'Our chances of survival would be next to zero, and you know it. Besides, it's still dark outside. We wouldn't stand a chance.'

'Maybe it won't come to that,' Jim retorted. He was surprised by Ben's fierce reaction. He had never seen his friend act like this before, and he and Ben had never argued. Until now, he couldn't even have imagined arguing with Ben.

Jim decided not to press the issue and glanced askance at Greg. 'I'm doing my best, Ben,' was all he said.

It was 5:15 and *Princess* was gradually losing altitude. The lower their altitude, the slower their rate of descent. When all four engines were still working, about five minutes ago, they had flown at 30,000 feet. Now they were at 24,000 feet.

'I'm estimating we have another twenty minutes, maybe a few minutes more,' Jim said. He received no contradiction from Ben.

It would be another hour and a half before morning dawned in this part of the Pacific, assuming the world as they knew it was still down there. The sea remained hidden beneath a blanket of clouds, as it had been all night – another bizarre occurrence. The only light visible outside was afforded by stars and a three-quarter moon.

Jim listened intently to the silence. He had never experienced anything like this before and couldn't have dreamed of what flying would be like without the distant thrum of engines.

Now the unthinkable had become the reality. The passengers wouldn't hear anything, either. And for them the silence had to be far more surreal and frightening.

Suddenly he had a desperate urge to contact *someone* out there in the world. He did not want to be alone. But there was no point transmitting radio messages. It would be like talking into an empty space.

Besides, he wasn't alone. Hundreds of people would live or die, depending on what he was about to do.

This was the moment of truth. He had to put everything out of his mind except what needed to be done. Could he do that? Could he handle it? He had thought he could, just a few minutes ago. And he resolved to survive whatever or whoever was responsible for this pending catastrophe.

Murderer! Jody whispered in his ear.

He ignored her.

'Engine one is not responding,' Greg reported. 'I'm going to try number four.'

'All right,' Jim said.

The air in the cockpit was getting so thin they were having trouble breathing. Jim considered strapping on his oxygen mask, but decided against it. The same was true for Ben and Greg, assuming they had even considered it.

They still had electrical power in the APU and – Jim assumed – in the ram air turbine, a small propeller that automatically deploys from the belly of an aircraft in the event of engine failure.

Greg devoted his attention to the fuel valves and the evolutions needed to restart the engines. Everything depended on it.

By 5:20, their indicated air speed had dropped to 250 knots.

'When IAS reaches 230 knots I'm going to give flaps, otherwise I can't fly anymore,' Jim said. 'But we'll have to be below 20,000 feet before we can do that.'

As Jim said that, Ben noted that their altitude had dropped to 22,000 feet.

'I'm going to try and slow us down by lifting the nose a bit.'

'Right,' Greg said.

'Transmit one more message. It probably won't make a bean of difference, but try anyway. Besides, it's procedure.'

Greg nodded and placed the microphone close to his mouth. 'Mayday, Mayday, Mayday. This is Oceans 5-8-2 . . .' He paused briefly. 'Mayday, Mayday, Mayday. This is Oceans 5-8-2, transmitting blind. Our current position is unknown. Our destination was Sydney. Total engine failure. We have lost all navigation and communication and are preparing to ditch. This will occur at approximately 12.45 Zulu time, twenty minutes from now. We have 353 people on board a Boeing 747-400. I repeat: we're preparing to ditch because we have lost engine power. Oceans 5-8-2 out.'

Princess descended to 20,000 feet. Jim again considered whether he should attempt a general restart, as Ben had suggested.

Again he decided against it. Too much had gone wrong during this flight, and it was a stretch beyond sanity to believe that anything would start going right. If they couldn't start the engines manually, it was likely this last effort would also fail. Instead of a belly landing, the plane would smash head-first into whatever was down there.

Eighteen thousand feet. Breathing was still difficult but easing a little. They would need to be below 10,000 feet before the air pressure stabilized. Now that he had decided what he would do if Greg couldn't restart the engines, Jim had some time to consider other matters such as saying a silent goodbye to his daughters, Cara and Natalie.

He could see their sweet faces in his mind's eye. If Ben was right and the plane was going to crash, he would never see them grow up; he would never have an opportunity to lecture them about the unreliable and ill-mannered boyfriends they would surely bring home. Maybe it was for the best – for those boys, anyway. Because none of them could ever measure up to his daughters. Not by a long shot. He loved his daughters and yearned to protect them from all the evil in the world.

I don't want to die tonight.

From the corner of his eye, Jim watched Greg's fruitless efforts to restart the engines.

'Keep going, Greg,' he urged.

He turned toward Ben. 'As I said, I'm not going to risk a general restart. If this doesn't work, I'm going to ditch. I'll inform the purser first, then the passengers.'

'Are you sure?' Ben asked.

'Very sure.'

Ben didn't argue. Someone had to make the decisions, and on this flight that responsibility fell to Jim Nichols. Ben accepted that, at least for now. His bleak expression betrayed his doubts and fears, however.

At 5:30, Jim phoned the purser. 'We have lost all our engines and are trying to restart them,' he told Aaron. 'I don't know if it will work. Prepare the cabin for an emergency landing. You have ten minutes. We're trying everything we can here, but ditching seems the most probable outcome.'

'I understand,' Aaron said.

'You know what to do.'

'Anything in particular I need to consider?'

Jim gave it some thought, then, 'Yes, move the Business Class passengers to the main deck. That will improve their chances of survival. Evacuate through the front sections, the back ones will be submerged. Take positions at the inflatables and appoint a couple of ABPs. Report back to me when you've done that.'

After they broke off, Jim realized he had forgotten to ask about the conditions in the cabin. No matter, he had a pretty good sense of what those conditions were. *It's up to me now*, he thought.

Despite his best efforts, he could not resist thinking about his rage on the previous day. Again he wondered what, if anything, he had done to Jody. The last thing he would have wanted to do was kill her. She had been a good wife in many respects. Especially in the early years of their marriage.

Don't work yourself up. You haven't killed her. She's alive and kicking.

Jim half expected 'Jody' to contradict him at that moment, but she did not.

Heaving a heavy sigh, he addressed the passengers. 'Ladies and gentlemen, this is your captain speaking. I'm sorry to report that we have a serious problem. All engines have failed. We are doing our damnedest to restart them. As a precaution, the crew will start preparing the cabin for an emergency landing. Please follow their instructions and remain calm. Be assured that we will do whatever we can to bring us down safely.'

Jim couldn't think of anything to add so he switched off the public-address system.

Greg shook his head. 'They're still not working. I've tried everything.'

'Don't give up,' Jim said. He tasted warm blood in his mouth.

He *had* drawn blood biting his lower lip.

Their altitude fell to 9,000 feet.

We're taking you to our destination, Jody suddenly said.

His breath faltered. He peered out the cockpit windows into the night.

'Destination?' he whispered to himself. '*What* destination?'

Jody went silent again.

Jim hadn't given a thought to their destination. He had only focused on the possibility that he might need to ditch the plane. But that was hardly worthy of the term *destination*, not on a subconscious level, or on *any* level, for that matter.

So he had *not* heard this last thought from within him.

But who then had spoken to him?

Jim began to realize something horrible.

Jody, what the hell are *you?*

TWENTY-SIX
Pursuit

A t 5:20, Sharlene stared wide-eyed at the open door of the dimly lit toilet stall. Of the corpse, she espied only one foot. If she wanted to see all of Jerrod Kirby, she needed to take three steps forward. But she was afraid to take them.

Because the body of the deceased man was not the only thing in there.

Sharlene staggered backwards, and the foot in the stall disappeared from view.

Then she found herself standing beside Cassie, who was again looking at her. *That man was murdered*, Sharlene thought she read in the girl's mind. *You know that, don't you?*

Sabrina and Evelyn also turned their attention to Sharlene. 'What on earth is going on?' Cassie's mother asked, rubbing her hands nervously. 'Why is it so *quiet* all of a sudden?'

Sharlene had to tell her something, and all she could think to do was stick to the story Aaron and her colleagues were telling everyone else.

'We're experiencing technical difficulties,' she managed.

Sabrina shook her head in disbelief. 'We're going to crash, aren't we?' she whispered nervously. 'We're all going to *die*.'

Evelyn shot her a shocked look. 'Don't say that. You're scaring me!'

Evelyn either didn't believe what was about to happen, Sharlene speculated, or she was in denial. But a part of her must realize an airplane flying without engines cannot stay aloft for long. All people on board were undoubtedly well aware of that basic law of gravity.

Sharlene could summon no words to reassure Evelyn. She glanced around, hoping to see Aaron returning. But she only saw the toilet stall.

The door to the stall was now closed.

She drew a startled breath. This was so odd that for a split second she wondered if the door had ever been open. But then she remembered that Devin Felix had witnessed the same freakish thing.

Had someone quickly closed the door? That was certainly possible, although the only other crew members in the aisle were Joyce and Michelle, and they were further away, past the toilet and the main galley, engaged in talking to passengers. None of the passengers could have closed it. They were all buckled in their seats and facing forward. Sharlene couldn't imagine any of them volunteering to confront a corpse stretched out on the floor of the stall.

She suspected that besides herself, Cassie, and Devin no one had even noticed that the door to the stall with Jerrod Kirby inside had briefly sprung open.

Her heart racing, Sharlene looked back at Cassie, who sat with hunched shoulders, looking tense, helpless, and vulnerable. *Do something, please, do something!* she seemed to be on the cusp of crying out.

'It *is* going to be all right, isn't it?' Evelyn asked in a pleading voice. The hefty woman was clutching Sabrina's hand. What she wanted was confirmation, and Sharlene had to give it to her.

'Of course it is,' she said, as if to a child. But as she said it, she could not meet Evelyn's eyes. Instead, she glanced toward the bathroom again.

The door remained closed.

It was up to the captain to determine if everything would be all right, Sharlene silently posited, and right now she wouldn't hazard a guess as to whether Jim Nichols was even in command of the plane.

As Sharlene walked away, Cassie watched her go with sad, mournful eyes. It was as though she were saying goodbye.

Sharlene saw passengers murmuring prayers, holding hands, or just staring vacantly ahead. Some of them called out to her, but she didn't pause to acknowledge them.

According to her watch it was now 5:23. How long could the *Princess* stay airborne without engines? Not long, was the obvious answer. If she were going to do something, it had to be now.

She paused before the curtain separating Tourist Class from the nose of the plane. Behind this curtain were the stairs leading to the upper deck. Did she dare go up them, alone?

She should ask Aaron to come with her, but she hadn't seen him during the past few minutes. Nor did she have time to search for him. Besides, she didn't *want* to retrace her steps, because that would mean having to approach the toilet stall again.

Sharlene decided to dash up the short flight of stairs. She would soon land on the upper deck, surrounded by people and close to the cockpit.

If she felt that chill again, she would just keep going. That was all she had to do – keep moving.

Drawing a breath, she swished the curtain aside and hurried toward the steps. She took them two at a time.

And then she was on the upper deck.

Nothing had stopped her or pursued her.

As she looked in Business Class, she noticed Ray Jacobstein talking to one of the passengers.

Now all she had to do was continue on to the flight deck, just a short distance ahead. Behind her, she heard the curtain of the upper-deck galley being drawn aside.

Was it Mara? Wasn't she supposed to be here with Ray in Business Class? Maybe she had stepped into the galley to secure the trolleys.

Then Sharlene felt a hand on her shoulder.

For a fleeting moment she convinced herself it was Aaron, following her to give her the support she so desperately needed. She prayed she would hear his voice.

Go on in, see Jim. Tell him. Tell him that three hours ago, during the turbulence, we passed through the door of your nightmares. We're now in a world where there is no Sydney. Something evil from that world has come aboard. They want us. You were here before, when you were dead. Now we're almost at the end of our journey. But Jim is taking us home. Didn't he promise you that? He'll always get you back home.

As soon as she realized it was not a hand on her shoulder, Sharlene felt chills besiege her body. Before she could cry out, something seized her and dragged her backwards into the galley. Her head bumped against the outside of an oven.

She blinked, and saw an essence standing there, as forbidding and threatening as the darkest of nights.

TWENTY-SEVEN
Searching

The bathroom door, ajar a few minutes ago according to Devin, was now locked. Aaron thought Sharlene was behind it.

He unlocked it and pushed the door open.

He saw nothing except the body of Jerrod Kirby, looking the same as it had before, with one leg stretched out and the other raised, his hands folded in his lap, and his head resting against the bulkhead. He looked as if he was simply taking a nap.

As Aaron closed the door, Rosette came up to him.

'I've got Jim on the phone,' she said. 'He wants to talk to you.'

'On my way,' he said. 'Where?'

'Main galley.'

He expected to hear the worst, and he did.

'Aaron,' Jim Nichols said, 'we have lost all our engines and are trying to restart them. I don't know if it will work. Prepare the cabin for an emergency landing. You have ten minutes. We're trying everything we can here, but ditching seems the most probable outcome.'

Aaron felt a sinking feeling in his stomach.

'I understand,' he acknowledged.

'You know what to do,' Jim said.

'Anything in particular I need to consider?'

'Yes, move the Business Class passengers to the main deck,' Jim answered. 'That will improve their chances of survival. Evacuate through the front sections, the back ones will be submerged. Take positions at the inflatables and appoint a couple of ABPs. Report back to me when you've done that.'

Aaron hung up.

While he was preparing himself for what was to come, Alexandra came in. Just seeing her made him more worried about Sharlene. Then he heard Jim Nichols' voice addressing the passengers.

'Ladies and gentlemen, this is your captain speaking. I'm sorry to report that we have a serious problem. All engines have failed.

We are doing our damnedest to restart them. As a precaution, the crew will start preparing the cabin for an emergency landing. Please follow their instructions and remain calm. Be assured that we will do whatever we can to bring us down safely.'

He sounded as if worse had not yet come to worst. When Aaron left the galley, he briefly entertained the illusion that Jim had been able to convince the passengers that things *could* be worse. The cabins went quiet and the silence was eerie.

But as a professional purser with many years of flying under his belt, Aaron understood that bewilderment reigned supreme in these kinds of circumstances. The passengers now fully understood that they were living in a nightmare, and that waking up from that nightmare was not an option.

The entire crew except for Sharlene and one or two others gathered around Aaron, who forced his mind to focus on what needed to be done. Time was short.

'You heard the captain,' he said hoarsely to the crew. 'Take positions at the exits, except in sections D and E. They'll be submerged after we ditch. Mara and Ray, move the Business Class passengers down here. Devin, select a couple of ABPs. I've got one to recommend. I'll point him out to you in a moment. Make sure everyone puts on their life jacket and then demonstrate the brace position. Secure everything that's loose and take duty-free bottles out of the storage bins. Get rid of them. You know what to do. Questions?'

There were none.

'OK, people,' he said. 'Let's get to work. We have ten minutes.'

The crew spread out, as directed.

Only Devin stayed with him. 'You were going to point someone out?'

Before an emergency landing, the crew often selected a few strong men among the passengers, able-bodied persons, who could offer a helping hand during the evacuation. As one such volunteer, Aaron wanted the man who claimed to have flown a Cessna.

He grabbed one of the flashlights in the galley, switched the light on, and aimed it at the broad-shouldered man.

'There he is,' Aaron said.

'I see him,' Devin responded and started walking toward the man.

Aaron's motto was that if people remained calm and proper procedures were strictly followed, the odds of everything turning out all right rose exponentially. Now, however, he feared that this situation would end very badly. He held out slim hope that Jim Nichols would be able to restart the engines. In fifteen minutes or so, he would have to ditch the plane. How could *that* possibly turn out all right?

Aaron tried to not answer his own question, deciding instead to take a quick look in First Class and on the upper deck, to see if he could find Sharlene. He realized he belonged with his crew, but at the moment he had Sharlene on his mind. And in his heart.

He strode quickly toward the nose of the aircraft, pointing his flashlight this way and that, checking the galley and bathrooms. Nothing in First Class. That left Business Class. He ran up the stairs and into the throes of chaos.

Mara and Ray were telling the passengers to get up and find seats downstairs. Aaron noted that Danny DeVito was making trouble, blathering all kinds of rude and fatalistic remarks. Other passengers took steps to avoid him, treating him as though he were a leper.

When Danny spotted Aaron, he pointed at him and seemed about to storm toward him. Aaron was in no mood to argue with him or anyone else. He turned his back on the man and walked back down the stairs.

In the Tourist Class section, many passengers had already donned lifejackets. They stared ahead hollow-eyed, each lost in the horror of his own thoughts like prisoners on death row in the final moments before execution.

Aaron had searched the entire plane. He hadn't found Sharlene, and she hadn't been present during their most recent briefing, minutes ago.

She was letting down the rest of the crew.

Either that, or something bad had happened to her.

The only thought left to Aaron was that she had collapsed and had gone back to the crew bunks. It was the only place on the aircraft where he had not yet searched.

But when he went to check out the crew bunks, he found the area deserted.

By now he was truly worried.

Something *had* happened to her.

Think. What did I miss?

He had last spoken to her just after the engines failed. No, he corrected himself. He hadn't spoken *with* her then. He had spoken *to* her. *She* hadn't said a word. He had last heard her voice when he told her about the navigation and communication problems in the cockpit. At that time he had no idea the engines were about to fail.

Later he had been stopped in section E by the stout man who claimed to be a pilot; and after that, for an inexplicable reason he had started feeling queasy. Devin had seen her by the bathroom stalls. And after that, she had apparently disappeared into thin air.

Despite himself, Aaron still entertained the notion that Jerrod Kirby had grabbed her and somehow disposed of her. It was an utterly ridiculous notion, he realized – but what was not ridiculous was that on more than one occasion tonight he had sensed that Sharlene had seemed to want to tell him something. She had wanted to confide in him, but for some reason she hadn't.

Because she thought I wouldn't listen, he thought fleetingly.

It wasn't that far-fetched.

I didn't listen to Pamela when she needed me most, and I didn't listen to Sharlene, either.

Suddenly, Aaron felt consumed with guilt.

Pam's situation had spiraled out of control in a terrible way. He had sworn that would never happen to him again.

But apparently it had. And Aaron had no solution or inspiration about what to do next. None at all.

He returned to the passenger cabin. The empty seats in Tourist Class were being occupied by Business Class passengers, who were coming in one by one. He hadn't yet spotted Danny DeVito.

The pressure on his ears increased. *Princess* was fast losing altitude. Aaron glanced outside, but couldn't see the ocean through the window.

He had no idea what was down there.

We shouldn't be here.

Ray approached him. 'We're ready, Mara and I. The upper deck is empty.'

'Well done,' Aaron said. 'How did it go with Danny?'

'Who?'

'The short guy with a big mouth.'

'Oh, him. It took a while, but we finally convinced him to come along.'

'That must have been a trick, since he's such a prick. Did he say anything?'

'If he did, I wasn't listening.'

Aaron put his hands on his hips. 'Have you seen Sharlene?'

'No,' Ray answered. 'Can't you find her?'

Aaron sighed. 'No.'

He checked his watch: 5:39. The time the crew had been allotted to prepare for a crash landing was nearly up. Despite the movement of passengers into seats, the cabin remained eerily quiet. The engines had not come back on. That meant that Jim would soon be initiating an emergency landing and it was likely there would be casualties. Worst case, the impact would kill them all.

Rosette reported all preparations complete.

'Then take a seat and strap yourself in,' Aaron said. 'It could happen any moment now.'

He crossed to the nearest phone and called Jim Nichols. 'The cabin is secured.'

'Good,' Jim said. 'The engines haven't responded, so we're going to ditch. I estimate we have another six or seven minutes. One minute before we ditch, I'll give the emergency stations order by blinking the seat-belt sign twice . . .' Jim hesitated. 'Provided *that* button still works, of course.'

Now that he had spoken with the captain, Aaron realized how little time was left to find Sharlene. Worse, he didn't know where else to look. He had searched everywhere. She was no longer on board.

That's impossible.

Was it time for him to start stepping beyond his own boundaries?

Something about the plane made her disappear.

He was deadly close to believing that.

He picked up the PA handset. 'Ladies and gentlemen, we'll be landing in a few minutes. About one minute before we do, the seat-belt sign will flash twice. Please assume the emergency position as soon as you see those two flashes. Lean forward with both hands on top of your head and brace yourself against the seat in front of you. After we have landed, immediately leave the aircraft through the emergency exits. Leave all personal items behind. And please don't inflate your life vest until after you have left the plane.'

Even now there was no sign of panic or hysteria among the passengers. Some of them were praying, others were writing goodbye notes or just staring in horror.

For the first time, Aaron allowed himself to consider the

possibility that he could be dead in a few minutes. He was going to have to accept the unacceptable, that he would be unable to say goodbye to Sharlene. She was the love of his life, although he had known her for so brief a time.

He used the final seconds to do a quick check. He noticed that one of the female passengers hadn't taken off her high heels. When he spoke in no uncertain terms to her, the frightened woman quickly removed her shoes. Aaron stuffed the pumps in an overhead bin.

Then the seat-belt sign dinged once. Twice.

Aaron ran to his station, sat down, fastened his seat belt, and in one movement took the phone of the public-address system. He looked up, opened his mouth to yell 'Brace!', but—

A soaking wet figure stood in the dim light in the aisle, right in front of him. She was pale as old snow and had long ebony hair. He thought he saw small sparks of fire in the depths of her charcoal-colored eyes.

'You abandoned me,' Pamela Drake gurgled, and more muddy water poured from the corners of her mouth.

Aaron's throat became clogged and he squeezed his eyes shut.

'*Brace!*' he screamed, finally, into the public-address system. '*Brace! Brace! Brace!*'

He kept his eyes closed, waiting for the horrific impact.

TWENTY-EIGHT
Destination

When the *Princess*'s air speed had dwindled to 190 knots, Jim Nichols extended the flaps. Their altitude was 8,000 feet. Any moment now they would clear the cloud cover, and then he would finally be able to see what awaited them down under. Jim decided not to further delay his final briefing.

'Greg, Ben, here's what we're going to do.' He cleared his throat and struggled to keep his voice calm. 'We'll keep trying to restart the engines until we reach 3,000 feet. If that doesn't work, and I doubt it will at this point, we'll focus on our landing. Greg, switch off the air conditioning and close the outflow valves on my signal.'

The air-conditioning system employed two outflow valves to control air pressure inside the cabin. Since these valves let the air out of the plane, they had to be closed before ditching to prevent water flowing in. After ditching, if all went well, the Boeing 747-400 would function as a boat; and with any luck it would stay afloat long enough for the passengers to get out.

'I'll bring the nose further up, reduce our speed to 140 knots, and extend the flaps to maximum position. After we've determined wind direction from the waves, I'll turn our nose into the wind. When we're almost down, I'll lift the nose about ten or twelve degrees to stay airborne for as long as possible, to allow us to hit the water at minimum speed. I'll try to land parallel to the waves. After that, there's not much more I can do beyond trying to keep the wings horizontal.'

Jim bowed his head and continued. 'The tail end will hit first. The drag of the water will cause the nose to drop. If it becomes submerged . . .'

He left the remainder of the sentence for his copilots to finish.

'What happens after that is a mystery,' Ben commented grimly.

'We could have fires breaking out on the wings,' Greg warned, 'caused by lashing power cables. And we might have flames on the water as well.'

Jim shrugged. 'I don't think there's much chance of that.' He paused, then he said, 'You know what? I'll eject the fire extinguishers into the engines while we go down. That way we can be sure it won't happen.'

'OK,' Greg said.

'Other questions?'

The copilot shook his head.

'You, Ben?'

'No,' he said tersely. How that one word was spoken conveyed Ben's deep frustration that Jim had not opted for the general restart.

Am I going to be the murderer who kills everyone on board after all? Jim wondered bitterly. He was expecting Jody's voice to answer that question in the affirmative, but she said nothing.

'Greg, keep trying to get the engines going.'

The copilot continued giving it his best efforts. The brief silence that followed was interrupted by a piercing series of beeps: *You're flying too low,* it screamed in alarm, *and the landing gear has not been deployed.*

'I'm turning off the alerts,' Jim said.

He pushed a few buttons. 'Ground-proximity gear override. I've also selected the flap and terrain override,' he said when he was ready.

The phone rang.

'The cabin is secured,' Aaron Drake reported.

'Good,' Jim said to him. 'The engines haven't responded so we're going to ditch.'

That wasn't entirely true, because Greg was still working on it, but he was no longer expecting a miracle. 'I estimate we have another six or seven minutes. One minute before we ditch, I'll give the emergency stations order by blinking the seat-belt sign twice . . .' He groaned softly. 'Provided *that* button still works, of course.'

Soon after his conversation with Aaron, *Princess* cleared the cloud cover.

Jim held his breath.

The aircraft shook slightly. For a moment they saw nothing through the cockpit windows but an indistinct mass of steel-gray.

What in hell is down there?

Jim didn't want to imagine the catastrophe that would befall them if what was beneath them was land and not sea. The fatal crash that would inevitably ensue would be one that even God in all his omnipotence could not prevent.

But what were the odds that they would find, at this precise moment, a stretch of land in the immense Pacific? It would be like finding the proverbial needle in a field of haystacks. Then again, this night had been one of multiple surprises and implausible outcomes.

A black surface loomed.

Ah, Jim thought, *just the sea, after all.*

He heaved a sigh of relief.

Greg hadn't seen it. He kept working the fuel valves, trying valiantly to restart the engines. With no success.

At 3,000 feet, Jim called it quits.

'You can stop trying now, Greg.'

'Dammit!' the copilot cursed in despair. It was the first time Jim had ever heard him swear.

'Air conditioning and outflow valves,' Jim said.

Greg executed the evolutions. 'Air conditioning off, outflow valves closed.'

'Flaps 20.'

'Flaps 20,' Greg confirmed.

The aircraft shivered as the flaps extended even further.

Jim decreased their speed to 140 knots, the minimum flying speed. The sea drew closer and Jim believed he saw white foam on the crests of waves. A few more seconds and it would be over.

In those last few desperate moments, Jim envisioned his home and garden. He saw himself, outside in the sunshine, with Cara and Natalie. Laughing as young girls do, they were chasing each other and a bouncing ball, playing some kind of game he didn't recognize. In recent months he had noticed that his daughters were intent on things he couldn't fathom.

I'm coming home and then you can tell me all about that game of yours.

Cara and Natalie were side by side now, smiling radiantly.

Then, suddenly, their smiles vanished and they fell over. Dead.

A woman appeared behind them.

She looked like Jody, but she wasn't.

Murderer! She growled, and he heard the word as distinctly as if she had shouted it at him from a few feet away.

Jim felt like he was waking up from some sort of nightmare. He glanced outside into the early morning darkness.

Look at the water. Whatever else you do, don't let waves wash across the nose. If that happens, it's over. I'm not going to let a wave get on the nose. I'm going to land on top of the waves.

He pressed the button to illuminate the 'Fasten seat belts' light twice.

Suddenly he jerked forward in his seat. Not far ahead, in line with where the aircraft was going to strike the water, he spotted something.

Jesus, *what* was that? He felt spasms of panic coursing through him.

They were going toward it no matter what, all 353 souls on board.

The *Princess of the Pacific* could no longer remain airborne.

And Jim Nichols had just spotted their final destination.

Interlude IV

The woman in the bathroom mirror had sunken cheeks, and dark circles beneath her glassy eyes.

She saw the woman take a small white bottle from the shelf beneath the mirror and twist the cap off. Dozens of pills were inside. The woman in the mirror cocked her head for a second, listening to 'Going Home', a favorite song emanating from the stereo system in the living room.

The woman in the mirror would not waver. She had resolved to do it as soon as the song ended.

She saw how the woman in the mirror put the bottle to her lips, lifted her chin, and spilled the pills on to her tongue.

The woman swallowed them all.

For a while, nothing happened. The living room was silent. The song was over.

The woman in the mirror considered playing it again, but suddenly she started feeling very ill. She couldn't breathe. Her fingers cramped as she clasped them around her mother's necklace. Then she collapsed.

Suddenly it was completely black around her. From somewhere, she couldn't determine where, she heard a sharp rumbling as if from a looming thunderstorm. She was not alone.

Where was she? What was hidden inside this darkness?

She wanted to get away from here! She needed to get away from here!

She felt herself sliding backwards. It simply came over her, beyond her control, and immediately afterwards she moved from the darkness into a brightly lit sterile room.

She could see herself below, in a hospital bed. Three doctors were standing around her. There were computers, monitors, all sorts of medical implements.

Light as a feather, she floated beneath the ceiling.

As soon as she realized this, she collapsed on top of her own body, lying there with eyes closed. Upon impact, she felt a small electric current . . .

. . . and she took a gasping breath.

The doctors she had just seen from above were now gazing down at her. They started chattering excitedly, and one of them stuck a hypodermic needle into her upper arm. She felt pain, but was too dazed to cry out.

Later, she learned what had happened after she swallowed the pills. Her friend Nance Partington found her. If Nance hadn't had a key to her apartment, and if she hadn't come by when she did, Sharlene would have died. As it was, the fact she survived was a miracle. Although the doctors pumped out the contents of her stomach, they briefly lost her. For fifty-seven seconds she was clinically dead.

Eight months later she talked about this incident as a patient of Dr Richardson, while he listened and took copious notes. He sat across from her, his legs crossed, his pen poised over paper.

'And that's when the nightmares started?' he asked.

'Yes,' she confirmed. 'They started when I was still in the hospital. In my dreams I go back to that rumbling darkness. There are things in there that can see me. I run away every time, but I never get away. I know they're pursuing me. Every time I think they're going to grab me, I start awake.'

'Hmm,' Richardson mumbled.

'Later on, I experienced another but similar kind of nightmare. I'm in my mother's Tupperware room and the door is closed. But something is kicking it in. Suddenly the lock breaks, the door opens, and behind it I see that same darkness again, and they're there. I'm sure of it, even though I can't see them.'

Stretched out on the burgundy couch, she gathered her courage and told Richardson what she thought the nightmares meant.

'I was dead,' she whispered. 'I can remember being dead.'

Richardson sighed and shook his head. 'Sharlene, I understand what you're saying. You've been through quite an ordeal. But . . .'

There was that word again.

'But . . .'

Resigned, she let the torrent of words pour out of him.

As she lay there, he talked about her mother and father, and he talked about Todd. Todd had raped her in the dark, and that's where her anxieties originated. What she had experienced after taking *those pills had only compounded her fear of the dark. Dr Richardson called it 'nyctophobia'. Her dream about the Tupperware room, he maintained, was related to the psychological terror her father had foisted on her. At the same time, it was connected with her love for her mother, whom she dearly missed.*

Sharlene did not believe him. She hardly listened to him. She understood what he was trying to say, but unlike her he hadn't been there.

She had *been on the other side.*

There were demons there. And they were still with her.

Every time she found herself alone in the dark.

V

5:47 A.M. — LATER

TWENTY-NINE
Alone

Sharlene opened her eyes to the dark, and for a blissful moment felt nothing. Then she screamed.

Something was crushing her legs. And her head started pounding, as if her skull had been split open. At length, after her screams were reduced to whimpers, she began to take stock of her surroundings.

She was on her back, on a floor. Something of consequence was lying across her legs, binding her. Whatever it was, it was rectangular in shape and the source of the horrendous pain savaging her body.

She struggled to get it off her. Tensing her stomach muscles, she held her breath, clenched her teeth, and pushed up with all her strength as another heart-wrenching cry split the night. Shards of glass littering the floor had cut deeply into the palms of her hands.

She slumped back down.

Were those snakes she saw dangling from the ceiling?

Her final cry stuck in her throat. She opened her eyes wide.

Using her injured hand, she felt around the inside pocket of her uniform jacket. Did she still have it? Or had she lost it?

Searching desperately, she found her flashlight and pulled it carefully out of her pocket. She couldn't let it slip from her bloodstained hand and roll away into the gloom. When she flicked at the switch, however, the light refused to go on.

A frustrated growl rose up in her throat, and then the flashlight responded, shedding light on her predicament.

To her relief, what she'd thought were snakes dangling from the ceiling turned out to be power cables.

The lead weight on top of her legs was a trolley. She was in the upper-deck galley. Around her was chaos. The floor was strewn with dishes, bowls, cutlery, food scraps, shards of glass, broken china and various other pieces of debris.

Sharlene touched her throbbing right temple and felt a large,

painful bump. Her hands and the side of her head were bleeding.
The trolley was still crushing her legs.

She heaved herself up, pushing the ponderous cart with all the
strength she could muster. It refused to budge. She fell back and
gasped for breath. Tears welled in her eyes and overflowed down
her cheeks.

From somewhere deep beneath her she heard a shrill, grinding,
screeching noise that sounded like tearing metal. Then she felt the
floor start to give way.

She had to get out of there. But first she had to get the trolley
off her. One of its sharp edges was cutting into her skin like a dull
butcher's knife, and she could no longer bear the pain. She could
think of only one thing to do – try to lift the end of the trolley a
little and at the same time draw her legs out from beneath it.

Clutching the edge of the trolley with both hands, she pushed it
up as though her life depended on it and managed to lift it enough
to free her right leg. But then the heavy cart dropped down on her
left leg, igniting another round of excruciating pain. She had no
choice; she had to keep going. She had to free her other leg and
there was no one to help her. She made another attempt to lift the
trolley, wrenching her leg at the same time. Her pants tore and a
bloody welt appeared on her thigh, as if she had been cut with
a scalpel. She held her breath, bit back the pain, and kept doing
everything she could to save her left leg, even though she knew she
was tearing flesh and perhaps even veins.

At agonizing length, she succeeded in getting her leg out from
beneath the lead weight, only to have the trolley almost land on top
of her right hand. She managed to draw it back, just in time, before
the trolley crushed her finger bones into powder.

Free at last, Sharlene lay there, panting.

She had once seen the movie *Saw II* with Todd Bower. The scene
that had stayed with her involved a heroin addict falling into a pit
filled with hypodermic needles. Repulsed, Sharlene had wondered
how much something like that must hurt.

Now she knew.

'Oh, *shit!*' she groaned.

After a few dreadful minutes, the pain began to ease and she was
able to consider her situation. What was the last thing she
remembered?

Being yanked backwards.

That dark shape. What did it do to me? And to the plane?

She racked her brain, but she hadn't a clue.

What time was it? she wondered. Sharlene aimed the flashlight at her watch: 5:56. She had been out of commission for half an hour.

She glanced around, taking in the extent of the wreckage surrounding her. She could be wrong, but it felt as if the *Princess* was no longer airborne.

If that was true, where had Jim landed?

And when had he landed? Where was he? Where was Aaron? Where were the passengers? *And where is that thing that was here with me?*

She shone her light this way and that around the galley. No doubt about it. She was alone.

The floor beneath her shifted again. It felt as though she was on the deck of a ship on a choppy sea. And it was quiet. She heard no trace of passengers, crew members, or anyone.

Sharlene pointed the flashlight at her left leg. Blood was welling up along both sides of the long rip in her pants. She lunged to her right when the left side of the galley began to shift. She heard a high-pitched metallic grating noise, which she feared might be the death throes of the *Princess of the Pacific.*

Now what? What was she going to do?

The destruction in the galley suggested that the plane had suffered a rough landing.

Where *was* everyone?

Were they all dead?

They wanted us, and they succeeded.

But Sharlene was still alive. She had no idea how that was possible.

Another gut-wrenching shriek of tearing metal sliced through to the core of her being.

Princess was breaking up. Any moment now a piece of roof or bulkhead could collapse on her. In the ebony darkness surrounding her, the metallic moans and shrieks were all the more ghostlike and terrifying.

If she stayed here, she would be buried in falling debris.

She needed to act, to do something.

But *they* lurked in the darkness behind the galley curtain.

Maybe she would be safe here after all, at least for a while.

The temptation to stay put grew stronger. This was not a safe place, but for the moment anything was better than having to confront the unknown outside the galley.

She remained motionless until a massive chunk of metal fell from the ceiling of the plane and landed beside her with a heavy thud. Had it come down slightly to the right, it would have crushed her skull.

Crying out for help, Sharlene tried to get up. She realized it wouldn't be easy, and it wasn't. When she put pressure on her left leg the pain nearly undid her. Her other leg didn't fare much better, nor did her head. It pounded unmercifully, she felt light-headed and dizzy.

The movie *Saw II* again came to mind. Why would people subject themselves to the most gruesome torture just for a feeble ray of hope? Why didn't they just accept their fate and settle for a swifter, less painful death?

She understood now. The instinct for survival outweighed any degree of pain or suffering, assuming a person *wanted* to live.

When she had taken those pills, years ago, she had lost all hope. She had no longer wanted to live. But since then, circumstances had changed. She was a different person now.

Sharlene grabbed hold of the edge of the counter, using both arms to hoist herself up, trying to keep her weight off her bruised leg.

She had to open the curtain. What horror would it reveal?

Holding her flashlight like a weapon, she pushed aside the curtain and shone the light into the dark space beyond it.

She saw no one. Nothing.

She dared to take a breath. A quick search revealed no passengers, and no members of the flight crew. The upper deck was deserted.

The Boeing must have made an emergency landing, Sharlene reasoned. But *where* in God's name were the passengers?

Maybe downstairs, in Tourist Class. Everyone was still there, they *had* to be. Hundreds of people could not have vanished into thin air.

She limped toward the stairway, doing everything possible to keep pressure off her left leg. Every step forward counted. At the top of the stairs, she stared down into the dark depths. She could make out very little. She did, however, hear the sound of water lapping against the body of the airplane and she saw the wash of water at the bottom of the stairs. For an instant she thought to shout for help.

She didn't, because if she did the demon or whatever it was that haunted the plane could emerge once more from the darkness. It was no longer a nyctophobic hallucination. It was the ugly truth.

She had to find Aaron. He had to be still on board. He wouldn't leave her behind, would he? No, her heart told her, unless he were no longer alive . . .

Hesitantly, she clutched the handrail with both hands and stepped down one step on the stairway.

As she made her way awkwardly down the steps, the sounds of sloshing and sucking water grew louder.

Nothing reached for her from the darkness.

Where, oh where in God's name are the 350 passengers and crew?

Except for the sounds of sloshing water, it remained quiet. It was as though she was on a ghost ship adrift on the Pacific Ocean.

Sharlene sensed that she was truly alone, the last living soul on board the *Princess of the Pacific*.

But then she heard a cry from below.

It started as a low, guttural sound, but it swelled into a blood-curdling wail. Sharlene had once heard a hyena howl, and this sounded a lot like that. She felt goose bumps break out on her skin.

I'm behind the door. Maybe I'm dead after all, along with every-body else.

That was probably it. After she had taken those pills, she had managed to return to the physical world with the assistance of highly trained medical staff. This time she had no assistance from anyone, and now there was no chance of making it back. She was trapped here.

Afraid to step further down the stairway, Sharlene suddenly felt an inexorable urge to go back up. As she turned around, her foot slipped and she fell over backwards. Her head hit something hard, igniting immediate and excruciating pain. She felt dizzy and faint. But she managed to roll over and get up on her hands and knees, then crawl up and away from the stairway.

The howling from below died away, but the *Princess* erupted in a new round of horrifying screeches. Her nose tilted up as though taking off from a runway. Sharlene feared that this time the fuselage would surely rupture, but the tilting eased and along with it the metallic screeching.

Silence. Blessed silence.

Did she still have her flashlight? she wondered. She worried that she had lost it. But to her ultimate relief she found it still clenched in her right fist.

The pain in her left leg and in her head tormented her, and she had to fight hard to maintain control of her senses.

In that same moment, Sharlene heard a stamp of feet on the stairs.

Something or someone was coming up.

She forced herself upright. Wobbling, struggling for balance, she pushed aside the pain of her injuries. The emotional fear of what might be coming at her transcended physical pain. She bit her tongue and limped away as fast as she was able.

The only egress open to her was forward, so that was the direction she went. She was too afraid to look back. She kept on going, her tormentor seemingly gaining on her. In her mind's eye, she could see a black-garbed creature reach out a sharp claw and rip at her back.

'*Do it!*' she heard herself cry out, her voice gravelly and choked. 'What the hell are you waiting for? *Do it!*'

Sobbing, she limped on past another seat, onward to who knew where. She no longer cared.

Suddenly the noise behind her ceased. Was this it?

Sharlene squeezed her eyes shut, awaiting the end of life as she had known it.

This was not where she wanted to spend her final moments.

An image of paradise took root in her mind.

She is stretched out on the white sand and Aaron is caressing her. Overhead, the sun is shining like fire in the clear powder-blue sky. He is kissing her and will make slow and passionate love to her.

Sharlene returned from this rapturous dream to the cold, dark nightmare that had become her reality.

She was tempted to catch a glimpse over her shoulder.

Only then did she realize that only ten yards separated her from the flight deck. And the door was open. She aimed her flashlight at it and saw no one inside.

She took a deep breath and another step forward. She didn't care about the pain. Another step. And another one. Just one more.

Incredibly, whatever was behind her did not try to grab her or ravish her.

She started a short sprint, her jaws clenched, one hand on her bleeding left leg, the other clutching the flashlight as if for dear life.

She reached the cockpit, stumbled inside and pushed the door shut behind her.

The nose of the aircraft tilted further up. Outside was darkness. She spun around and found that she was alone.

Someone started banging on the door. Then she heard an ear-splitting crash, followed by a second one. In the bright light from her flashlight, she saw dents appearing in the metal door. The lock was about to give, just as it had when her father had pounded the door down.

But she wasn't finished. Not yet. Sharlene slung her arm around the armrest of Jim's seat. With a wild cry of exhortation, she hauled herself up a final time.

A third crash. The door was on its last hinges, she believed.

Then it stopped. For a span of time impossible to determine, all was silent. As she looked around the flight deck, she dared to relax her arm and leg muscles. More seconds ticked away.

'Sharlene!'

She heard the voice, muted through the door.

'*Sharlene!*'

The voice came louder this time, and it belonged to Aaron.

At least, it *sounded* like Aaron. But it couldn't be him. It was impossible.

She hesitated an instant, driven by whatever shards of hope she had left, wanting to grab hold of them like someone grasping at straws while dangling over an abyss.

But then the straws snapped in two.

Aaron was no longer on board the aircraft. Either that, or he was dead, like all the others. This had to be the voice of the demon that had chased her into the cockpit, and the demon was not human.

'*Leave me alone!*' she screamed hysterically. '*Leave me the hell alone!*'

Another silence. Then she heard him shout again.

'Sharlene? Are you in there? *Is that really you?*'

The voice *did* sound a lot like Aaron.

'Open up! It's *me!* It's Aaron!'

'No, it's not you,' she said quietly, to herself.

The doorknob rattled and she heard renewed pounding on the door, but with less strength and determination than before.

'I can't open the door from this side. *You have to do it, Sharlene!*'

She didn't answer. She was frozen in time and place.

'Open up!' Aaron cried, his fist pounding on the door. 'For God's sake, if you can, *open the door, Sharlene!*'

Sharlene stood teetering on the tilted floor. She braced herself, swallowing the pain.

This wasn't over yet. *They* wouldn't let her go. And she knew the door was going to collapse – with the same inevitability as death.

But she was resolved to fight and not go quietly into the night.

She was no longer the vulnerable girl she once was.

She jammed the flashlight into the inside pocket of her jacket to free both hands, and then began frantically searching the cockpit.

Where was it kept?

Then she remembered. It was behind one of the overhead panels.

She found the compartment where it was kept, pulled it out, and gripped the wooden handle in her right hand. She stared down at it, as the incessant pounding on the door suddenly continued.

'*Open up, Sharlene. Hurry! We don't have much time.*'

On one end of the handle was a sharp blade, on the other end a pickaxe. It was a tool that every plane carried in the cockpit.

Sharlene planted her feet in front of the door and raised the axe.

'Come on in,' she murmured. 'You're in for a surprise.'

The demon on the other side could not possibly have heard her. But no . . . it had. The sounds died away. The shouting ceased. The demon was *listening.*

Sharlene had another brief reprieve. It was still night, and she was inside the unlit cockpit of a Boeing 747-400 that was bound for hell.

She had an idea. Quickly she unclasped her necklace and clutched the gold crucifix in the palm of her hand. It felt warm. It *radiated* heat. It was as though her mother were right there with her in this instant that would decide her life.

A cockpit door was impossible to open by brute force. But, as she had expected, this time it not only flew open, it happened in a heartbeat.

She heard a last inhuman, destructive crash. In the next moment the door was hanging by its hinges, crumpled and ajar.

Now there was nothing to stop whoever or whatever was behind the door from entering the cockpit. Sharlene gripped the axe with both hands and raised it high over her head. Wrapped around the shaft of the axe was the crucifix.

Like a viper seeking out its prey, she was ready to strike.

Then a shadow emerged in the open doorway.

She sliced down hard with the axe.

THIRTY
Ditching

At 5:47, Jim Nichols witnessed the end of the world.

A few miles ahead, where he would need to ditch the 747, he saw the leading edge of something that looked to be a black . . . *nothingness.*

He could still see the ocean in the silver glow of the moon, right up to the edge of . . .

. . . Of *whatever* it was. Not a shred of light penetrated inside it, and it stretched as far and wide as the eye could see. There was no avoiding it.

Jim's first thought was that he had lost his mind, and with it any lingering sense of reality. What was out there hidden in that darkness? Was *any*thing in there?

He fought to keep his wits about him. Maybe it was just a thick bank of fog. But no amount of fog could create the illusion that he had reached the end of the world – like ancient sailors who believed the earth was flat and that if they sailed far enough they would inevitably fall off the edge into . . . *What?*

So what in the name of God *was* this? Jim wondered as he stared rigidly ahead.

He was gliding at an altitude of 300 feet. Two minutes at most was what he had left to keep the aircraft airborne. But by then they would be swallowed up by the vast abomination that lay dead ahead.

There was only one way to avoid being swallowed up. He had to ditch and he had to ditch *now*. He had to slam the 747 into the water and damn the consequences.

Jim understood all too well the consequences of doing that. If the plane touched the water with the nose down, at this speed, it would break apart. Most passengers would be killed.

But if that darkness spelled certain death for all, ditching now was still a better option. At least *some* of the passengers and crew might survive.

Suddenly he remembered – why did he think of this *now*? – the promise he had made to Sharlene that night long ago, somewhere in Asia, when she had told him she had lost her mother in a plane crash.

I'll get you home safely, Sharlene.

He had acted oversentimentally, but the hour was late and he had pumped aboard a few drinks. He didn't want to think about that promise now, nor about a host of other promises made to those he once held dear. But one thing was certain: he was *not* going to get Sharlene home safely tonight.

What to do? What to do? Sweat beaded his forehead.

Jody kept quiet. Would she – whatever or whoever she truly was – be waiting for him inside that pitch-black darkness the plane was rapidly approaching?

He couldn't act. His brain went dead. He knew he had to do something, he had to ditch and quickly. But he *couldn't*. If he did, he would kill his passengers and crew, exactly as Jody had predicted.

Greg and Ben said nothing. Jim glanced askance at Greg and noticed his copilot, never much of a talker, staring ahead, mute and wide-eyed. Seated behind him, Ben seemed to be muttering a prayer, and he too only had eyes for what he could see coming at them through the cockpit windscreen.

But *neither* of them could see the nothingness. Jim was somehow convinced of that.

He checked the radio altimeter. *Princess* was now gliding 170 feet above the Pacific.

Jim decided not to ditch. Not this moment, at least. If the only way to avoid that awesome darkness was to recklessly crash the plane into the sea and maybe kill them all, he would have none of it. If he were about to die, then so be it. He would not be responsible for the death of his passengers, who had entrusted their lives to him. He may have reached the end of this world, and there was nothing for it but to discover *what* lay behind what he had always known to be the border of reality.

Everything that had happened since the turbulence had been pieces of a puzzle leading them to this destination.

'I know you can do this, Jim,' he heard Greg utter in a hoarse voice. '*Do* it.'

Until the very last, Greg stayed true to himself and to his fellow pilots.

The area in front of them – darker than the night itself – loomed ever larger.

Come to us! Jody yelled.

From whatever dismal, dark cavern she had disappeared to, she had now returned, her voice sounding more dire than ever. And this time Jim was convinced, without a shadow of a doubt, he hadn't just heard her inside his mind. She had spoken loud and clear, to all in the cockpit, possibly because they had come so close to what might be *her* realm of existence.

In a panicked reaction, Jim almost shoved the nose down after all.

'Shut up, bitch!' he screamed, without thinking, surprising himself more than his colleagues. But it was a liberating outcry.

Jody said nothing in reply.

'You're the devil!' Jim shouted out loud.

If that were true, his muddled brain told him, then in front of him was hell.

'Jim!' Ben also screamed, behind his back. 'Keep your act together! For God's sake, you *have to* now!'

Greg remained silent. He might be looking at him, confused about Jim's outburst and questioning his state of mind, these final seconds before ditching, but Jim didn't notice.

He saw nothing anymore, except for that darker than dark endlessness in front of him, which was now *very* close – and it *did* seem that neither Ben nor Greg were able to see it, as somehow he'd known. If that were true, they presumably hadn't been hearing Jody either.

That which sounded like his possibly dead wife was talking only to him. And—

Too late. Suddenly, the blackness surrounded him and the plane. He had crossed into it.

As of this moment, Jim thought, he *was* in hell.

Where are you? Jody, where the fuck are *you?*

For the moment he didn't hear or see her, and Jim did the only thing he could think of doing. Maybe Ben had inspired him with his last words, which he had almost spat out.

He started praying. 'Dear God, help us,' Jim murmured. 'Deliver us from evil, Holy Father, *save us . . .*'

He checked the altimeter again. The *Princess* was no longer airborne.

'This is it, guys,' Jim said, his jaw clenched.

It was 5:49.

The tail of the 747 grazed something solid, and the frames of the cockpit windows shook slightly. The belly of the aircraft slid along the surface of what was down there.

Then everything seemed to happen at once. With a jolt, the *Princess* slowed dramatically. Jim heard loud banging noises, like cannons firing. He had no time to question their source; he could only hold on to the controls as tightly as possible to prevent the airplane from swinging wildly to the right or left and perhaps flipping over.

I need to keep this crate in one piece, he thought desperately.

'We've arrived,' he announced with a growl. 'We've come to where *you* wanted us.'

He wasn't addressing Greg or Ben, but who *was* he talking to? Jody? The *Princess*? It wouldn't even entirely surprise him if they were one and the same. Nothing on earth could surprise him now.

'God, help us!' he yelled. 'Please help us!'

Princess continued her wild bumpy ride, jerking and jolting. Jim braced himself, expecting the wings to crash into something and be clipped off.

Water splattered across the windscreen as if it was pouring rain outside.

Was that the Pacific? Jim wondered. *Did the ocean continue on beyond the end of the world?*

Strangely, he noticed even the minutest details of the gauges, lights, and numbers on the instruments on the display panels. Beside him, Greg sat squeezing his thighs in a braced position. Their speed was dropping swiftly. In a matter of seconds the 747 would come to a complete stop.

Suddenly the cockpit went even darker, as if a massive wave had washed over the plane and entombed it. Jim screamed. After a gut-wrenching jolt, the plane came to rest.

Jim blinked. He was still alive. So were Greg and Ben.

Jim let go of the controls and stared slack-jawed at his colleagues. 'Go,' he yelled at them. Go, *go!*'

The three pilots quickly unfastened their seat belts. Ben opened the cockpit door and was the first one out, followed close behind by Greg.

Jim started to run after them, but on the threshold he hesitated.

Despite the unimaginable that had just occurred, he could not resist taking one last look around the place that had served him so well for so many years.

He knew this had been his last flight.

Much worse was the realization that he would never see his daughters again.

Where had he taken all the people on board – at least those still alive?

He glanced out the side window and, to his astonishment, saw the glow of the moon. He also saw silvery waves. He hadn't expected that, but it didn't relieve him. To him such visions no longer served as confirmation that they resided, after all, in the world he knew.

It didn't matter. For now, he had to do everything he could to help get the survivors off the aircraft. Very soon the water would flood in and the plane would start sinking. He didn't have time to stand there and do nothing.

They would just have to see what was outside the *Princess*.

At 5:51 he left the flight deck and ran after Greg and Ben. The Business Class section was empty. The passengers there had been moved to the main deck, as per his orders.

Jim hurried past Sharlene without realizing that she was lying unconscious under a trolley behind the galley curtain.

The three pilots ran down the stairs into the unwelcoming arms of a general panic.

Passengers crowded the aisles, desperate to exit the plane. Men and women, spurred on by a survival instinct, were jostling each other and shoving each other out of the way. It was dog eat dog, a stampede. A man's fist lashed out and caught the jawbone of another man, who slumped down, semi-conscious.

Despite the reign of chaos, Jim was relieved to see that so many people had survived. At first blush he spotted no casualties except for the semi-conscious man.

And, despite it all, his head cleared a little. His thoughts about

Jody and the end of reality seemed more distant. He felt his brain coming alive again.

Then terror struck with a vengeance.

THIRTY-ONE
Evacuation

After Aaron screamed '*Brace, brace, brace!*' into the public-address system, an icy silence settled over the cabin. He held his breath. When would the end come? *How* would it come?

He was afraid to open his eyes. Pamela stood before him in the aisle. Her cold, deathly pale face was just inches away from his.

At 5:49, the *Princess of the Pacific* shook from the impact of an enormous crash. Aaron felt as though his head was about to explode. Then his entire body started trembling from the shock of impact. The seat belt cut into his skin and air was squeezed from his lungs.

He did open his eyes. His sister was no longer there. A black Samsonite bag flew through the air and struck the head of a passenger sitting across from him. The passenger slumped over. From inside the nearest galley a trolley rattled, upsetting dishes and glasses, which smashed into slivers and littered the floor. Oddly, he saw a pair of eyeglasses flying as if they were a bird. He didn't know if Pamela was still *somewhere* here and he didn't care. At that moment, he had only survival on his mind.

All the passengers, as far as he could see, were doubled up in their yellow lifejackets and braced against the backrests of the seats in front of them.

The nightmare kept on churning. Aaron's stomach twisted. He gagged repeatedly as he rode out the pitching and yawing until either it stopped or the windows blew out, or the fuselage ruptured and the plane was destroyed. Somehow he had injured a finger and pain shot up through his hand into his arm. He cursed out loud, joining a chorus of other people moaning, screaming, and swearing – a cacophony of misery, fear, and horror.

Finally the worst seemed to be over. The plane continued to slide and shake, but it had slowed to a manageable speed.

And then *Princess* came to a complete standstill.

Aaron unfastened his seat belt and groped for the flashlight that, amazingly, was still in his pocket. He switched it on and rose from his seat. Passengers and other members of the crew slowly followed suit. With his free hand, he pulled the lever of the emergency exit in section B, but the door leading outside wouldn't budge. Warm blood oozed from his nose on to his lips and he licked it away. Passengers in various stages of shock started crowding around him.

He put the flashlight down and pulled the lever with both hands, but still the door refused to open. More passengers filled the aisle. An older man standing near Aaron was pushed over, and cried out in alarm and pain when he was stepped on by hysterical passengers pushing and shoving in close quarters. No one tried to help him up or offer assistance of any kind. It was every man for himself, and only the fittest or most cunning could hope to survive. Aaron again pulled down on the door lever, to no avail. It was as though the damn thing was rusted shut! Passengers were now climbing toward him across the seats. Even in the murky light he could clearly see the dread and terror etched on their faces. A few people had ignored instructions and inflated their life vests inside the craft; they were now jammed into their seats or blocking the aisles. The screams cut through Aaron like a butcher's knife. Thank God, he thought, there didn't seem to be many fatalities, at least as far as he could see.

Aaron kept pulling the handle, but the massive door refused to yield. Mara squeezed through the throng of people toward him.

'Here, let me help you!' she cried out to him. Together they pulled hard on the lever, with no results.

Then Jim Nichols appeared beside them. Passengers nearby gave him room, either in hope or in deference to his uniform, or both.

'It's not working!' Aaron shouted at him. '*I can't get it to open!*'

'I can see that!' Jim yelled back. 'Move aside. Let me try.'

The captain started yanking the lever. Aaron felt the floor beneath his feet moving, as if he were on a ship at sea. But the plane *was* acting like a ship at sea, one that was about to flounder. There wasn't much time. Only now did he realize that *no one* was getting out, not here and not through any of the other exits. Were they still closed as well? That was impossible, wasn't it? He craned his neck.

Yes, everyone still seemed to be on board.

The *Princess* was not letting them go. It was as though the aircraft was cursed and was determined to take every last one of them down with her to her watery grave.

Suddenly, a shrill screeching sound echoed through the cabin. Aaron froze. It was the unmistakable sound of metal tearing apart. The nose of the *Princess* lifted into the air, and the tail end sank deeper into the sea. Passengers toppled over, screaming.

Shaking off the daze that had momentarily engulfed him, Aaron gripped the door lever again and added his strength to the captain's. The plane kept grinding and groaning, tilting up further and further. Passengers and crew members were standing, sitting, or lying down in the front three sections. There was no curbing the chaos. It was out of anyone's control.

And then a great cheer rose up. Aaron let go of the lever, stood on tiptoe and saw that people were finally able to disembark from section C.

He stared at Jim. 'Let's try again.'

He gave another yank on the lever, and cried out when the heavy door finally gave way and the evacuation slide popped out behind it. Aaron inhaled the sweet scent of sea air and pumped his fist. He then beckoned to the passengers.

'Jump! Jump!' he shouted. 'One by one! Easy now! Stay calm!'

A horde of people obeyed his first order and ignored the others. Almost knocking over Aaron and Jim in their frantic efforts to get out of the doomed aircraft, passengers fell and jumped on to the rubber slide serving as a raft afloat on the waves. Danny DeVito was among the first to bail out. The crew had given express orders to evacuate women and children first, but Danny and others of his ilk didn't give a damn. Within seconds, twenty-five people were sitting on the slide, its maximum occupancy. 'Hold on! *Hold on, everybody!*' Aaron roared.

Jim disconnected the slide from the hull of the aircraft. After he pushed it off with both hands, it floated away into the darkness.

'Here!' Aaron heard someone yell. '*Here!*'

A large man was elbowing his way to the front. It was the Cessna pilot, now acting as an ABP. When he pulled the lever on a panel in the roof of the aircraft, a yellow package slid down. As large and brawny as he was, he needed both arms to catch it. Jim and Aaron took it from him, and pushed it out the door and on to the sea. An inflation cylinder automatically activated and transformed the yellow package into a hexagonal inflatable boat, with a small ladder and a towing line. Aaron quickly tied it to the hull.

'Good job!' he shouted at the man.

His relief and satisfaction intensified as he got to his feet. At other exits, passengers were jumping out of the plane one after another. Outside he could see the lights of three life rafts already at sea. Many people had indeed survived.

Then something went terribly wrong. When a woman, dressed in black from head to toe tried to step into a rubber boat, she slipped and keeled over into the water. She quickly disappeared into the ocean depths.

The Cessna pilot did not hesitate. He dived headfirst into the water and went after her. When he finally surfaced, he had his arm cradled around the chest of the spluttering and coughing woman. Those in the boat reached down and dragged them both aboard.

'God bless that man,' Aaron said softly to Jim.

There were still dozens of passengers inside the cabin, among them a number of injured people. An elderly man with a white beard had taken a blow to his head and seemed confused. A young blonde woman with an ashen face pressed an arm against her chest – it must be broken, Aaron mused, or the shoulder dislocated. An old woman, breathing heavily, held both hands to her chest and seemed to be suffering from a heart attack. Aaron went to her aid.

The plane suddenly bucked, and passengers started screaming. Aaron released the old woman, and as he staggered back to the exit door he bumped into someone who had nothing to hold on to and who was on the verge of being bowled over.

The tail of the aircraft sank deeper, the weight of seawater pouring in lifting the front end of the hull higher. Aaron stood by the door with Jim. 'I'm going back into the cabin. There are more people who need help.'

Jim nodded. 'Go ahead.'

Aaron squeezed past the throngs crammed near the exit.

The next two emergency exits, in section C, were no less chaotic. People were climbing on top of each other, screaming. Fistfights had broken out. Passengers *were* getting out, nonetheless. Soon everyone would be out.

'Help!' a voice called out, audible despite the din. '*Somebody please help us!*'

In the murky glow of the few cabin lights that remained functional, Aaron saw several women still strapped in their seats. He
made his way toward them. Sitting between a girl with a ponytail
and a young brunette was a hefty older woman, her neck and chest
stained red from blood running from her nose. She had an addled
look about her. The young brunette had cried out and was now
beckoning Aaron urgently.

'I can't get this woman to an exit,' she shouted to Aaron when
he was at their row of seats. 'She's too heavy.'

'I'll get her,' Aaron yelled.

He extended his hand toward the girl with the ponytail. 'Come
on. You stand over here for a moment, so I can help this lady.'

She took his hand and dutifully rose from her seat.

Aaron grabbed the hefty woman beneath the armpits and hoisted
her up. He helped her toward the nearest exit in section C, shuffling
backwards clumsily, as though he was dragging a dead weight. The
brunette and the girl followed behind, their eyes wide with fear.

At the door, Aaron had to wait until the remaining passengers had
left the aircraft. Then Michelle and Joyce, who were overseeing the
evacuation at this station the best they could, took over from him.

'As soon as you're ready, jump out,' he yelled at them.

Aaron now had a clear view into sections D and E. He noted
that they were deserted.

It had gone quiet. Now that nearly everyone had left the *Princess*,
there were no more screams. The sudden calm made the cabin feel
more like a tomb than the innards of a once grand aircraft. How
much time had passed since the doors had been opened and the
evacuation started, he could only estimate. It was probably no more
than two minutes, though it seemed an eternity.

Aaron checked his watch: 5:53.

He heard water sloshing somewhere at the rear of the aircraft,
indicating a breach in the fuselage. The mortally wounded Boeing
747 had not long to live.

Making his way aft, he saw water gushing toward him. He
searched for the breach but was unable to locate it. By now he was
ankle-deep in water and the water was rising precipitously. It dragged
at him with such force he had trouble maintaining his balance. Cabin
luggage floated around and past him – duty-free bags, attaché cases,
coats, shoes, soggy children's toys – and amid that debris, the first
dead body. It was a male floating face down along the aisle until

his arm became entangled beneath one of the seats. The man's torso twisted sideways, and his leg became jammed beneath another seat. The body rested motionless, seawater washing around and over it.

Aaron looked askance and found himself staring into the eyes of another man who had died in his seat. He was staring up, open-mouthed, disbelief registered in his unseeing eyes.

'Sir!' Aaron yelled at him, knowing it wouldn't do any good. *'Sir!'*

The man remained silent.

There was nothing Aaron could do to help him, and he couldn't remain where he was.

His thoughts returned to Sharlene. Although he still had not seen her, he remained convinced that she had not left the plane. It was a gut reaction, nothing more, but she *had* to be on board somewhere and his time to find her was rapidly evaporating.

Desperate, he turned and started sloshing back through the rising water. By the door Jim Nichols was gingerly helping an injured woman, whose arm looked to be broken, into the life raft secured to the hull. Apparently she was the last passenger in the aircraft. Everyone else had been evacuated within less than three minutes. Only a handful of crew members remained on board.

Outside, on the ocean, lights bobbing up and down with the waves indicated where the life rafts were positioned. Men at the oars paddled as far away as they could from the *Princess*. When she went down, the suction could take anyone nearby in the water down with her. Just as on the *Titanic*.

As more water flooded into the tail section, the nose of the plane rose higher. By now, most of the midsection was submerged. Aaron and Jim, still inside the aircraft, had to brace themselves against the heavy listing.

The last of the crew members were jumping out from the next exit. Greg Huffstutter and Ben Wright followed them. Only one lifeboat remained, and that was tied fast to the *Princess*.

'You're next, Aaron!' Jim shouted.

Aaron stared at his captain. 'Where's Sharlene?'

Jim gave him an odd look.

'What do you mean? Out *there* somewhere!' He pointed out to sea, toward the lights on the boats.

Aaron shook his head. She hadn't left the aircraft. He had never been so sure of anything in his life.

'Did you *see* her leave?' he shouted at Jim.

The passengers in the last life raft screamed. Their little boat was lifted so high on its rope attached to the *Princess* that the rope jerked taut and knocked several of them over just as another terrifying screech of tearing metal pierced their ear drums.

'Jesus Christ Almighty, Aaron, we don't have any more *time!*' Jim roared. 'The plane's breaking up and the boat's about to capsize. Get in the boat. *That's an order!*'

Aaron's gaze swung from Jim to the passengers in the boat. Over the groans of the aircraft, he made up his mind.

He grabbed Jim Nichols by the shoulders and pushed him into the life raft. Caught off guard, Jim landed on his back on the bottom of the boat. Before he could get to his knees, Aaron was untying the rope.

'What the hell are you doing?' Jim cried.

Aaron said nothing. He gave the boat a shove and it floated away from the stricken plane.

Jim kept yelling. '*Aaron, you can't do this! Aaron!*'

As the raft began to drift away, Aaron took a deep breath, turned around, and ducked back inside the plane.

Forcing himself to implement his professional training and stay calm, he resolved not to leave the aircraft without Sharlene. He would not leave her behind to be swallowed by the Pacific Ocean and sink into its depths.

But where to look for her? He had searched just about everywhere. For sure she wasn't either on the main deck or upper deck. He had thoroughly combed through those areas.

Still, she must be somewhere.

It was 5:55 and the *Princess* was slowly slipping beneath the waves. Water pouring in from the tail section had reached his knees, and the water carried with it three more bodies. Two were women who looked as though they had been trampled, and the third was the body of a man in a yellow lifejacket still sitting in his seat with his seat belt fastened. Only the dead remained on board, Aaron thought grimly. He was the only one left alive.

Is she dead?

No, his heart told him she wasn't dead. But his brain thought differently. After all, she could not have disappeared without a trace, and she would never have stayed behind voluntarily.

Aaron's heart pumped madly. This couldn't be true. Not his Sharlene!

Where to look for her?

He needed to keep the flame of hope alive, even if for only another flickering moment before it was forever extinguished by a cascade of seawater.

I'm going to search for her, just as long as . . .

'As long as what?' he asked himself aloud. As long as it took for this aircraft to disappear beneath the waves?

Yes, he answered his own question. Without Sharlene, life was not worth living. Besides, the Boeing was still afloat. As long as it remained afloat, the flame of hope still burned. Aaron waded forward through knee-deep water, away from the emergency exits. It felt like climbing a steep hill. Further on, toward the nose of the *Princess,* the floor was dry. However, it wouldn't be much longer. He arrived in First Class and saw no one there alive or dead. Still, he checked row after row, the toilet stalls, and the small galley. When a thorough search convinced him that the entire section was deserted, he cursed under his breath. He didn't know where else to look. He wondered if he had time to go back downstairs. The water was rising more precipitously now. He felt like a man shipwrecked on a tiny island with a rogue wave poised to swamp it.

So he had been wrong – everything hadn't turned out fine after all. In fact, it couldn't have turned out worse. He had lost the two women he loved and soon he would be joining them, wherever they were.

He needed to hurry back to the emergency exit and, if possible, swim to the nearest raft. If the *Princess* didn't sink before then, it could drag him under if he got out too late.

At 5:58, Aaron started walking back toward the exit he had manned earlier with Jim. Suddenly he heard a sound that chilled him. It wasn't metal tearing or warping. It was an animal sound, like the howling of a wolf – a growling, guttural sound, gradually intensifying.

What in the world was *that*? Whatever it was, it set his nerves on edge and went on for perhaps thirty seconds before fading away. It was followed by more groans from the Boeing 747-400, as the tail end dragged the *Princess* deeper into the ocean. It couldn't be long now, Aaron thought.

In the ensuing silence, he heard another sound. It resembled the sound of a large animal charging, but he didn't see anything. Whatever was producing those spine-chilling noises was coming up the stairway to the upper deck.

Aaron made a decision not to leave the *Princess*. He had to discover the source of that god-forsaken commotion, whatever it was. He could only pray it would somehow lead him to Sharlene. Things had happened on board this flight that for the life of him he couldn't understand. But these sounds *were* real. He had to follow them.

It was the only card he had left to play.

Aaron climbed the first few steps, and the noise abated. The stairway was pitch-black. He hesitated.

Seawater was sloshing around his feet. If this was just an illusion he was chasing, it would be tantamount to suicide. Even if he found Sharlene on the upper deck, how on earth were they going to survive?

It doesn't matter, I'm going on.

It wasn't as dark in Business Class. There was a light on somewhere, but he saw no one – not man or woman or beast.

The nose of the plane lifted higher. To stay upright, Aaron had to hold on to the headrest of a seat. Fleetingly, he entertained the insane notion that the cockpit instruments were magically being restored, as in a rewinding movie, that all systems were being re-activated, and that the *Princess* was rising up from the ocean like a phoenix rising from the ashes.

Aaron lost his final remnants of hope when he heard what sounded like an explosion coming from the nose of the aircraft. Still, he hobbled toward it and, as he did so, he heard stentorian banging noises at short intervals, as though from a demolition ball. Then all was quiet.

He reached the door to the flight deck, but found it closed – and severely damaged, as if a bull had rammed it. A bull surely hadn't done this, but never mind that now. What mattered was why the pilots would have bothered to close the door behind them when they evacuated the flight deck as soon as the plane came to a standstill.

Aaron pressed 1 on the code lock and then ENTER. Following that, a gong would sound inside the cockpit. If Sharlene *was* in there, she could open the door. Assuming she was able to.

When he heard no response from the other side of the door, he punched in the emergency code 345 and pressed ENTER again. If the system still worked, the door would open automatically in thirty seconds. The time delay gave the pilots inside the cockpit the opportunity to override the code and keep the door closed. Those were the longest thirty seconds of Aaron's life.

The time delay ran out, but still nothing happened. It could mean one of two things. Either the system was down – a real possibility, maybe probability – or there *was* someone inside the cockpit intentionally keeping the door closed from the inside. But Sharlene would never—

'Aaron,' he heard a frail voice call out.

He turned his head sharply.

Beside him, sitting against the wall, was Pamela Drake.

She reached out a festering arm, and when she spoke water sloshed from her swollen, peeling lips. 'Help me,' she said, her voice thin and fragile.

Aaron stood rooted to the floor.

'You're not going to leave me, are you?' she begged. 'I can't leave here. Please, help me.'

More water poured from her mouth.

Aaron's flesh broke out in goose bumps. He was too stunned to say or do anything.

'I've been waiting for you,' Pamela continued. 'I thought you'd come, but you didn't.'

He glanced back toward the cockpit door.

Suddenly he was convinced that Sharlene was behind it.

She was the only one who mattered. The apparition beside him was trying to prevent him from doing what he had to do.

'Sharlene!' he yelled.

There was no answer.

'*Sharlene!*' he shouted again, louder this time.

He waited, but still no answer.

'I'm taking you with me. *Both* of you,' Pamela growled. She sounded different now, like a cornered wolf. From the corner of his eye, Aaron thought he saw the drowned figure rising up, but he dared not look at her.

A second passed. Another. And another. Fear and horror were paralyzing him.

'Leave me alone, *leave me the hell alone!*' a voice from behind the door shouted.

It *was* Sharlene!

Relief washed over him in waves, rendering him momentarily speechless.

'Sharlene? Are you in there? *Is that really you?*' he yelled. 'Open up! *It's me, Aaron!*'

She didn't comply immediately. *Was* she unable to? Was she hurt? Was there something in there holding her back, just as Pamela was trying to hold him back?

He pushed against the closed door, rattled the doorknob, and pounded the metal plate separating them.

'I can't open the door from this side. *You have to do it, Sharlene!*'

If she didn't open it, and soon, they would be separated until they drowned. The door remained shut.

'Open up! For God's sake, if you can, open the door! *Sharlene!*' he yelled, pounding the metal with his fists, feeling utterly powerless. A cockpit door, once locked, would not budge even if struck by a battering ram.

He heard not another sound. His relief veered to fear. Mortal fear.

It paralyzed him. Thoughts about death overwhelmed him. His own death, and hers. He'd done everything possible, but in the end it had led him nowhere. This Boeing 747 was going to be his grave. He'd be buried together with Sharlene – and the thing that looked like his sister.

Time passed. He just stood there, as if frozen.

Then a last cry, either of utter despair or frustration, rose from somewhere deep within him.

'*Open up, Sharlene. Hurry! We don't have much time.*'

He pounded the door anew with his fists, but then dropped them again. If she wasn't trying to open the door by now, then she *really* was incapacitated. She could never open it.

What state was she in? What had she been through?

More seconds ticked away. Long, agonizing seconds.

Then Aaron heard a snarl beside him.

Pamela, he thought.

What happened next was too overwhelming to comprehend.

Something, not him, pounded on the cockpit door with superhuman strength until it hung crookedly from its hinges and stood ajar.

Aaron expected that Pamela, or whatever she was, would now break every bone in his body.

He tried to squirm his way in past the warped doorframe. What else could he do? He was at the mercy of evil aboard the *Princess*, but he was here for Sharlene and he wanted to take her into his arms, even if it was only for a dance of death.

Aaron stepped across the threshold and saw her.

He also saw the axe slicing down at him.

THIRTY-TWO
The Axe

The moment Sharlene saw the dark form in the doorway, she hacked down hard with the axe. Her mind went into overdrive. Suddenly she saw with crystal clarity, unburdened by the dark filter of her anxieties, that the person entering the cockpit was not some sort of evil force. It was Aaron, and she was about to split his skull open and spill his brains over the cockpit.

He stopped moving. He didn't try to lunge out of the way. He stood there frozen, staring at her like a startled deer caught in the glare of a car's headlights.

No! she screamed silently.

Then the axe hit home and he cried out.

But not because she had buried the axe in his head. Her aim was thrown off at the last split second and the razor-sharp blade had grazed his right shoulder and narrowly missed his leg. Blood spilled from a wide gash in his uniform jacket.

Grimacing in pain, he pressed his wounded arm to his side and bit down on his lower lip.

How could I have missed? she wondered, stunned beyond measure.

He was injured, but he was alive.

It was incomprehensible to them both. The blade of the axe should have hit him right between the eyes. He hadn't moved, and following that brief flash of recognition she had been unable to stop what she was doing or change the direction of her swing.

Aaron should have been lying at her feet, dead or dying. The fact that the blade had simply glanced off him had nothing to do with quick reflexes.

Something *else* must have happened.

Horrified, Sharlene tossed the axe away. Her body was trembling, and her throat felt dry and vacant, as if her vocal chords had been severed.

Aaron felt the world spinning around him. Had it not been for their catastrophic circumstances, he would have gladly succumbed to blissful unconsciousness.

'We need to get out!' he croaked. 'The plane's breaking up.'

Sharlene opened her mouth, but was still too shocked to speak.

'*Does that side window still open?*' Aaron yelled frantically.

Sharlene turned toward the small window beside the pilot's seat.

It *should* open, she thought in a daze. It was the only way to leave the aircraft from the flight deck, other than going out the door. Until now she hadn't given it a thought.

The nose of the plane heaved upward, like a bow of a ship minutes before taking its last fatal plunge. Sharlene staggered backward and fell into Aaron's arms. When she did so, the filter of evil returned in a flash of terror. For that brief moment she again became convinced he was a demon sent out from the underworld to do her in.

You should have killed me when you had the chance, you stupid bitch. Now I'm going to kill you.

But he did nothing of the kind. He wrapped his injured arm around Sharlene's waist and used his other hand to support himself on Jim's seat. Then he dragged them forward a step, toward the side window. There was a lever beside it that he needed to pull.

'Let me,' she mumbled.

She had finally found her voice.

Would this work? Would they be able to leave the aircraft through the window, the only egress available to them? Or were the satanic powers inside the *Princess* determined to keep them locked inside this tomb forever?

She pulled the lever – and to her relief the window slid open. She breathed in the salt air.

The nose cone of the plane made a sudden dip downward. Water splashed against the cockpit windows. Sharlene could clearly see white-crested waves swirling around the outside of the aircraft. The *Princess* was on her way into the abyss.

They had seconds before the ocean waters would come raging in through the open window and devour them.

Aaron pushed her.

'What are you doing?' she moaned.

'*Go!*' he screamed hoarsely.

She felt his hand on her neck as he forced her to lean her head out the window. As he did so, water surged up against what little remained of the aircraft above the ocean's surface.

Suddenly her abdomen was resting on the window frame, and her feet were dangling inside the cockpit. Aaron had his hands on her buttocks and was pushing her out. How he had managed to do that with his injured shoulder, she could not imagine. Then she fell out, and hit the water and went under.

When she bobbed back up, spluttering, she opened her eyes and saw the window right beside her, just above the surface. The rest of the 747's formidable nose cone, like the great underwater mass of an iceberg, was out of sight in the depths below.

'*Aaron! Where are you?*' she screamed.

He was still inside the cockpit, but he had stuck his head out the side window. She could see the terror and pain in his face. Their eyes met, for the last time.

A black shadow loomed up behind him.

Sharlene tried to warn him. Her lips parted, but she swallowed a wad of salt water. She gagged, and tears came to her eyes.

Then suddenly it felt as if the same demonic power that had groped her in the main and upper galleys was pulling at her ankles. She went down, together with the *Princess*. The immense aircraft was dragging her down with it.

Sharlene felt a crushing pain from the pressure on her ears, worse by far than what she had experienced when the trolley crushed her leg.

She no longer had the strength to resist.

She was drowning.

THIRTY-THREE
Zone

Just like everyone else in the life raft, Jim Nichols witnessed the demise of his beloved *Princess*. He had a front-row seat, because his boat was closest to the aircraft. As she made her final plunge, he stood up straight as if saluting the plane.

He was close enough to see someone falling from the side window of the cockpit.

Jim caught a glimpse of the body in the light of his flashlight. It was almost as if the Boeing shed one last tear before it yielded to the inevitable. The dome of the aircraft disappeared beneath the surface, and the ocean waters lapped over where it once had been.

A large, dark wave curled toward his little boat, lifting it up and almost capsizing it. That wave was followed by a number of smaller ones, sloshing against its rubber sides. Salt-water spray stung Jim's eyes and wet his clothing.

Using the flashlight, Jim searched for the body, but he found none in the choppy water. He turned back toward the passengers in his life raft and counted fifteen heads, the last of those who had escaped from the doomed aircraft. Most of them were injured. One passenger had a broken arm bone; a boy who could not have been more than ten years old had a broken nose; and a red-haired man had what looked to be a fairly serious head wound. But among them were four men who seemed unharmed.

'I need your help,' Jim called to them. 'We need to start rowing, that way.'

He gestured toward the place where, a moment earlier, he had seen the nose of the *Princess* disappear beneath the surface. Who had tumbled from the window? Had it been Aaron?

The purser was the only one who had stayed behind, as far as he knew. He didn't believe Sharlene was still on board, as Aaron had claimed, although he couldn't discount it completely. In the chaos of the evacuation he hadn't noticed her leaving the Boeing.

Or did I see Jody leave the plane?

The four men grabbed the four oars in the boat and started pulling toward the area indicated.

Silence settled over the little craft; even the injured passengers seemed to be holding their breath. Jim was not surprised by their reaction. They had all come face to face with death, and *that* was a life-defining experience for anyone.

How many passengers had he lost? During the evacuation, Jim had noticed a handful of fatalities, but there must have been more he hadn't seen. No matter how bad it was, it could have been a lot worse.

Maybe it still will be. Where *have I taken us?*

He would worry about that later. Now he needed to find whoever had fallen into the water.

Jim shone his flashlight this way and that, wishing dawn would finally break – assuming there *was* such a thing as dawn here. His light found a gray piece of debris. Behind it, a floating suitcase. But no body. Aaron must have been dragged under by the suction of the sinking aircraft and drowned.

But then the flashlight picked out a body lying face-down in the water. He pointed at it.

'There!' he shouted urgently. *'There!'*

The four passengers pulled on the oars.

Jim kept his light trained on the body. The little boat approached, and then he suddenly saw a mass of long blonde hair and realized it was Sharlene.

When the life raft came alongside, Jim and another man leaned across the bulbous rim of the inflatable boat and each grabbed an arm. Carefully, they hoisted Sharlene up and over the coaming until she slid backwards across the rubber floor of the boat. Jim crouched beside her. Her eyes were closed and she was not breathing. He felt her pulse. No sign of life there, either.

Jim leaned over her and started mouth-to-mouth resuscitation. Then he folded his hands over her heart and pushed downward in short, hard bursts of pressure. He breathed into her mouth again, and then repeated the pressure on her chest.

She suddenly turned her face to the side and coughed up water, spluttering and coughing. Then she opened her eyes and Jim cried out in relief. Sharlene looked up at him as if he were a complete stranger. She blinked her eyes and then closed them again – this time, he feared, for good. His body went ice-cold.

'What's *that?*' he heard the man ask who had helped haul her aboard.

Sharlene coughed, spitting out salt water and mucus. Her throat opened and she was able to breathe again, drawing air deep into her tortured lungs. She was on her back, exhausted, lying in what felt like a water bed. It was rocking, not unpleasantly.

She opened her eyes and saw people peering down at her. Across from her was a middle-aged woman hugging two girls, neither more than eight or nine years old. A lanky boy about the same age with a bloody nose and mouth was sitting beside her, leaning his head on her shoulder. He was staring at Sharlene as well, as if she were some kind of celebrity.

Around the edges of the giant water bed was a woman, white as a sheet, sitting hunched over with her chin on her chest. Next to her Sharlene noticed a man grimacing in pain, his arm pressed stiffly against his body. A red-haired gentleman in a rumpled business suit sat staring into space, with a makeshift bandage wrapped around his head.

Only then did she realize that her left leg had been swaddled. At the same time she felt a sharp sting of pain beneath the bandages, and she hissed between her teeth. Salt water had seeped into her wounds and the pain was intense.

And she realized there was light. Overhead was blue sky and a yellow sun. Then she made another discovery. Jim Nichols was on his knees beside her, with his back turned, tending to the woman with the two girls. He gestured and said something to someone at the back of the water bed, although she realized by now that it was actually a rubber life boat.

She became aware of someone else sitting beside her, and he had his hand on her shoulder.

'Are you OK?' a familiar voice asked, although it sounded some-what hollow and raspy. She turned her head toward him.

It was Aaron.

His shoulder, the one she had grazed with her axe, had been wrapped in white bandages. 'How . . .? How . . .?' she stammered.

In her mind's eye she saw a brief flash, as if from a camera. She saw a mental image of him with that black shadow behind him, inside the cockpit.

He couldn't have gotten out.

Her heart leapt with joy, but this could not possibly be him.

Jim Nichols turned around, saw that she was awake, and shuffled toward her on his hands and knees. He had removed his tie and opened the top button of his shirt. His sweaty face, now bright red and with more lines than she had ever noticed before, split in a wide grin. His tired eyes lit up.

'Glad to have you back among us, Sharlene!' he exclaimed.

Before she could respond, Aaron brought a plastic bottle of puri-fied water to her lips. 'Here, drink this,' he said. 'It will do you good.'

Her throat was parched and she drank greedily.

'Easy, easy,' Aaron warned. 'Don't overdo it.'

He slowly removed the bottle and twisted the cap back on. The fresh water did wonders to revive her. Already she felt better.

'Help me up,' she said.

'No, you need to lie there for a little while longer,' Aaron cautioned. 'Take your time. There's no rush. We're not going anywhere anytime soon.'

'No,' she said decidedly. 'Help me up.'

Shaking his head, he assisted her to a sitting position. Dizziness washed over her and her head ached. But she was alive and sitting up, and with the man she loved. And now she could look out above the rim of the little boat.

There were ten other lifeboats floating on the water, close together, most of them crammed full of people. The Boeing 747 was gone. Sharlene couldn't see land anywhere. The sea stretched to eternity in all directions. The sun was bright in a blue sky with nothing but a few dots of fluffy white clouds. There was no wind at all. She looked back toward the other people in her boat, toward Aaron and Jim.

'Where are we?' she asked.

Jim shrugged. 'Your guess is as good as mine.'

'That's comforting,' Sharlene said with a slight smile.

Aaron wrapped his good arm around her shoulder and pulled her close. 'You're still here,' he whispered in her ear. 'Wherever we are, we're here together.'

Sharlene had so many questions, she didn't know where to start.

She started with the most obvious one. 'What happened?'

'I'd like to hear your version of that,' Jim countered.

'You first,' she said adamantly. 'I blacked out while we were still airborne.'

Jim arched his eyebrows. 'I'm sorry, I didn't know that.' He paused, then said, 'I had to ditch the plane. Because the *Princess* had such a capable crew, we were able to evacuate all survivors within minutes of hitting the water. The aircraft sank shortly after six o'clock this morning. A few minutes later we pulled you from the water.'

She vaguely remembered segments of that account as if from a dream she'd had a long time ago.

'Fortunately we also spotted Aaron floating not far from you and were able to drag him on board as well.'

'It was a close call,' Aaron agreed, adding, 'When the cockpit filled with water, it felt like I was swimming against a waterfall. I held on to the window sill and somehow managed to pull myself out. I'm still not entirely sure how I managed to do that.'

Sharlene was tempted to ask him about the figure she had seen behind him, but for the time being kept that unsettling image to herself.

'We've counted nineteen fatalities, all passengers, and a few dozen injured,' Jim continued. 'It's 10:15 now. We have to see it through until someone picks us up. Fortunately, our beacons are working, transmitting on all available frequencies – 121.5, 243, and 406 megahertz.'

'Do you think someone will come for us?' Sharlene asked tentatively.

'Yes, of course,' Jim said firmly. 'It might take a while, though. This is a big ocean. But we have everything we need right here. Emergency rations, tarps, thermal blankets. We also have fishing rods, and tablets for turning salt water potable. And we can take care of the injured. We have first aid kits with bandages, medication, splints. If necessary, we can survive out here for days. That is, unless a bad storm hits.'

He must have told the passengers the same thing, probably in the same words. But did she believe him? He wouldn't look her in the eye. In both her professional and personal life she had had dealings with people who said one thing and thought another; they gave themselves away when they refused to look you in the eye. That was her litmus test and Jim had just failed it.

Should she blame Jim for not being honest with her? No, this was hardly the time, she decided. She had to consider the other passengers on the lifeboat who desperately needed to believe what Jim had told her – and them.

She nodded pensively and looked at Aaron.

'Your turn. How did you find out I was inside the cockpit?'

'I'd lost you,' he said. 'After the evacuation was complete, I didn't want to leave without you. I knew you had to be somewhere inside. I don't know how I knew it. I just *knew*.'

He gently squeezed her arm. 'What's your story, Sharlene?' he asked. 'What were you doing up there in the cockpit?'

Sharlene took another sip of water and decided not to keep anything from him. She resolved to tell him everything she had gone through, every detail, no matter how insane it sounded.

She started with what she heard from Cassie, the woman in black, and the Latino. She even told him about her conviction that the turbulence had launched the *Princess of the Pacific* into another reality, and intruders from that world had taken over the plane. She explained that she had been on her way to see Jim but got only as far as the galley on the upper deck. The last thing she'd noticed was that dark shape. Then she blacked out, and only regained consciousness when the plane had already crash-landed in the water. She described how she dragged herself into the cockpit. She had thought some horrific apparition was pounding on the door, and raised the axe in terror when the door buckled.

Her voice broke. She needed to drink more water before she could continue. 'That's about it,' she concluded as she wiped her lips with the back of her hand. 'Go ahead, tell me I'm nuts. I've heard it before, I can take it. Hell, maybe I *am* nuts!'

Tears welled up when she touched Aaron's wounded arm. 'I'm so sorry,' she said, choking on her words. 'I thought . . . I thought you weren't . . . *you*. I would never, ever do anything to deliberately hurt you.'

'I know,' Aaron half whispered, and held her hand, caressing it.

'I saw Pamela,' he said – sounding so casual she thought at first he was talking about one of the passengers.

He shrugged. 'So either we're *both* nuts or . . .'

He didn't need to finish the sentence.

As the meaning of his words started to sink in, her jaw dropped. It took a moment for her to gather her wits.

'Was *she* the one I saw behind you inside the cockpit?' she finally asked in a hoarse voice. 'I saw something . . . There was something or someone . . . in there with you.'

'Could be,' he said. 'I was thinking only of my survival, and praying I'd be able to make it. She could have been there with me. Or whatever she was. It wasn't Pamela herself, that's for certain. Pamela is dead.'

His voice sounded slurred, as if he had taken medication. Aaron had changed during the night. He was no longer the man he had been before the lift-off of Flight 582.

Jim scooted closer to them. 'Sharlene, we now know there are

other passengers who experienced the same kind of phenomenon
. . .' He hesitated. '. . . Including myself.'

She stared at him, open-mouthed.

'I distinctly heard a woman's voice in the cockpit,' he said som-
berly. 'It was Jody, my wife. She was talking about a destination
. . . I . . .'

He cast his eyes briefly down. 'I thought we were going to disappear into thin air. Just like you, it made me doubt my own sanity.'

Sharlene nodded knowingly.

'What did you do?' she asked after a moment.

'I prayed,' Jim whispered.

Aaron did the same, she thought.

'And now we're here,' Jim said. 'Someone will come to our
rescue. I have to keep believing that. We'll talk about all that other
stuff later, once we're out of here. Whatever it was that happened
last night, we have to push it aside. Right now there's not a lot we
can do, except make the best of our situation. And help those who
are looking to us for their salvation.'

'I understand, Jim,' Sharlene assured him. 'You can count on me.'

'I always have,' he replied.

She stared out across the vast ocean, fearing there was no one
out there to respond to their beacon signals, just as had happened
with their onboard equipment.

She was overcome by a suspicion – no, a conviction – that the
bright sun and the blue sky were nothing but illusions. None of this
was real. They were lost, in every sense of the word, in a place they
weren't supposed to be. In another world. In a different *zone*.

Hours elapsed. The heat became oppressive and there was inadequate
protection from the effects of the scorching sun. Passengers crawled
into what scant shade the tarp shelters provided in the boats. Especially
for the injured, finding shade had become a matter of life and death.

Sharlene thought about Cassie, the woman with the sunglasses,
and the Latino. She searched for them, and finally spotted both
Cassie and the lady with the Ray-Bans in another boat. She hoped
the Latino had also made it safely out of the aircraft, just as he'd
escaped the Grim Reaper after the other crash he'd survived.

For her and these other three passengers, the door to the other
world was open. Apparently, the same was true for Aaron and Jim.
She thought she knew what had caused it in Aaron's case. He had
lived through the tragedy with Pamela. But what kind of scar was

on Jim's soul? She didn't know, but it apparently had something to do with Jody, his wife.

They had revealed themselves to those who could see them, assuming the characteristics of their deep-seated anxieties. In the end, in the upper-deck galley, she had seen the demonic-looking black figure. What was the meaning of *that*?

It seemed obvious to her – now.

It showed itself to me as death, my *greatest fear.*

What could their real faces look like? What did they want from the survivors of this ill-fated flight? Why had the plane and its passengers been brought here?

Maybe time would tell.

The survivors exchanged stories, and the stories traveled from boat to boat. The most poignant was the story of a mother grieving for her lost baby.

For hours, Sharlene sat staring out across the ocean. Aaron, sitting beside her, did the same. Beneath the burning sun, she remembered their hotel room at the Tokyo Grand Hotel, room 534. They had fallen in love that night, and she had hoped their love would close the door to her past, permanently. She had wished for everything to be better for her and for them in the future.

It seemed she would be denied her wish.

The boat starts rocking more violently. She sits up and looks out across an utterly flat ocean. Night has fallen again. Everybody is asleep. Aaron, Jim, the passengers.

How is this possible? There is no wind, the surface of the sea is smooth, but still the boat rocks as if pushed by choppy waves. She realizes there's something moving below in the water.

A few yards ahead, a black claw breaks the surface. She can see it very clearly in the moonlight. The claw cuts through the water like a shark fin, coming toward the small boat. Sharp talons bury themselves deep in the thick rubber.

A black figure, death itself, levers itself up and slithers across the bulbous rim, like a snake.

'Sharlene . . .' it growls.

She woke up screaming, sitting bolt upright.

It was still dark. She flailed her arms wildly, in full-blown panic, until she heard Aaron's voice and felt his arms around her.

'Sharlene! Jesus, darling, what's wrong?'

She stared at him wild-eyed. 'These things,' she said, shivering. 'They're still on board and *they're coming back for us.*'

Jim had been awakened by her screams, as had everyone else on their boat. He shuffled over on his knees to her and Aaron. 'That Boeing is staying at the bottom of the sea,' he promised. 'I'll make sure it will never, *ever* be salvaged.'

Tears ran freely down Sharlene's cheeks. She pressed her face into Aaron's chest.

The night passed without further incident, and a new day dawned.

During the next few hours the air turned stifling in the desert-like heat, just as it had the day before. Sharlene's face felt hot and she was deathly thirsty. Jim Nichols had ordered strict rationing of water, no exceptions.

Two passengers on another boat, both well into their seventies, complained of feeling ill. Some of the injured were in bad shape. A few were approaching a critical condition.

Sharlene had no doubt that more people would die during the next twenty-four hours. And none of them would last several more days, especially if the water supply ran out. The weakest would be the first to go – one of the harsh laws of nature. All that the others on board could do was hope and pray.

But then, when the sun was at its zenith, it happened.

They suddenly heard a rumbling high above them. At first Sharlene thought there was a storm brewing. Then she spotted a tiny dark dot in the sky.

THIRTY-FOUR
Butterfly

The rumbling intensified and the dark spot in the sky grew larger. Sharlene peered at it, unable to believe it was a helicopter until she could see the machine clearly. It hovered over the life rafts, and then slowly descended to just above the glassy surface of the ocean. The chopper rotors fashioned circles on the water. The helicopter door slid open and a man tossed down a rope ladder.

The survivors of Flight 582 stared up open-mouthed, as if witnessing a visit from aliens in a mysterious spacecraft.

Sharlene's boat was rocking violently. Around her, people started shouting.

'It's going to capsize, we'll drown!' a man cried.

'Here! *Here! Help us!*' another screamed.

Their desperate cries were drowned out by the deafening noise of the helicopter blades. Sharlene herself was exhausted. She let it all happen with utmost calm, as though she was going through motions in a dream. She hardly heard the chomp-chomp of the helicopter engine.

They were being rescued. Incredibly, against all odds, everyone in the boats was going to survive this ordeal.

The man in the helicopter climbed down the rope ladder, stretching out an arm to the first survivor he reached. It was a woman and he pulled her in. Then the next one. And the next.

When maybe two dozen passengers were on board, the helicopter left and silence returned.

But not for long. Some two hours later the helicopter came back. Sharlene saw the aircraft reappear as a giant black insect in the sky. More passengers were taken aboard and flown away, to wherever the helicopter base was.

The machine came back for the third time, and again, and again after that. The rescue lasted all day – until after the blood-red evening sun had dipped into the ocean and the last fiery remnants of daylight had disappeared – and well into the night.

Aaron never let go of her, and together with Jim they were the last ones to be picked up. When the helicopter with her in it lifted off, Sharlene looked at the sea spray and for the last time stared at the spot where the Boeing had gone down. It seemed as if the nightly ocean was blacker there; a grave for dark forces.

Sharlene snuggled close to Aaron as the helicopter conveyed them away from this cursed place.

There *was* more out there than just everyday reality, she thought. She had known this ever since she crossed its boundaries the first time.

This near catastrophe marked the second time she was leaving the other *zone* behind. She devoutly hoped the evil that existed there would remain forever locked up inside the wreckage of the *Princess of the Pacific*.

She worried, nonetheless, that her hopes and prayers would be in vain. Last time, she had returned to the realm of the living alone. This time *they* had come with her. The metal shell of the Boeing would not be able to keep them inside forever, if the nightmare Sharlene had the previous night on the raft was any indication.

But she had gained something in return: a renewed faith. Maybe Jim and Aaron's prayers had made the difference between life and death, between that other world and this one.

Faith was something she could hold on to. Maybe, just maybe, she would discover a world of hope she didn't yet know existed.

Maybe she and Aaron could discover *that* world together.

Sharlene squeezed his hand and wished she was a butterfly.